Checking the clock, which showed 12:07 a.m., he heard the loud sound again and this time he opened the door and picked up a huge brick by the side of the house. If a thief was trying to break in, he would be in for a thrashing. Unashe recalled hearing about the burglaries in various homes in the neighborhood as he walked slowly towards the gate, avoiding the wet puddles and mud. He heard the sound again as he got closer, but it sounded weaker this time. He heard a sound like a woman sobbing, and threw the brick down and inched closer to the gate.

When he opened the peephole, he nearly died of shock. It was Priscilla, and she was soaked from head to toe.

She practically fell into his arms.

THAT WHICH HAS HORNS

MIRIAM SHUMBA

Genesis Press, Inc.

INDIGO VIBE

An imprint of Genesis Press, Inc.
Publishing Company

Genesis Press, Inc.
P.O. Box 101
Columbus, MS 39703

Copyright © 2010 Miriam Shumba

ISBN: 13 DIGIT : 978-1-58571-430-8
ISBN: 10 DIGIT : 1-58571-430-5
Manufactured in the United States of America

First Edition

Visit us at www.genesis-press.com
or call at 1-888-Indigo-1-4-0

DEDICATION

To my fearless and remarkable sisters, my best friends: Doren, Lucky, Emma, and Laura Denenga.

To my mothers and little mothers, Agnes, Christina Jessica, Martha, Georgina, Beatrice, and Hilda.

I would also like to dedicate it to the memory of my amazing grandmothers, Theresa Manoah and Miriam Denenga.

ACKNOWLEDGMENTS

God provides people, ideas and wisdom in the right time, and in writing this book, the Lord brought many people to help when I needed it. I want to thank my entire group of advisors that helped me in the process of writing Priscilla's story.

First, my husband, Gabriel, has always been there with answers to many questions about business, life, love and God. He is my biggest fan.

My mother has always been the first editor to my work, giving valuable feedback in her wisdom and knowledge. Her input has added richness to the story that would not have been there.

Theresa Mhangami was so kind to edit my Shona words so they were accurate.

I also received feedback from many friends and family members who gave me courage to complete and submit this book. They are Lucky, Eunice, Emma, Michael, Aaron, Angelica, RayElle, Madeline, Chaka, VaNgwenya, Maryam, Nellie, Nura, and Netsai.

The people at Genesis Press were amazing during the publishing process and I am grateful to them.

I am also grateful for Washe G Shumba my baby and Nathan Denenga my father, for being in my life and enriching my writing with the love and joy they bring.

PROLOGUE
Ngano—Stories

When she was nine, Priscilla learned and accepted truths that later formed the philosophy of her life. Some of these truths came from the mythical tales her grandmother, Mufaro, would tell every time she visited her in the village. After a day of hard work in the corn fields alongside her grandmother, there was nothing else to do at night but sit by the fire and listen. Her grandmother's stories always had the effect of terrifying Priscilla and her three sisters into obedience, as was Mufaro's intention.

Those stories mostly made Priscilla afraid. But those folktales were not the only stories Mufaro would tell them. Her grandmother had tried her best to pass on a part of herself in those tales, some true and some made up. And the stories became as much a part of her granddaughters as the blood that flowed in their veins.

Though each of her three older sisters revealed something about life, Priscilla learned her biggest life lessons and truths by watching her sister, Vimbai stumble into mistake after mistake. Years after Mufaro's tales had ended, Vimbai served as the agent that scared Priscilla into a life lived in the shadows. Priscilla would always remember the night the most important of those truths was seared into her mind.

That night she had gone to bed early sleeping uncomfortably next to her older sister, Rutendo. Rutendo slept deeply, because she lived hard each day, often angry at the injustice of life in their small house in the township of Glenview, not far from Harare's city center.

Priscilla was happy that it was Vimbai's turn to wash the dishes and wipe the floor on her knees with the torn dishrag that their mother insisted they use for the task. Priscilla had left her older sister in the kitchen and had fallen asleep immediately, dreaming of her grandmother. She dreamt of the village, because she hated going there to work in the fields alongside her grandmother. The work was not as bad as her grandmother's dissatisfaction with her. She could never do anything right, and was constantly a burden to her. Her unhappy dream would have continued, but something woke her.

Priscilla heard the yelling. Her father's shouts came storming into her room like intruders in the night. Rutendo continued to sleep deeply next to her. Oliver didn't usually shout unless Priscilla was somewhere in the room, but now she heard it and wondered if somehow the angry words were directed to her.

"You have disgraced the family," Oliver Pasipano yelled. "What will your sisters think when they hear what you've done?"

There was silence, thicker than Oliver's roaring voice. Priscilla sat up, her nightdress slipping off her to reveal her scrawny shoulders. She put her feet on the ground, curiosity and fear urging her out of bed.

Of all the Pasipano children, Priscilla was the one Oliver seemed to hate the most. Of course, he loathed the fact that he had fathered only girls who couldn't keep his name going, but Priscilla knew that of all the girls she was somehow the one who ignited his anger with just her appearance. She always wondered if being the youngest was the reason, or perhaps it was the fact that after she was born her mother had not been able to have any more children. She knew this because she would eavesdrop when her grandmother and aunts were talking. They would say that she ruined her mother's ability to have sons. The guilt wore heavily on nine-year-old Priscilla. She believed that was why her father was always angry at the sight of her.

She realized the moment she opened her bedroom door that she should have stayed inside her room with Rutendo.

"Priscilla! Come out here," Oliver shouted, his bearded face lined with anger. His usually clear eyes were red and the lines on his forehead deep like a muddy road, carved by tractor wheels. Priscilla walked into the short passage on trembling legs. She tried to take in the scene in front of her, but it took a moment for her eyes to adjust to the light in the room. Vimbai, her 15-year-old sister, stood next to the bathroom holding her stomach. Her face was drawn and covered with tears. She shivered on the cold floor. Her mother stood a few steps from Vimbai, looking down sadly, as if she had caused whatever problem they all faced.

"This child has disgraced the family. She is pregnant!" The words made Vimbai flinch as if she had been slapped. "And this wife, this mother of yours, tried to keep it from me. That's why they say for a goat to eat cabbage tree leaves is to imitate its mother. You are just like your mother," Oliver yelled.

Priscilla looked from her mother to her father, wishing she had stayed in bed and pretended to be asleep. She was confused and she wondered if she was still sleeping, her dream of her grandmother's village now truly a nightmare.

"I'm going to punish all of you for this terrible mistake. You! Vimbai. Tomorrow we take you to the man who is responsible."

Vimbai looked up, terror in her eyes.

"And you, so you never do this, you are going to sleep outside tonight," Oliver said, pointing to Priscilla. Monica looked up with shock but quickly looked down. "I won't have my children being impregnated by any man that I have never heard of. You all need to learn from this," Oliver said, looking directly at Monica. "I hold you responsible, mother of my children. You are the one who failed to protect your daughters because you are too busy sewing, baking . . . for whom?"

Then Oliver turned his angry eyes on Priscilla. "You go outside, now," Oliver said and stepped forward and began to push Priscilla towards the door. Her bare feet slid on the shiny, polished cement floor. She had no shoes and she knew it was freezing outside. Monica lifted her hand to stop Oliver, but he ignored his wife's gesture.

"Ma," Priscilla pleaded, but Monica just shook her head. Tears were in her eyes. At the same time, Vimbai began to sob softly. Her crying sounded like a trickling waterfall. When thrust outside, Priscilla huddled in a corner of the veranda and wrapped her skinny arms around herself. She felt terror, as she imagined being attacked by the witches and thieves of her grandmother's folktales. She heard an owl shriek and huddled closer to the wall.

I'm going to die, Priscilla thought, and somehow thinking that filled her with peace. She wouldn't have to live in fear anymore. Fear of her father's hatred and anger that was an invisible force, like the heat of the sun or the sound of thunder.

She heard the door open, wishing it was her mother coming to call her in. It was Vimbai. Her older sister crouched beside her then gave her the blanket from her bed. She put it around Priscilla and sat next to her. Priscilla opened up the blanket and allowed Vimbai to share its comfort. They didn't dare say anything. Speaking might wake their father and increase his wrath. They fell asleep, keeping each other warm.

The next morning, the two young girls woke up to a chilly sunny June day. Outside the gate they could see people walking to work, others carrying wares to sell at the market. They looked at the street quietly for a while. Vimbai turned to look at Priscilla.

"What's going to happen?" Priscilla asked her older sister. Their closeness made life bearable. Vimbai always tried to protect Priscilla, wiping her tears when her father was angry or bringing her food when Oliver had forbidden her to eat.

"I think I'm going to be leaving." The announcement terrified Priscilla. Priscilla saw the tears fall down her face.

"Is that what happened to Hope?" Priscilla asked. She was too young to remember how their oldest sister left home.

"*Akatizira*," Vimbai said, and, seeing Priscilla didn't understand, added, "She eloped. It means she found out she was having a baby and ran away to go to the husband before Baba knew she was pregnant."

"Was *Baba* angry?"

"Of course. She still hadn't finished form four. And Baba had paid for her exam fee. At least he hasn't paid mine or he would have been angrier."

Priscilla nodded, still not sure she understood. Running away or being chased away, all seemed just as bad.

"I better go and get dressed. I don't want to make *Baba* angrier."

"No. Don't go. I want you to stay," Priscilla cried, her heart breaking at the prospect of not being with Vimbai.

"Don't make it worse, Pripri. Don't cry," Vimbai said, glancing fearfully at the door, reverting to the nickname she called Priscilla when she was a baby. Priscilla took gulps of air and tried to stop her crying. She shut her eyes tightly. Fresh tears stopped, but she still had the old ones that Vimbai wiped with her hand. Vimbai seemed to be building up strength for what lay ahead. Vimbai got up and went into the house, leaving Priscilla alone outside.

A few hours later, the family stood outside in a formal, stiff line. Thirteen-year-old Rutendo had been told the details by a grim Monica. Rutendo's eyes darkened with anger as she stood next to Priscilla. Vimbai was dressed in her favorite yellow dress with red flowers. She wore her school shoes with white socks and looked even younger than her fifteen years. Oliver stood straight like a pole next to her as he gave money to his second cousin, *Sekuru* Peter, who was to deliver Vimbai to the man who had made her pregnant. There was no yelling that morning just a sad acceptance of what was to be done. Outside the neighborhood was coming alive. Priscilla could hear a man chanting as he made his way to the market to sell his wares.

"*Muriwo werepi, matomatisi onions.*" He passed by everyday singing his wares out to all who would hear. Today, even he seemed to be moving slower and the burden of his merchandise, dark green leaves, tomatoes and onions, seemed to wear him down. Later another man rode by on his bike selling eggs, yelling "*mazai apo*" at the top of his voice, the wheels of his bike spinning and picking up dust on the red gravel road.

"*Chienda.* Go. Go," Oliver commanded, pushing Vimbai towards the car. Priscilla looked at her mother, wanting her to say something or do something, but Monica just stood there, her expression unreadable. It was one of the most difficult things she had ever done, but Priscilla kept her sobs locked up deep inside as she watched her sister get in the car. Oliver folded his arms across his chest and seemed satisfied at his perfect punishment for his wayward daughter.

Part I

Deception—Nhema

CHAPTER 1
Muchato—Wedding

When Priscilla woke up the day of her parents' wedding, she didn't know that her life was about to change forever. There is a saying in Shona that would always remind her of that day. *Rine manyanga hazviputirwe,* that which has horns cannot be wrapped up. On that day the truth did come out, and it shook Priscilla's life.

Why were they having a wedding anyway, she wondered. What was the use? They had been husband and wife for over thirty years, and, as far as Priscilla was concerned, it had not been a happy marriage.

Lately in Zimbabwe, the new trend had been to get married again, in church with the priest, the white dress and bridesmaids. To her thinking, her mother should've been running away instead of making new commitments to Oliver in front of people and God, too. Besides, her father had always upheld traditional values, shunning the western culture like a disease. This wedding seemed so against his nature.

What stood out for Priscilla from the wedding were the words she heard after the celebration was over. How can seven words change your life so easily? The words obliterated everything that happened before the wedding, hours spent cooking beef stew and grilled chicken. She completely forgot about the night she'd spent decorating the hall with red balloons and plastic flowers with her sisters and women from the neighborhood. She barely remembered the brick church that was packed with invited and uninvited guests, and the walk from the church to the school hall where the reception took place.

The wedding was over and her parents drove off in a flurry of goodbyes and drumbeats. The women sang and danced with joy. Priscilla didn't join in. Oliver and Monica didn't go home, but had booked a hotel for the night. Their bags were in the trunk of the car taking them to the Nyamayaro Hotel.

Priscilla felt a little joy trickle in her heart as she began to take off the tablecloths that had been donated by one of her mother's friends. She would have to wash them before returning them the next day.

Her surprising joy gave her energy as she continued to work, though she had hardly slept the past two days. Priscilla walked over to her sister.

"For old people it wasn't such a bad wedding," Rutendo said, taking out a tube of lipstick and applying it to her full lips. Rutendo had left home as soon as she had a job. Priscilla recalled Oliver screaming and shouting for weeks after Rutendo left. She was the rebel of the Pasipano daughters, and was very proud of her reputation.

"I know. But we have so much work to do now," Priscilla said, looking around the hall. There were many people helping to clear the food and sweep the mess on the floor, but more hands were needed. Yes, after months of planning, the wedding was now over and it had been more fun than Priscilla had expected.

"You do it, Priscilla. I'm leaving soon," Rutendo said.

"Why are you leaving us to do everything?"

"I have a date," Rutendo said and rushed off, not caring that the rest of her sisters had to help with the cleaning. Priscilla was about to call out when Vimbai walked over to her.

"Leave her," Vimbai said. Priscilla was about to argue when she noticed a deep sadness in Vimbai's eyes. Besides, it was hard to argue with Vimbai. She had a gentle way about her that made it hard to say even a cross word to her. She was the total opposite of Rutendo, so considerate and kind in her words and actions. Rutendo had always wanted to do her own thing and not follow any traditional protocol, especially the way women had to work at every event until their hands and feet hurt. Rutendo didn't care what anybody said about her. She would not be that kind of woman.

"Didn't Gilbert come?" Priscilla asked about her sister's husband. Even saying his name left a very bitter taste in Priscilla's mouth. She had witnessed too much of Gilbert's poor treatment of Vimbai to feel kindly towards him. Even when Vimbai lost the first baby and then the second, Priscilla had always blamed it on his cruelty.

"No. He said he would come, but I think he was too busy at work . . ."

"Vimbai. I'm your sister. What's going on with you two? Gilbert never visits us, and the few times I've seen him he has been very disrespectful to you."

"That's how marriage is," Vimbai said meekly, picking up empty Coke bottles and putting them in the crates. Priscilla's face twisted in disgust.

"Men are supposed to be that way?"

"Most men. They don't know any better," Vimbai said.

"Is that how your life has to be?"

"You'll see when you get married."

Priscilla shook her head. "If marriage is having a man cheat on you, beat you up and treat you like dirt, then it is not for me."

"He's nice sometimes," Vimbai said half-heartedly, but there was sorrow in her voice. She started taking off the white tablecloths from the tables and folding them into neat squares.

"Let me take the cloths to the inner room, and then I'll come and help pile up the chairs," Priscilla said, walking away from Vimbai and thoughts of her husband. She walked towards a smaller room at the back of the hall with the pile of white tablecloths.

With the door closed tight, she had to put down the tablecloths before it. There were some distant relatives talking in the kitchen and she recognized some of them to be her father's cousins. She listened with dismay as she heard Oliver's half sister, Beauty's voice.

"Did you see the way Rutendo was dancing?"

"She is a whore, that one. Living in the Avenues and dating a married man."

Priscilla felt heat build up in her with her rage. How dare they? No matter how Rutendo lived her life, hearing her relatives call her names infuriated her.

"You know what they say. The son of a snake is a snake. Aunt Monica is not an angel herself."

"I never thought he would have a wedding with her," Beauty said.

"Ah. Sometimes I wonder about your brother. That woman put him through so much. And that Priscilla child is not even his, but Monica forced him to look after her as if she was. She never gave him the son he wanted and still . . ."

Priscilla stood frozen for a second, unbelieving, and then afraid someone would see her. She quickly opened the door and stumbled into another tiny room stacked with empty crates. She closed the door and let the words she had just heard sink in. Swiftly her anger was replaced by shock.

'That Priscilla child is not even his.' No! It couldn't be.

Priscilla closed the door and leaned against it, her heart beating with the shock of the few simple words that could change everything, if true. Before she could even think or digest what she'd heard, she heard footsteps approaching the room. She quickly opened the door and met Vimbai, who was holding a crate of drinks.

"Oh, Pri. I was wondering where you'd gone. There are more tablecloths out there. Can you get them?"

"Oh. Sure," she replied in creaky voice.

"Are you okay, Pri? You don't look well."

"Tired. You know last night we didn't sleep while we were busy decorating the hall and then cooking the chicken by the fire. I think I'm now feeling the lack of sleep." Priscilla lied with difficulty, but she did feel tired.

The energy she had felt a few minutes ago was gone, replaced by cold dread and weariness.

She tried very hard to push what she'd heard out of her mind, but the words kept repeating over and over in her head. She couldn't stop hearing them, and the more she thought about them the more she believed them. Those words explained everything.

That Priscilla child is not even his.

CHAPTER 2
Hupenyu—Life

Vimbai arrived at her home in Gweru a day after the wedding. She had enjoyed the wedding, but would have been happier if Gilbert also came. It wasn't that she enjoyed his company; she hated it when everybody kept asking her where he was. When she told him he laughed, saying he wouldn't waste his time driving to Harare to the wedding of the man he hated. Gilbert still resented her family for making him marry her.

It wasn't easy traveling with two young children, but Chipo and Max always behaved well. It seemed they knew that their mother had a lot on her plate and didn't want to add to her burdens.

Her tiny home in Middlebelt was dark when she arrived. It was as if nobody was home. When she opened the door, the first thing that greeted her were bottles of beer on the kitchen table. Some was spilled on the tiled floor. Her heart sank at the sight. The sink overflowed with dirty pots and plates.

"Sit down here," Vimbai whispered to three-year-old Max. He nodded understanding. After putting the bag on the floor, Vimbai pulled Chipo from her back. The little girl slept deeply. Vimbai laid her on the sofa and stretched her back. She walked gingerly down the narrow, short passage. It was almost 7 o'clock. The bus was delayed in Kwekwe, so she arrived much later than she wanted to.

She reached the bedroom she shared with Gilbert and opened the door. Gilbert was sleeping on his back, but she almost screamed when she saw movement under the covers. She gasped and clutched her chest. Gilbert opened his eyes. She could see they were blood shot. A woman sat up and looked at her with surprise.

"What are you doing here?" Gilbert asked and burped.

Vimbai didn't answer as she stared at the stranger in her bed, shaking with shock and fear. Gilbert demanded again. "I said what are you doing here, woman?"

"I-I am back from the wedding," Vimbai stammered, her eyes veering from Gilbert to the woman next to him.

"Who told you to come back today?"

"You said I shouldn't stay too long. I . . ."

"You are a stupid woman. Get out of here!"

"Gilbert. Please. The children are in the house."

He sprung up, making to strike her, his hand held high in a familiar gesture. Vimbai jumped back.

"If you don't leave now I will hit you! Go and sleep with your children. I'm busy here."

Tears sprung to Vimbai's eyes as she walked away quickly, afraid of being hit again. Max was still sitting where she had left him. She took his hand and went to pick up Chipo. She went into the spare room, made a floor bed and laid down with her children. It was all too familiar. Her mother had been through the same treatment. She wouldn't cry in front of Max, but her blood had turned to tears.

Priscilla had spent a miserable week. She couldn't talk to anyone about her feelings, or the shock of what she heard at her parents' wedding. Vimbai had left soon after the wedding, so she couldn't talk to her sister. She wasn't close to Hope and Rutendo at all. So she made her way to the bus stop to visit her favorite aunt, Mukai, when the weekend arrived. She realized that she had to talk to someone.

During the week, she went to work and then home as usual on the city bus, hating being home and feeling trapped. She thought back to the way her father had treated her over the years. Her childhood had been horrific because of him. She had spent all her school years trying to please him, trying to make him stop resenting her, but no matter what she did he always treated her like a dirty, unwanted child. She always felt that it was her fault, but was it really? Was she his wife's bastard? Did he hate her and punish her because of that? Questions filled her mind.

If he is not my father, then who is? Is he alive? Does he know about me and miss me?

Priscilla sat alone on the bus wondering how the day that was supposed to fill her with so much hope for the future had turned out to be the day that shook the ground she stood on. She always hoped each stage of her life would be the start of a new and beautiful phase, like the butterfly shedding its past.

When she started first grade she wanted to do well at school, hoping her father would start to look at her with pride instead of distaste. When his expressions didn't change she looked forward to high school. In high school she went away to boarding school, and she imagined he would miss her so much that when she came back home he would welcome her with open arms and realize how much she meant to him. When that didn't happen, getting a great job had been the next big step. But all that brought were more grunts and disgruntled comments.

When she heard her parents wanted to renew their vows by having a real wedding ceremony, Priscilla's hopes rose again. Weddings were romantic and joyful events; it could only bring her family the harmony that was lacking during all the years as she had grown up. The day came and went, but the opposite happened.

She looked out the dusty window as other passengers boarded the Zupco bus. Women carried babies on their backs as well as grocery bags and baskets of vegetables. She watched an old woman gather her three full bags and try to get on the bus.

Glenview had been her home since she was born. It was a highly populated neighborhood started just after Zimbabwe won its independence from the United Kingdom. Somehow over the years almost all the people who had started building their homes had never completed them. She studied all the homes as the bus chugged along, halting at various bus stops to add more people to its green seats.

She was now used to the sight of these homes. Some houses had no windows, others were not painted and others only got the foundation done before the money ran out. So it was rare to find a house that was complete in most parts of Glenview. She also knew that in most of those homes, more than one family inhabited the small space. It was not surprising to find a family of six using three rooms and another family of four using the other two rooms and then sharing the kitchen and bathrooms.

The scenery began to change as they moved out of Glenview and other similar but older neighborhoods. After that, the factories emerged. She could smell the chemicals in the air as she passed one factory that manu-factured soap and cooking oil, right across from another residential area. She passed a trucking company, a cereal company and then an ice-cream company.

Finally, they reached the downtown area. The build-ings there appeared shabby, but, as you got closer to the city center, the skyscrapers became more attractive high rises with shiny glass windows. Fast Mercedes Benzes and pick-up trucks overtook the bus she sat on.

After almost an hour-long journey, she jumped off the mini bus and walked towards Mukai's house. The neighborhood was peaceful with half acre to acre homes. She walked past the servants' quarters, the cottage and the garage. She knocked on the kitchen door and the maid opened it with wet soapy hands.

"*Hesi*, Sisi Ruva. How are you? Is Auntie home?" Priscilla asked the older chubby woman. Ruva had worked for Aunt Mukai for over fifteen years and she was like a family member, a grandmother to Priscilla.

"*Hesi*, Priscilla," Ruva greeted her, smiling. "Yes. She's in the lounge."

Priscilla walked in and her aunt, who had been sitting on the sofa reading a book, looked at her and smiled.

"Pri, my child, hello." They hugged tightly and Priscilla felt her eyes fill with tears. She blinked them back.

"How are you?"

"Very happy that you are here. You won't believe who's here, too."

"Who?"

"Unashe."

"Really? He's here?"

"Yes. He was on the phone in my bedroom. Go and tell him to get off. He'll run up my phone bill."

Priscilla walked with excitement towards her aunt's bedroom. She opened the door and peered at Unashe, who lay on the bed with his shoes on the pristine white duvet cover.

He smiled, sat up and waved.

"Hey, I have to go. Can I call you later tonight?" He was now looking at his feet. Priscilla stood there watching him, arms crossed. He hung up the phone and got up. As he strode toward her, his gorgeous grin lit up his handsome face.

"Priscilla, is that you?"

"Yes. And you, Unashe, you have changed."

She walked towards him and they hugged briefly. When she looked at him, Priscilla had completely forgotten her troubles of before. She was just so happy to see him.

"So. You have finally decided to come and visit your ma and the rest of us," Priscilla scolded him playfully. The last time she came to visit Mukai, Unashe had been working in Bulawayo. Even though it was only six hours away by bus, Unashe rarely came to visit. She took his arm and led him out of Mukai's bedroom and towards the living room.

"Come on, your mother told me to get you off the phone. Who were you talking to?"

"A friend."

"A girlfriend? Is that why you don't come and visit your ma?"

"Just a friend who is a girl. I came last year but I couldn't get to see everyone. I had to get back to work."

"You know how sons are. Work and fun is more important than their mother," Mukai complained as they entered the living room. Priscilla could tell by the smile on her face that Mukai adored her son. She looked at him as if he was a miracle, unable to believe that she had such a handsome, intelligent son. Unfortunately, she seemed to overlook his lack of ambition.

Unashe walked to his mother and put his arm around her. "Mum, at least now you know I'm not going back there again. Working for Uncle Tim was okay at first, but relatives take advantage of you and don't give you any time off work. And managing a clothing store is not really what I want to spend the rest of my life doing."

"And what do you want to do?" Priscilla asked him as she studied him standing next to his mum. He was so tall, and had developed muscles revealed by the vest he wore. The last time she had seen him he had been a skinny boy with a long, thin body. Things sure had changed. Still he was the same person who she had always been able to talk to about anything, and he had always listened with such understanding.

"I think I just want to get out of this country and study some banking or business. I'm working on it," Unashe said.

"It's more like I am working on it," Mukai said sitting on the sofa. "Una. Why don't you bring us some juice? Priscilla looks thirsty."

"I'll help you," Priscilla volunteered, walking towards the kitchen with Unashe closely behind her. Unashe took the glasses while she took the drink from the refrigerator. "It's good to see you. It's been a long time."

"It's nice to see you, too, Cilla."

"You still call me Cilla. Nobody calls me that."

"They call you Pri. Cilla suits your personality better. That name suits a girl who gets bothered by guys on buses."

"Please. It's very irritating. Today it was Takesure."

Unashe laughed. "Takesure? What kind of boys do you attract?"

"Rude and annoying. What about you? Are you still dating Chantel?"

"Oh, Chantel. It's over already. When I left here I told her to forget about me," Unashe said, holding the glasses out and really showing off. Priscilla laughed. Unashe smiled, and that made his eyes disappear. He had the most sensitive and caring eyes. Mukai was an attractive woman and her son was the same way, with defined cheekbones and full lips. Priscilla knew many girls liked him and wasn't surprised he was breaking hearts all over Harare.

"Oh, you are heartless. Why couldn't you keep in touch? She liked you a lot."

"I don't think I ever want any woman to come between me and my career plans. It's too important. You know how you women are. Too demanding," Unashe said. "I just want a girl when it's convenient for me."

"You are mean, but you are right, too. Relationships can take time. With my work schedule I don't have time for men and don't want any relationship to come between me and my job."

"That's my girl," Unashe said, nodding his head in agreement. "Come, we better take the drinks."

Mukai was standing watering her plants. She looked at them as they walked in. With her glasses lowered, she reminded Priscilla of one of her science teachers.

"You took your sweet time," Mukai said. "Were you squeezing the oranges?"

"Just catching up," Unashe said, putting two glasses down without a tray.

"Aren't you having a drink?" Mukai asked when she saw the two glasses. She picked up each one and placed it on a coaster. She wiped her table with her fingers, making a disapproving sound that Unashe totally ignored.

"I have to go. I'm meeting a friend who has been in the UK."

"Oh," Mukai said.

"I better go. Cilla, I'll see you a lot more now that I'm here with nothing to do."

"So you are leaving already? Bye, then."

Unashe laughed and disappeared into his bedroom. When he appeared a few minutes later, he'd changed. He left with a wave.

"Are you glad he's back?" Priscilla asked her aunt as they sat having a drink in the comfortable living room.

"Oh yes. I miss him so much when he's away," Mukai said, leaning into her cushions. "And now he's talking of leaving the country."

Priscilla could understand her sadness. As soon as Unashe had walked out of the room, she'd missed him, too. He was full of laughs and energy and when he left it was as if the room got a little dimmer. Besides, talking to him helped her to lighten up, to forget things.

"Are you sad?"

"Mixed feelings. I want him to experience all there is out there in the world, but I wish he could stay," Mukai said. "How are your parents, anyway? The newlyweds?"

Priscilla felt the lump in her throat and suddenly tears filled her eyes.

"What's wrong, Pri? I know something upset you at the wedding, and I wished you could tell me. I know my side of the family can be mean. They talk rubbish,"

Mukai said, putting her glass down. An expression of concern was all over her face. Mukai's expression broke Priscilla and she sobbed.

"Aunty, you won't believe what it was. I just don't know what to think of it all."

"What? What happened?" Mukai asked.

"Is *Baba* my real father?" Priscilla asked her eyes red and full of questions. Her heart beat with dread as she watched the shock on Mukai's face. The shock changed and turned to sympathy.

"How did you find out about Oliver?"

"Oh, my God!" Priscilla stood up, covering her mouth, realising that it must be true.

Mukai stood up and pulled the crying girl into her arms.

CHAPTER 3
Amai—Mother

Priscilla looked at her mother, seeing her as if for the first time. It's true she had always talked to her, spent each day with her, but did she really know her?

Monica was in her garden, pulling up annoying weeds from her precious vegetables, her blue dress covered by a huge flowery apron. Priscilla was not far from her, picking up the green leaves of ripe vegetables to be cooked for supper with fried *matemba* fish.

The neighborhood was enjoying a cool summer day and all around her she could hear people talking, music playing from little radios and the children next door playing *pada*. Priscilla could hear the little girls throwing rocks and imagined the crudely drawn boxes that they jumped in to pick up the rock. She had played the same game of hopscotch with Vimbai, so long ago.

Priscilla wanted to ask her mother about what Mukai had told her, the long story, the dreadful things Oliver had done in the name of love. However, she knew she couldn't. Monica wasn't one for confidences, even with her children. Monica's thoughts were closed tight, hidden behind her serene eyes.

"Is that all we are eating tonight?" Monica asked, looking at the five dark green leaves in Priscilla's hand.

"Oh, sorry," Priscilla said and gave a short, strained laugh. She began to pick more of the vegetables in the way she had been taught. Starting from the bottom and not picking up the new leaves, her mind going back to what Mukai had told her, remembering each word as if Mukai was speaking to her in her mother's garden.

"Before you were born, your father, Oliver, kicked your mother out as if she was a dog. He took another wife, Lindiwe. He hoped your mother would be destroyed and unable to fend for herself, but he was wrong. That's not your mother. She got a job very quickly and soon suitors were knocking down her door. That's where your real father came in."

Real father, Priscilla thought, still reeling from the possibility of a loving father somewhere. Mukai's voice came back to her again, filling in all the missing pieces of Monica's life.

"I believe she fell in love with him, and when your father heard this he went completely berserk with jealousy. He forced her back to him and kicked Lindiwe out. You see if your mother had been miserable and unhappy he wouldn't have wanted her back, but her success and happiness led him to take her back again. He wanted to contain her in a nice, neat little box that he could keep and control. He would only bring her joy when he felt like it."

Now Priscilla took a deep breath and looked at Monica. She wondered why her mother had stayed with Oliver if he treated her so badly. Why?

She had asked her aunt the same questions. "He who has not carried your burden does not know how it weighs," Mukai had said.

Besides the news that Oliver was not her father, she realized that Mukai wasn't her real aunt, either. Not that she was Oliver's sister. The only reason that Mukai was close to the Pasipano family was because when Oliver's mother couldn't look after him after she remarried, Mukai's mother, who was Oliver's aunt, had taken him in and raised him until Oliver left to pursue his own life in the city. Still, she was very hurt by the fact that she didn't share any blood with people she had thought the world of. She recalled what she said to her aunt at the end of the revelation.

"Ever since I have known you, I've been proud to be related to you. Just knowing that you are my blood and you had accomplished so much just gave me hope. I admire my mother and love her dearly, but you are the only one who stood up for me when *Baba* was cruel to me. You stood up to him and told him that he was being unreasonable. You helped him see reason so I could go to college to pursue my programming course. I felt like I could get some of your courage and independence. And now. We are not related. You are just someone who has no connection with me at all. We are not kin."

"Priscilla, that doesn't matter."

"It does, though."

"Not to me, it doesn't. I'm not a traditionalist who only helps those who are my blood relatives. I do what I want and I think for myself. I choose what's fair, not what's always been done or what the elders want. I've known since you were born that you were not my blood, but I loved you when I saw you in hospital. You were so pretty, so calm and sweet. Your parentage was the biggest known secret of the family. We all knew, but we just never talked about it, like it was taboo."

Back at home, Priscilla went to the kitchen and started cutting the vegetables, small and even, the way Monica said Oliver liked them. But Mukai's words had shifted something in her. If she had any chance of escaping the kind of life her mother lived, she would have to take hold of her destiny.

One thing was certain. She knew that she couldn't live at home any more.

CHAPTER 4
Shamwari—Friends

Chamunorwa Tengani made his way in the elevator up to the sixth floor of the twelve-story building. Once there, the eager receptionist led him personally to the programming department. Everybody knew him at Computer Management Solutions (CMS). He and the modernization of the companies he owned was one of the reasons CMS was so profitable. He was CMS's biggest client. As he entered the software department, his eyes spotted the reason he'd chosen to do business with CMS and he felt his heart rate quicken.

Priscilla sat by a computer in her office with her back to Chamu. He tapped gently on the open door and she turned to him with a smile.

"Good morning, Mr. Tengani."

"Call me Chamu. Remember, we went to school together."

Priscilla had been in charge of his payroll program for some weeks, and now he looked forward to hearing her progress as much as a child anticipated going to

Greenwood Park to jump on the trampoline. He'd known her in high school, but though they talked he'd never had the courage to ask her out. He saw how other young men were burned when they tried to get to know her, and he laughed at them while at the same time being relieved she had let them down. He shook his head at the memory of how unsophisticated he had been in high school. Now he was sure he had the confidence to get closer to her.

"Okay, Chamu. I just finished checking your program. Do you want to take a look?" she asked, pulling a chair up for him.

He cleared his throat as he sat next to her. She looked beautiful in her dark blue striped skirt and soft white blouse. Priscilla reminded him of a fresh morning after a gentle rain. She was perfect and unspoiled. Her smile astounded him. She worked fast on the computer, and soon her program appeared on the screen.

"This is for your car rental company. I included all the features you requested and added extra modules that I thought would be helpful," she explained, her eyes on the screen and her long, elegant fingers working on the keyboard. "As you can see here, you may also use the same program for sales management and even for your payroll."

Chamu watched her, enjoying her voice, her face, and her busy hands. Yes, she was like that wild plum turning red on the tree to attract attention. He had noticed her and wanted to reach out and taste her. Her milk chocolate skin was smooth, and he knew it would be soft and satiny to his fingers. She was respectful and intelligent, and he would do anything to get her.

Chamu didn't believe in luck or superstition. If he wanted something, he went out and got it. The Shona people were generally known for being passive, in history having endured other tribes stealing their women and raiding their livestock without fighting back even when they had more people. He didn't like his people's reputation, and in his own life did some of his own raiding but avoided stealing. If there was something to be taken, a company or woman, then by all his ancestors he wanted to be the one taking, not losing. He knew he had the advantage over most of the young people who worked with Priscilla. Most of them didn't have much to offer a woman like her. But now he had the wealth, the confidence and the smarts to win her.

He glanced at her, then back at the screen, trying to focus on her words. She explained all the different programs and demonstrated some examples of the new software included in the package. After almost an hour, she had gone through the whole program. His questions and desire to understand everything stretched what should have been a 30-minute demonstration. But she didn't mind. Her bosses would be very happy if Chamu Tengani was happy.

"What do you think?" she asked finally, looking at him with steady eyes. He could tell she wanted to please him, and that made him feel good. What amazed him was that she seemed not to be aware of the effect she had on him.

"I thought it was splendid. What I wanted and more," he said, and almost laughed when he saw how happy she looked. She seemed relieved and the smile that brightened her face fascinated him. If only she knew. "I think you deserve a special lunch from our company, and I will be delighted to take you somewhere nice."

"Lunch? I still have plenty of work to do," Priscilla said, looking at her watch.

"Go for lunch, Priscilla. You deserve it." Priscilla turned, surprised to see her boss, Ryan Cronsby, standing behind her. His red hair was cut close to his scalp, and there was a smile of welcome on his red, sun-burned-face.

Chamu shook Ryan's hand, annoyed by the interruption.

"How are you, sir," Ryan said with respect. Priscilla enjoyed seeing the man grovel for a change. He was not a nice person to work for. He didn't believe in breaks, and that included lunch.

"It's lunch time. After such a great job your boss knows you deserve to take a break," Chamu said.

"To be perfectly honest I rarely have the chance to eat lunch, but since I've finished your program I can spare a few minutes before I plan the next step of installing all your information. We have hired data captures to do that for you," Priscilla said, looking at Ryan, who nodded with approval.

"Take your time, Priscilla. You did a great job on this account. I'll give you a call later, Mr. Tengani. Enjoy your lunch."

"Thank you."

Chamu could barely contain his excitement as he watched Priscilla pick up her jacket and purse.

As they drove to lunch in his silver Mercedes Benz, Chamu explained how he had become so successful at such a young age.

His father, Jonathan Obert Tengani, had given him his businesses to manage when he fell ill. Chamu had moved from owning one shop to owning a bottle store, and had then decided to leave the retail business. Now he was in many different business ventures ranging from car rentals, taxis and a chain of furniture stores. Priscilla knew about some of his businesses because she'd worked on developing computer software programs for most of them. She also knew his businesses were flourishing. She listened intently, wondering if he could offer Unashe a job. Unashe was interested in finance, but she decided she would ask him about it later.

At the charming restaurant away from the busy downtown, the waiter dressed formally in black and white led them to their table.

"Well I hope you'll like this restaurant," Chamu said as they reached their seats. He pulled her chair for her and they sat down facing each other. Chamu watched Priscilla closely, noting how much she enjoyed being treated like a lady and suspecting that she never gave many men the opportunity to do so. He was lucky because he had known her in high school. She felt quite comfortable with him. and of course, that clown Ryan Cronsby may have helped him get this lunch date, too. She asked about his other sister who had been a year ahead of her at Goromonzi High School.

"Chido is now married."

"Is that so? It's hard to think that people I went to school with are already married."

"You could be married, too."

Priscilla laughed, taking a sip of her orange juice. "What about you?"

"Not yet found the right woman," Chamu said, keeping his gaze on the menu. "So what made you decide to get into computers? You are really good at it."

"I heard that computers were becoming important and I could get a good job. I think it was my science teacher who told me."

"Mr. Madziro?"

"Yes. Did he teach you, too?"

Chamu nodded. "Oh, yes. A very angry man."

"And Mrs. Madziro taught me math. She didn't like me."

"What? Somebody didn't like you?"

Priscilla laughed. "Actually Mrs. Madziro didn't like anybody. She told all the girls they wouldn't amount to anything because they gossiped too much and danced with boys at the disco."

"I never saw you at the disco."

"I had to study. I wasn't that smart. It wasn't easy for me to stay in Goromonzi. I think I only got in because we had family connections."

"Really. The year I got in, they were choosing people according to height. They lined us up and the head-master walked down the line looking at us."

Priscilla laughed and Chamu continued laughing, too.

"The guys on either side of me were sent away. One was too tall and the other was too old. He just said to them 'too tall, too old, no, you won't do' and he sent them out the door."

"So you were the right height and didn't look too old."

"That's right," Chamu said.

"How about dessert?" Chamu asked at the end of the meal. Priscilla declined, putting the white napkin on the table.

"I must get back to work. Today I can't work as late as I'd like to. I'm looking for a flat."

"Oh. I can take you if you like," Chamu offered graciously, uncertain how he felt about her living in a flat. He would have to think about it. It could be a good thing if he played his cards right. He could tell Priscilla was quite surprised at his offer, but after a while shook her head.

"No, it's all right. I must do this on my own."

"I don't mind. Do you have a car to drive around at night?" Chamu asked.

"No . . . I-I'll manage. Actually, my aunt will be quite happy to take me around."

"Are you sure?" Chamu persisted, trying to hide his disappointment.

"Absolutely. We better go."

Chamu stood up reluctantly. Spending time with Priscilla was the highlight of his whole year, no, make that his whole life, and she wanted to end it too quickly. But her laughter and her smile as he told her his stories would keep him going until he saw her again.

CHAPTER 5
Koromoka—Fall Down

Unashe heard the loud bang outside his window. He cocked his head to the side, wondering what the sound could be. The air was damp from the drizzle outside and he wondered if what he heard was lightning and thunder. He heard the sound again, and this time it sounded unmistakably like somebody was hitting the thick metal gate with something hard. Heart racing, Unashe put on a shirt and picked up the umbrella he had put by his door when he left the main house to come and sleep at the cottage, alone like an independent man. He had to check what the problem was. He was the only man of the house and it was up to him to protect his mother, who slept peacefully in the main house.

Checking the clock, which showed 12:07 a.m., he heard the loud sound again and this time he opened the door and picked up a huge brick by the side of the house. If a thief was trying to break in, he would be in for a thrashing. Unashe recalled hearing about the burglaries in various homes in the neighborhood as he walked slowly towards the gate, avoiding the wet puddles and mud. He heard the sound again as he got closer, but it sounded weaker this time. He heard a sound like a woman sobbing, and threw the brick down and inched closer to the gate.

When he opened the peephole, he nearly died of shock. It was Priscilla, and she was soaked from head to toe.

She practically fell into his arms.

"What happened?" he asked looking around to see if she had come with anybody else. All he saw was an empty street lighted by one single bulb on a high pole.

"It's crazy," Priscilla said, breathing hard. He could feel her heart beat fast beneath his arm. "You won't believe what happened." Priscilla's mind went back a few hours before she found herself outside Unashe's house.

Monica Pasipano cooked supper as her husband read the paper in the sitting room. Her lovely face looked peaceful and serene as she stirred the pot, but she was actually worried about Priscilla, who wasn't home yet. She heard the rattle of the gate. She wanted to run and check but she decided not to as Oliver would think she was worried and then become upset with Priscilla. Oliver had changed since the old days, but some old habits were hard to lose. One was his attitude towards Priscilla. She walked in and greeted her father as Monica listened from the kitchen.

"Good evening, *Baba*," Priscilla greeted Oliver.

"Good evening," he replied in a gruff voice. The living room was small but had all the necessary furniture, a four piece sofa set, TV and a framed photograph of the family on the wall. Priscilla wasn't in the particular portrait, as she wasn't born yet. It had her three sisters, mother, and father. Actually, there were no pictures of her on the walls. Now it all made sense to her.

She walked into the kitchen feeling the walls closing in on her. Unashe had dropped her off and left. He didn't get along with her father. Not many people liked Oliver. He would have lectured Unashe on his lack of employment.

"Good evening, Mama," Priscilla greeted her mother.

"Good evening. You are quite late. Were you still at work?" Monica asked as she busily wiped the stove. Priscilla watched her mother's movements. The stove was already spotless, but Monica wanted it to shine.

"Yes," Priscilla lied, but she didn't want to explain her whereabouts. At least not yet. Maybe after supper when she was sure she would be leaving this house for good in the morning she would explain where she'd been. She was so glad about how easy it would all be. The agent had told her she could move into her flat anytime after signing the lease agreement, and she paid the deposit and first month's rent. Normally half her income went to her father, but now she would be using it for her own place.

"You work too hard," her mother said.

Priscilla nodded and then sat on the kitchen chairs.

"Do you want help with anything?" she asked.

"No, my dear. You can go and change if you like,"

Priscilla walked into her bedroom and took off her earrings and work clothes. She put on her home dress and sat on her narrow bed. Her bedroom was very simple, with a dresser in one corner and a fitted wardrobe against one wall. The curtains were white with blue flowers and would not have been her choice at all. She couldn't live here anymore.

She didn't even feel like she belonged there. She left her bedroom and walked down the narrow passage and took water to the lounge for her father to wash his hands. He wore his shirtsleeves rolled up and had on grey trousers. Oliver was a dark man with a small beard on his chin. Though not very tall, he appeared so because he had a lean body. He had always worked as a labourer. Oliver had worked his way up to supervisor in the tire factory. His hands were rough and dark from operating the tough machines and handling tires and rubber. He washed his hands with the usual grim expression he reserved for her and his subordinates at work.

Oliver nodded to show he was finished, and Priscilla walked back to the kitchen to get the food. Her mother walked in with her plate also and they sat down to eat. Priscilla forced her food down, but all she wanted to do was throw up as she watched her parents. This man sitting next to her mother was not her father, and he hated her for it. How dare he? She couldn't stand to look at him, and she wondered how she was going to spend one more night at that house.

Chewing silently, she looked at her plate of food. She couldn't be in his presence any longer so she took her plate to the kitchen and stood there against the counter for a while trying to still her breathing.

"Are you okay?' Monica asked as she walked into the kitchen.

Priscilla shook her head. "No. I'm very tired."

"Take the beer to your father."

Priscilla walked with the big glass of Lion Lagar, his favorite, and put it in front of Oliver. She sat on a sofa. When her mother walked in she decided to tell them her plans.

"I have something to tell you," Priscilla said, looking down. Monica looked very worried as she watched her husband's expression.

"Now?" Monica asked, her eyes pleaded with her not to say anything.

"Yes," Priscilla said.

"What is it?" Oliver asked as he focused his gaze on Priscilla and smirked.

"I have found a flat and I want to move into it tomorrow," Priscilla said, though inside she felt terrified.

"What the hell?" Oliver shouted, standing up and putting the glass down so roughly the liquid splashed on the wooden table.

"Priscilla?" her mother questioned, but her eyes begged her to keep quiet.

"Yes. I would like to move out tomorrow."

"You slut! You want to go and live alone?"

"Yes. I think it's best." Priscilla shook from the way he called her a slut. It cut her down to the bone.

"How dare you sit there and tell me this in my own house. Get out now!"

"No!" Monica cried, standing up. Priscilla stood up, too.

"I'm going. I'll get my things." Priscilla's voice trembled.

"You go now." Oliver pushed her so roughly she hit the chair with her leg and cried out in pain. "Out now!" Oliver pulled the door open and pushed her outside, where she fell on the wet ground.

"I never want to see you again. You are no child of mine!"

Priscilla stood up on the lawn. Tears were pouring out of her eyes as she watched her mother crying and the angry expression on Oliver's face.

"I know." Priscilla mumbled and turned away. Oliver stood there, stunned, like a startled lizard.

CHAPTER 6
Nyaradza—Comfort

"Don't wake your mum," Priscilla begged in a croaky voice after Unashe closed the gate behind them.

"I'm sleeping in the cottage like you suggested so you can come here," Unashe said, helping her into the room that had the double bed he had just been sleeping in. She stood, soaked, by the door. He ran and took his towel from the bathroom and handed it to her. Absently she began unbuttoning her shirt. Unashe caught himself staring, and, when their eyes met, he flushed with embarrassment while she stared blankly at him.

"I'll wait in the bathroom," he said, then took his t-shirt from the cupboard. When he returned, she was sitting on the bed wearing his t-shirt. Her clothes were in a wet pile by the door. The towel dangled from her hand.

"I'll put these in the tub to dry," Unashe said, picking up her clothes. Priscilla just stared at him. He came back, took the towel from her, and wiped the water dripping from her hair.

"You are really wet," he said, shaking his head. She took the towel from him and began wiping her head more vigorously than he had been. She wiped her legs, and then leaned back against the wall.

Unashe took some water from the mini kitchen a few steps from the room. He sat next to her and gave her the water. She drank slowly then held the glass precariously in her hand. Unashe took it before she dropped it and put it in the sink. Her eyes were half closed and there was strain all over her lovely face.

"What happened, Cilla?"

The sound of his voice filled with concern and love brought tears to her eyes. She blinked rapidly and took a deep breath. "*Baba* kicked me out of the house," she explained, wiping her eyes and trying to stop crying. Unashe looked incredulous.

"Why? Why did he do that?" Unashe asked, putting his arm around her trembling, delicate shoulders.

"He's crazy, that's why. I thought he had changed. I hate him. I hate all men." Priscilla looked at his face. "Except for you. You are the only one who understands me. You are the only man I'll ever trust."

Unashe smiled. He wanted to hug her, but he just rubbed her shoulder quickly and then let go. He was so furious at what had happened to her that he couldn't even think straight.

"You are the best person I know, Cilla. Why would he kick you out?"

"Because I told him I was moving out tomorrow. And I think he just hates me."

"How could he? So—How on Earth did you get here?"

"I got a lift into town, and then I walked the rest of the way."

"What!"

"It's all right, Unashe. I'm okay."

"Damn him."

"I must lie down for a while," Priscilla said, leaning into the pillows. Unashe covered her with the blankets and in a second she was asleep with her hand still in Unashe's. Unashe gently moved away and stood watching her sleeping face with the long lashes covering her cheeks.

A strong feeling of protectiveness gripped his heart and spread all over his body. The feeling intensified when he saw the flimsy bedroom slippers she had been wearing. That bastard had kicked her out when she was ready for bed. How could he?

Unashe went and sat on his mother's old sofas that were pushed against the wall. He just sat back and watched her sleeping, and then he, too, fell asleep.

Monica Pasipano went into the kitchen and started tidying up the mess. Her heart was crying in pain because of what had just happened. It was all too much to come to terms with and through blurry eyes, she washed the plates and then started mopping the already immaculate floor. She just did not feel like talking to her husband who, after Priscilla had run off into the night, had gone into the bedroom and slammed the door after him. Of all the awful things he had done to her daughter, this was the worst. With shaking hands, she remembered what Priscilla had said when her father had shouted.

"*You are no child of mine.*"

"*I know.*"

She remembered the slice of lightning across the dark sky as she said those words.

What did she mean by that? Goodness, did she know?

Monica pondered as she poured the water into the sink that was located just outside the kitchen. The night was dark and the smell of the coming rain strong in the air. Somewhere it was already raining and her daughter could be walking in that darkness alone. She felt angry. Oliver had been unfair and irrational in his treatment of Priscilla, and this was so unnecessary.

Since the wedding several weeks before, and for years before that, he had tried to be reasonable and they had tried to talk things through. Now this.

After a long time in the kitchen, Monica had herself under control and went around the house making sure doors were locked and windows shut. Lastly she went into the bedroom Priscilla had been in just a short while ago and felt hysteria threatening to engulf her as she saw her black purse on the chair and her clothes for the next day on a metal hanger hooked on the wardrobe door handle. *Where are you, my child? What is going to happen to you?*

Monica felt a strong urge to go and look for her, but by now she would be far away. No. She felt a strong urge to leave this house forever, but she knew she would never do that. She would stay for better or worse and though most of her married life had been more on the worst side she was not the kind of person who ran away.

With steely determination, she walked into the bedroom and was not surprised to see that Oliver was on top of the blankets listening to a talk show on the little radio beside their bed. Oliver glanced at her and watched her as she gracefully changed into a cotton nightdress and started to put cream on her hands. She was not going to say anything. She would wait for him to start speaking.

"Did you know about Priscilla leaving home?" he asked in an accusing tone. The same accusing tone he had used when Vimbai had gotten pregnant out of wedlock many years ago.

"No. Tonight was the first time I heard it," Monica replied, sitting on her side of the bed.

"Are you sure?"

"Yes," Monica said calmly. She never showed her anger even though inside a volcano was erupting. Oliver shook his head, disbelief all over his face.

"I don't know what she was thinking. What kind of girl goes to live on her own? Why does she want to leave home?"

You are no child of mine. I know.

"I don't know."

"She's the worst of the lot of them. That's why I wished I could have had sons, not daughters. Problems, all of them. They are ungrateful and ignorant. You send them to school and they thank you by getting pregnant with the first useless man they meet or they leave home in the middle of the night."

Monica listened as her husband twisted events to take away his guilt. He would never admit that he kicked her out and as they settled in the double bed, they were both unable to sleep, but unable to say exactly what was bothering them. There were two things keeping them awake that night: Priscilla's safety and her paternity. But neither of them was going to say anything. At least not for a very long time.

CHAPTER 7
Vimba—Hope

The rain of the night before was gone and the sun shone brightly and chased away the dark clouds. The warmth filled Priscilla with hope as she leaned back in her aunt's car and watched the morning traffic. Mukai now knew all that had happened the night before and was just as upset as Unashe.

"What time do you start?" Mukai asked her.

"Eight. What about you?"

"You know me, Pri. I start when I get there. The joys of having your own business," she said, her voice husky.

"Lucky you," Priscilla said with feeling. She looked around at the houses they drove past. All seemed very secure with high walls and gates. Leaving the quiet residential areas, they entered the busy wide roads that lead to the city center. Priscilla could see the tall buildings in the distance.

The first major building was the gold Sheraton hotel that rose like a majestic jewel in the city skyline. Beyond that was the ruling government party headquarters, which had been recently finished. It didn't look that wonderful from the outside. It echoed the drab uniformity of most government buildings except for the symbol of the party, a black cork emblazoned into the grey walls.

The numerous traffic lights now slowed the traffic flowing into the city center. Impatient drivers hooted and rushed pedestrians were forced to run across the road as the drivers didn't give them way. Mukai double-parked and waited for Priscilla to leave the car when they reached Anderson House.

"Thank you, Aunty. I will return these soon," she said, looking at the clothes Mukai had given her.

"No hurry. Now, will you be okay?"

"I think so. I'm just excited about my new flat."

"It's exciting, isn't it? I felt the same way the first time I had my own place. Anything is possible after that."

"I feel the same. I better go."

"Okay. I'll get your clothes for you," Mukai said as Priscilla opened the door.

"Thank you. But please don't get into a fight with *Baba* on my account."

"Okay. But I was looking forward to a good fight," she said, and they both smiled.

Priscilla was about to step out when her aunt gave her a wad of money. She was about to refuse when her aunt spoke.

"You don't even have your handbag. Take it. How will you get home? What will you eat?"

She felt tears sting her eyes. She recalled how upset Mukai had been when she told her about her night's ordeal. She was grateful for both her and Unashe. "Thank you, Aunty."

Priscilla stood there for a while watching her aunt's car merge into the traffic. People rushed past her as she tried to compose herself, and she only moved when she realized people were looking at her strangely.

She got into the elevator, which took her to the sixth-floor reception area.

"Good morning, Priscilla," the young receptionist, Mavis, greeted her in Shona.

Priscilla responded and then walked into the office. No one was in yet, and as soon as she sat down the phone rang.

"Priscilla. It's Mr Tengani," Mavis said.

"Thank you. I'll take it," Priscilla responded.

"Hello, Priscilla. How are you?" he asked in a cheerful, happy voice. Priscilla wondered how he could sound so upbeat so early in the morning.

Priscilla really tried to match his enthusiasm, but she realized she probably sounded only slightly awake. She forced herself to sit up straighter. Mr. Tengani was an important client. She tried very hard to inject some enthusiasm into her voice.

"Good morning. I'm fine, and you?"

"Well, thanks. How is work?" he asked.

"Fine, fine. And how is business?"

"It's going well," Chamu said, picturing her sitting in her office. He really was excited to be talking to her. He felt his heart begin to race as her voice caressed his ears. A favorite memory of her always came into his mind as he remembered her many years ago in high school. She'd been much younger, but still as hauntingly beautiful. She had been on the high school netball team and though he never watched the sport, he remembered her walking to a practice in her short maroon games skirt.

She had stopped, and, while the others chatted, she had smiled at him and greeted him first. Being shy and awkward, he had only managed to say hello to her and nothing else as he watched her smile. Her eyes and everything about her remained etched on his mind forever.

Since then she'd been his ideal woman. He had never met any woman that he didn't compare with her. She was the only woman who could fulfil all his dreams. He came back to the present when Priscilla asked him if there was anything in particular he wanted.

"Oh, yes. I know you are still finishing off the rental car system but I was wondering if we could organize the training of some of my accountants to use your new accounts package."

"That can be arranged. Would you like me to get hold of our training department and talk to them or can you give them a call?" Priscilla asked. That wasn't really her area, and though she had studied the package herself there were other people employed to do the training. She just developed software for specialized clients and sometimes adapted existing packages to suit her particular client. Though she didn't really like teaching, sometimes her job required that she train her clients on the new software she had developed. To her that was the least fun part of her job.

"I'll call them, then. I thought you did everything," he teased her.

She tried to smile. "Not yet."

"Have you made any plans for lunch then?"

"I actually can't go out for lunch today. I have another deadline which I have to work on," Priscilla said, tapping a pen on her desk calendar.

"Maybe another time?"

"Maybe," she said and ended the conversation. After she hung up, she stared at her computer for a while. She had so much work to do and she knew that would keep her mind off her personal problems. Julia, her colleague and friend, soon arrived full of exciting stories and laughter. She lived near Rutendo and always seemed to know what was going on with her neighbors.

"Do you remember that girl I told you about? The one going out with the married man?"

Priscilla looked blank. She really couldn't keep up with all the names.

"That one, Tarisai. The one who is a receptionist at Dairyboard?"

"Oh, yes. I remember her."

"Well, last night the wife caught Tarisai and her husband together. She was screaming and hitting Tarisai. The husband was also in the flat. They were making so much noise."

The day went fast as they had meetings with the director, and, of course, Julia would always entertain them all while they worked. Finally, at 5 p.m., Priscilla was ready to go home.

Home.

Priscilla thought of what her home had been until a day before. She hadn't been happy there at all.

Joining the rushing crowds as they left their offices, Priscilla stood for hours in the queues until she finally got onto a bus. The bus was crowded with all sorts of rushed and impatient people. There were middle-class workers who couldn't afford cars and women carrying their babies on their backs and even those who sold their wares in the streets. It was stuffy and smelly and Priscilla was grateful she had sat by the window and kept her eyes outside away from the man, named Jealous, who was trying to strike up a conversation with her.

The bus stop was a short walk away from her new flat. She got there in about ten minutes. She climbed the polished wooden stairs and got to her door with her keys in hand. The key gave her trouble initially, but soon she had opened the door.

She stood looking at the bare room with patterned wooden tiles on the floor. She loved what she saw, even though it was going to need a lot of work.

"Well, this is my new home," she said, trying to smile even though she felt more like crying. Her voice seemed to echo back to her in the still empty room.

She walked towards the side glass door, which opened onto the balcony. She unlocked it and stepped onto the small empty space. From there she could see the gate and out to the street where the traffic moved and pedestrians rushed home to their families. The sun was setting, and some headlights from the traffic flashed at her. Priscilla stood there for a long time taking in her new life.

When it was getting cooler, she walked back into the house and went into the bedroom. She liked the big space and beautiful built-in pine cupboards. The bathroom came off the bedroom and was all white with a decent size white bathtub. As she opened the medicine chest with a mirror, she heard a strange sound. Feeling frightened she listened intently and heard it again.

Fearfully, Priscilla walked into the lounge and realized that what she had heard was a knock.

"Who is it?" she asked furtively.

"It's me. Unashe."

Smiling, she opened the door and there he stood holding blankets piled up to cover his face.

"Oh. You," she cried and pulled two of the top blankets from him and let him into the house.

"What are you doing here?" she asked, smiling broadly as she closed the door.

"I came to check on you," he said, looking around at the flat.

"Thanks. But I'm fine," she said.

"Fine. Where were you going to sleep?" he asked, then looked at the floor. "Here?"

"Well, I hadn't thought of that yet. Okay, I had, but I hadn't come up with any ideas," she said, though she was smiling.

"Well, I was thinking about it all day," Unashe said, still holding the blankets. "Where should we put them?"

"Well, the floor is quite clean. Let's put them in the corner."

They did that and then stood facing each other.

"Thank you Una. You are a life saver," she said, smiling up at him. He acted like somebody who wasn't serious about people or their problems, but he was one person who didn't just talk about caring, but actually did something.

"It was no problem," he said, still looking at her. Her eyes took him in gratefully. He wore a pair of jeans, a T-shirt and Adidas shoes. His defined and handsome features showed his concern and his dark brown eyes said a lot, though it seemed he chose not to say it aloud.

"Are you okay, though?" he asked her, strong arms folded in front of his chest. Priscilla nodded, moving to sit on the window ledge.

"I'm fine."

He came and sat next to her. "I mean about what happened yesterday."

"I'm trying not to think about it. There is actually more you don't know about," Priscilla said, looking ahead. She was biting her lower lip as she always did when she was worried.

"Tell me about it," Unashe said gently, his deep voice soft and filled with concern. He couldn't imagine anything worse than what she had gone through the night before.

She started talking about the wedding and what she had overheard. She related the complete shocking story to him, leaving nothing out.

"I should have known something. All these years he would look at me as if he hated me. I should have guessed," she said.

"There is no way you could have known, Cilla. He had no right to treat you like that. So you are certain he is not your father?"

"Yes. I told you what your mother said. It is sad, but true. She even knew," Priscilla said with a tired voice. She looked at him and caught him looking at her with so much sympathy.

"So who is your father?"

"I don't know," she sighed and looked back at him. Unashe reached for her hand and gently held it. It was so comforting, and she felt herself getting warm. She was not used to this.

"I'm sorry, Cilla," he said and slowly enfolded her in his arms. Surprised at first, Priscilla soon found that she felt comforted by Unashe's embrace.

CHAPTER 8
Mufaro—Great Pleasure

After holding her for a while without saying a word, Unashe spoke close to hair.

"Why don't I take you out and buy you something to eat? You don't seem to have a stove in here."

Priscilla smiled but stayed in his arms. It was a new and good feeling. She could not recall any man ever holding her like this, so tenderly as if she was a special treasure. Even her mother didn't hold her. Breathing in his scent, she held on tightly and closed her eyes, savoring the feel of his strong arms around her.

"You want to go out now? Are you sure?" she asked in a muffled voice.

"Come on," he said, standing up and bringing her up with him by holding her elbows. She reluctantly stood up, facing him.

"Thank you, Unashe. I'm so glad you are here," she said, not sure those words were adequate to explain the feeling of gratitude in her heart. And something else, too, a sense of comfort at his tenderness and caring.

"I like taking care of you," he said, though he seemed distracted to her.

Shyly, like a little child, she went into his arms again and put her arms around his waist. Unashe let her stay there for a while, and then pulled her head back so he could look into her face. She was lovely, standing there in his mother's work clothes looking like an angel. Her eyes were half closed and a small, dreamy smile on her lips. He found himself leaning down and softly placing his lips on hers. She didn't move away. He moved back and removed her hands from his waist, feeling guilty and embarrassed.

"I'm sorry," he said, rubbing his mouth. "I shouldn't have done that."

Priscilla giggled softly, pressing her lips together. "It was nice," she said, moving away from him, still looking down, her heart racing. Unashe could have kicked himself. What had possessed him to do that?

"Come, let's go."

They drove in silence to a small restaurant at the nearest shopping center. Priscilla looked out the car window, as he drove.

The name VINOLA'S shone brightly in red. There were a few people at the bar, but further inside she could see dining tables laid with gold tablecloths. When Priscilla stepped in, she was quite surprised at the restaurant's glamour and felt underdressed.

"It's nice here," she whispered to Unashe as a waiter in a richly embroidered waistcoat and black trousers approached them.

"That's why you are here," he whispered back. She gave him a quirky smile and stepped aside so the waiter could lead them to a quiet table in the corner past only three sets of other diners.

Unashe pulled out a chair for her in an exaggerated gallant way and she laughed. He sat down opposite her, stretching his long legs by her. He opened the big menu and peered at her over the top.

"Will this place do, madam?" His eyes danced with mischief. She smiled back. She felt like she was dreaming. She had never imagined the day before that she would be eating dinner with Unashe in this magnificent restaurant. And the way she was feeling inside made her wonder. He was making her feel so happy when she should have been sad. And the kiss.

Forget the kiss.

"Yes," she said. "I've never been here before, or to that many restaurants. Have you? Like with Chantel?"

"Not with Chantel. Actually I never went past the bar."

The waiter arrived to take their orders and they both ordered chicken grilled to absolute tenderness, with fresh vegetables and roasted potatoes. They ate slowly and talked. Unashe wanted to hear all about her work, and she wanted to hear all about his plans for the future.

"I'm going to be very successful," he said, "no matter what I have to do."

"That's nice. Do you have any ideas?"

"I just don't see myself making it in this country. Just as the British came here to explore and take our land, I want to go check out what they have to offer over there in Europe."

Priscilla smiled at his statement, amused by his logic.

"I get frustrated, and I want to see the world. You know, go overseas. Learn what the developed countries are doing. Just get out of here."

"Do you hate this country that much?" she asked, a bit disappointed. She never thought of leaving Zimbabwe, not that she would even know where to go. Many young people's only ambition was to go to England or to South Africa. They preferred to suffer in foreign lands. They wanted to go anywhere rather than stay in Zimbabwe. It shouldn't surprise her that Unashe wasn't any different, she thought.

"I don't hate it, but I don't want to be stuck here all my life. I want to enjoy life and I think Harare, which is the most happening place in the country, is actually tired. You know all my friends have left the country, especially the Prince Edward boys. They are doing well, getting degrees, driving BMWs in South Africa and stuff. I never applied to go to university, but now I regret it."

She watched his face intently, getting lost in his eyes. *Unashe, why would you want to leave?* She couldn't blame him, though. It seems everybody felt life could only be good if they left Zimbabwe. The economy kept getting worse, and the corruption was so bad everybody was out to get what they could from the country. It was hard to get anything done, including getting your passport and even your identity card unless you knew somebody.

"I think I'll be around here for a long time," she said, sipping her juice.

"It doesn't matter. You are doing well in your company. I wouldn't be surprised if you start running the company soon anyway."

"You think I can do that?"

"You seem like you can do anything. You are a very determined person."

"I was crying like a baby last time I saw you."

She had a self-mocking smile on her face, but he didn't find that whole night's episode funny at all.

"Anybody would cry," he said and took a sip of his root beer.

"So any luck on the job front?" Priscilla asked, eager to change the subject.

"Not yet, but I have some interviews lined up."

"You are lucky your mother is well off and can take care of you while things fall into place. That is a blessing."

"It can also be a curse, because you tend to relax and not have the drive to succeed that *you* have, for instance. She's great. She never puts pressure on me. I actually put more pressure on myself."

"I've always admired her independence. She's my role model."

"I should tell her."

"No. Don't. You know how big-headed she is."

They both laughed. The bill came and Unashe took out his wallet.

"I'm sorry I can't help you pay."

"Don't worry. When you get your stove you can cook for me."

"Any time."

He watched her smile and grinned back at her. "I have something to tell you," Unashe said.

Priscilla's smile froze at the serious expression on his face. "What is it?"

"Don't get mad," Unashe said as he held up a cautionary hand.

"Don't make me mad," Priscilla warned, leaning closer. "Just tell me."

"All right. I knew about Oliver."

"What do you mean?"

"I knew he wasn't your father. For many years. I just knew that we could never tell you."

Priscilla opened her mouth to speak, but then closed it abruptly. She shook her head, puzzled.

"Ma told me about it. I'm sorry I never told you."

"It's fine. It's just weird to learn that everybody else knew except for me. At least you could've told me. You knew how mean he was to me."

"I just never knew how to tell you. Mum said I shouldn't say anything, and your family seemed fine. And then I just forgot about it. The only thing I know for sure is that you and I were not related, not that we ever really were."

"I'm now not related to a lot of people. I don't even know who my real family is."

"I'm sorry, Cilla. I didn't mean to upset you." Priscilla looked into his sincere eyes. So warm, so inviting. She bit her lower lip again and regarded him suspiciously. The look in her eyes made him ask, "What?"

Priscilla leaned forward and spoke very quietly, as if somebody could overhear. "Unashe. So do you know who my father is?"

"No. I don't. I have no idea who he is."

"Are you sure? Did you ever ask your mum?"

"No. Maybe I did but she never told me. I don't know if she knows. Do you want to find him?"

Priscilla leaned back in her chair, only then beginning to think about who her real father might be. She had been so busy that she hadn't given serious thought to this man who was half of her.

"I don't know. I suppose I may one day want to see him. Not now, though."

"Are you sure?" Unashe asked.

She looked at him, a frown on her face, and nodded.

"Don't worry. I'm fine. Thanks for the dinner."

They didn't say anything as they made their way out of the empty restaurant. They had been the only people eating for a while and would have stayed if the manager hadn't started clearing his throat and turning off the lights.

As Unashe drove her home through the empty streets, they were both quiet and thoughtful. When they got to her building, it was after ten o'clock. He took out more items for her that were still in the car, and they both had armfuls climbing up the stairs.

"A two-plate stove. Wow," Priscilla exclaimed as she put the cutlery and curtains on the kitchen cabinets. She looked through the boxes as Unashe watched. The kitchen was tiny and, with Unashe's build and height, he practically filled it up.

"Yes. You know how Ma is. She wants to look after everybody."

"She has a heart of gold." Priscilla surveyed all that Mukai had sent with Unashe.

"We both worry about you. That's why she sent me here tonight," Unashe said, walking into the lounge. "Where are you going to sleep?"

She looked around the lounge then pointed into the bedroom. "In there."

"Let's try and cover the windows," Unashe said, picking up one curtain. "You can't sleep with the windows like that. You might wake up and find some strange creature staring at you," he said, and laughed when he saw the fear in her eyes. She looked out the window and shivered.

"Now you are making me scared," she complained, staring into darkness.

"Come on, we'll cover them." He put his hands on her shoulders and guided her into her bedroom.

"Don't worry. Nobody can climb upstairs and look at you."

It was quite an effort to hang the curtains precariously over the windows without the proper rods and equipment. Still, Priscilla felt better now that she couldn't see darkness. She tried not to think about being alone after Unashe left.

Unashe helped her to make her bed on the floor using all the blankets. The makeshift area looked quite comfortable when they were done.

"There you are, Cilla," he said, surveying his handiwork as if it was a work of art.

She smiled at him. "Perfect."

"Why did you decide to come here? Why didn't you go to your sister or even spend the night with us?" Unashe asked suddenly.

"I didn't think of it. I guess I should start being independent and not rely on others too much. You know what they say, 'What leads to living together is what leads to contempt.' Don't want to get on anybody's nerves."

"You know we don't mind," Unashe said.

"I know. I'll be fine, you'll see. I don't have to work tomorrow, so I can get my stuff together. I like the feeling of freedom, even though I don't have much."

Unashe watched her for a while, seeming to weigh her words. She knew what he must be thinking. He was still living with his mother and here she was, exactly the same age as him, making a life for herself.

"What are you going to sleep in?" he asked, looking at her work clothes.

"Unashe," she said in mock severity. "Don't tell me you didn't bring me something to sleep in."

"I'm so sorry, my queen. Please don't kill me," he begged, pretending to be so scared that she laughed. That was Unashe. He could make her laugh, even when her world was falling apart.

"Okay, I'll spare your life because you have been a good servant," she said. Then, smiling, she added, "So far."

"You are too kind, madam." They smiled at each other for a while.

"I don't want to leave you here alone," he confessed, suddenly serious. She matched his expression as she frowned.

"I don't want you to leave." They stood, the makeshift bed between them, and looked at each other.

"I better go," Unashe said and stepped over the makeshift bed towards the door. Priscilla followed close by, trying to think of something to say to make him stay longer. Her mind was blank. Of course he couldn't stay with her. What was she even thinking? She chose to live alone, and this is what she got.

"I'll see you soon," she said as she saw him to the door. She could hear the hope in her voice and felt confused.

"Yep. You'll probably get tired of seeing me," he said. Her heart lifted at his words, though he was wrong about her ever getting tired of seeing him.

"Lock up." She nodded at his command, and he stepped out. Priscilla turned the key in the door and stared at it for a while. She was heading towards the bedroom when she heard a knock. She just knew it was him.

"Who is it?"

"It's me." Of course it was Unashe. She unlocked the door and opened it, questions in her eyes.

"I couldn't leave you. I'll stay with you most of the night," he declared and stepped into her living room. She closed the door and locked it.

"I'm glad," she said, though she was a little apprehensive about the prospect. She walked towards her bedroom and crossed over to the other side.

"Do you want me to?"

She nodded. "Can you? What will your ma say?" she asked, worried, folding her arms across her chest.

"I'll tell her I went to a friend's house after I left here," he stated simply and leaned against the wall.

They stood silently for a while. It was so quiet. The neighbors were all fast asleep and there was very little traffic on the road outside. The silence filled with something shifting between them. Something that almost reminded her of the air before the rain, heavy and scented. It was almost tangible.

"I don't know . . ." she said.

"I couldn't leave you alone. I wouldn't be able to sleep," he said honestly.

Priscilla pointed to the floor. "You forgot a pillow."

"I suppose now I'll have to die, my queen," he said and sat on the homemade bed, grinning at her. She looked at him, shaking her head at his antics.

"You can lie on me," he offered, then watched her face as all sorts of expressions played across it. "I can be a pretty good pillow."

She didn't say anything, but slowly took off her blazer and gingerly sat next to him. He took off his shoes and she slipped her heels off and slid down on to the floor with him. Her heart was beating wildly as she looked up at the ceiling with the white paint.

"Come lie on my chest," he said softly. She wanted to refuse but knew that she would do as he said. She looked into his eyes silently for a while, and then slowly laid her head on his chest feeling his heartbeat and his chest rise and fall. Her heart rate had increased so much she was sure he could hear it. She swallowed hard, not sure she could trust her voice to say anything. Would she sleep? Would he?

"I'm just curious," Unashe said, breaking the silence. "Why did your parents have the wedding, anyway? What was that all about?"

Priscilla giggled, feeling some of the tension leave her body. This was Unashe. She shouldn't be tense around him. "I don't know. They do things that are weird to me."

"Tell me about it."

Priscilla shrugged. "Most people don't think our own traditional marriage is enough, you know."

"I hate that. Everything is becoming westernized."

"Some things need to be westernized."

"Like what?"

She relaxed when they began to share their opinions on their culture, dreams, their likes and dislikes, state of marriages, the corrupt government. Their voices were the only sound in the room until almost 2 a.m. when Unashe turned off the light.

She was awake for a few minutes before exhaustion took over and she fell asleep.

Before he, too, fell asleep, Unashe wondered what was happening to him.

He brought the blankets over them, covering her shoulders.

"Good night, Cilla," Unashe said.

"Good night, Una," she whispered, but she was already asleep.

It was early morning when Unashe woke up and gently nudged Priscilla. The light wormed its way through the thin curtain fabric and gave the room a strange, intimate glow.

"How did you sleep?" he asked in a hoarse voice. She had slipped away from him and lay with her head facing the wall. She turned and faced him slowly and her eyes looked unfocused and distant from dreamland. She blinked rapidly, her eyelashes striking against her skin.

She covered her eyes with her hands and looked at the ceiling while he still watched her, seemingly fascinated.

"Are you awake?" he asked again.

"Yes," she responded quietly, shyly. "Are you going home?"

"Yes,' he replied. "Come and lock the door after me."

She stood up, rubbing her neck. Her shoulders and back ached from the floor. This was now the second night they had spent together, but this morning was different. There was an awkwardness that wasn't there when Oliver had kicked her out of her home. She didn't seem as comfortable as she had been before. It seemed she had crossed some mysterious river and could not go back any more, or remember the best place to cross without drowning.

"You go back to sleep," he said, touching her cheek.

"I might," she said, not quite looking at him. "Thank you again, for everything."

"Don't mention it. I'll see you soon."

He seemed to want to say something more, but thought better of it. Then he left.

Priscilla checked her watch. It was 5 a.m. She rubbed her eyes as she sauntered back to her bedroom. With a sigh she lay back on her makeshift bed and thought of Unashe.

CHAPTER 9
Dana—Love

That first Saturday in her new place was a day of visitors for Priscilla. Her mother walked in with a serious expression followed by her sister, Rutendo, who was dressed in a tight black outfit and high heels.

"Mama," she cried, embracing her mother. Her mother was almost in tears as she held her youngest daughter.

"My Pri," she said, looking over her shoulder at the bare flat. Monica wore her church uniform, and Priscilla suspected that she had lied to her father that she was going to her church meeting with the women. It was a red belted jacket and black skirt with a white hat. A while back Priscilla had asked her mother why she always wore the outfit to church meetings, and Monica had explained that it was a uniform of sorts. Most traditional Zimbabwean churches had adapted the outfits for their female members, and they all seemed to embrace it.

"How are you, Ma?" Priscilla asked, looking at her face. She felt like she hadn't seen her mother in a long time, even though it had been just a few days.

"I'm fine. I should be asking the same of you," she said.

"Yes, Pri," Rutendo added. "Mukai told me what happened."

"I'm fine. I just need some of my things."

"I only managed to take a few things," Monica explained, taking out Priscilla's handbag that contained her bankbook and money. She also pulled a dress, which looked wrinkled from the bag, a bra, panties, her tooth-brush and her Bible from the paper bag she had brought with her. "Thank you, Ma."

Priscilla looked at her sister, who stared at her with both sympathy and a knowing look. Priscilla could tell that Rutendo was trying to guess why Priscilla had left home. Rutendo was proud that she left home as soon as she got a job in a bank. She'd started out as a lowly clerk at the bank, but she'd taken advantage of advancement opportunities. Rutendo was now a manager in training. She had been determined not to stay home with her over-bearing father.

Rutendo often complained that Oliver was just bitter that he had never had any sons, so she wasn't going to stay home and take his stupid laws and insults. Of all his daughters, Rutendo was the most single-minded and dif-ficult, at least according to Oliver. She answered back and refused submission. Priscilla had witnessed Oliver beating Rutendo with a belt, cutting all her hair off and banning her from talking to the rest of the family, but she remained as stubborn as a donkey.

Rutendo resembled Monica but lacked her quiet nature and reserve. Rutendo had her father's fire. She was attractive in the voluptuous, unabashed way that many

men found appealing. Rutendo could also dance shame-
lessly and make you laugh with her storytelling and
straight talk.

"We can't stay long," Monica announced, still
standing close to the door. There was really nowhere to
sit. The women stood in a circle around the empty room.

"I understand. Next time you come I'll have some
food and drink," Priscilla offered. She knew that being
hospitable was very important to her mother. Whenever
people visited, Monica went out of her way to buy drinks
for them and prepare food even if the family had just finished eating. Priscilla had seen her mother begin cooking
an elaborate meal at ten at night if guests should arrive
that late. Priscilla felt awkward with nothing to give.

"I'll bring you some stuff, little sis," Rutendo said,
putting another piece of chewing gum in her mouth.
"Our father will regret treating us this way."

Priscilla nodded. Rutendo had promised her many
things in the past, but had never really delivered.

*I will pay your fees for the computer course. I will buy
you the books, don't worry. I will come and see you this
weekend.*

"Don't talk about your father that way," Monica
admonished her daughter. Rutendo pursed her lips
tightly.

Monica and Rutendo left soon after that without
really discussing what had happened. Later in the day,
Mukai arrived with Unashe lugging a mattress, some
chairs, cutlery and clothes. Mukai was in a hurry to go
somewhere and had to leave with Unashe.

"I've got a soccer match, so I'll see you later," he said as they drove off.

Thanks to Mukai's donations, her flat was beginning to take shape. She still had some time to go before it was a home. She did not have an iron, towels, dishes and many other things. She would receive her salary soon, and the first thing she would have to do is go for some major shopping. Priscilla liked the feeling of independence that being at her own place gave her. She felt liberated. There was no going back now.

After the hell of being at home, constantly fearing rejection and torment, this feeling of choice was exhilarating. Now she understood how her Aunt Mukai felt. She was her own woman. Not like her mother, or her two older sisters. Actually many of the women she knew were under the thumbs of men who did nothing to improve their lives, who gave nothing to them but heartache and misery. When she asked to attend college, she remembered Oliver's disdainful tone as he admonished her.

"What do you think college will accomplish? Just waste my money anyway. You all get pregnant and run away. It will be a total waste of money. You just don't want to work."

The list went on and on, and her mother never defended her though she could see that Monica was upset. Monica was always trying to keep the home calm, though deep down she knew there was no peace at all. Deep down in all their hearts there was no harmony, a constant nagging snake kept the house in more turmoil than a country at war.

A knock on the door interrupted her troubling thoughts.

It was Unashe.

"How was soccer?" Priscilla asked him as she perched on the windowsill. It was warm there, and the sunshine streamed in like a seductive river. Unashe sat on one of her recently acquired chairs, dressed in his tracksuit and running shoes. As always, his dressing bordered more on the casual.

"Good. You must come watch some time. I actually scored two goals for you," he boasted, giving her his lop-sided, one-dimple grin.

"For me? How wonderful," she replied, feigning pleasure. Priscilla marvelled that they always talked like that, teasing each other and making each other laugh.

But his next question took her by surprise.

"So how come you don't have a boyfriend?" he asked, folding his arms across his chest.

"What?" she asked, not sure she had heard the question properly.

"A boyfriend? Where's he?"

Priscilla laughed briefly. He was looking around like there was a man hiding behind the walls.

"Boyfriends. What will they bring me? You know what it usually leads to, marriage."

"So? You have to get married some time," he said, challenging her.

"No, I don't. I can look after myself, thank you." Priscilla tossed her head in an almost childlike manner.

"I'm sure somebody has been interested in you," Unashe persisted.

"I don't have time to entertain such thoughts. I haven't seen anybody that is happily married. Except the men who enjoy other extra 'relationships' on the side. I totally hate African marriages. Completely. They just don't seem to have any love or romance in them."

"Aren't your sisters all married? Is it that bad?"

"Worse, Unashe. I've watched them for years, and they put me off marriage. Vimbai and Gilbert have been unhappily together for nearly twelve years. Vimbai is the sweetest person you could ever know, and Giri . . . Let's just say he's a monster in the making."

"Why did she marry him?" Unashe asked, puzzled. He shifted on the uncomfortable chair and finally found comfort when he stretched his legs.

"She was young when she met him. Gilbert lied to Vimbai, saying that she wouldn't get pregnant, and when she did, he had also been reluctant to marry her. *Baba* forced her to move in with him, basically just kicked her out one day."

Priscilla could picture the day Vimbai had gotten in the car and driven away, her heart constricting with pain. "I was there the day she left. Vimbai never worked since her first son was born, followed by a daughter. Both children died of malaria when he sent her to live in the village with his mother. Now she has two kids. She raised the children, tried to make the small two-bedroom house comfortable, and was constantly saying he never came home, how he never paid the bills, how she had no money for food.

"Once after I had just started to work I had to pay for their electricity to be turned on when Gilbert disappeared for weeks and Vimbai didn't know where he was. Only lately Vimbai started talking of taking a course, or doing something to bring money."

"That's tough. But not all men are like that, like this Gilbert," Unashe argued, leaning towards her.

"That's all I see. It just makes me so angry how her life is just wasting away."

Her vehemence shook him. For a while, they were both quiet, digesting what she had just said.

"My other sister is the same. I don't know her too well. She also married very young and moved away. Hope's husband actually acts like he owns her and we are not that important. We are not very close."

"That's too bad. And Rutendo?"

"She's okay. We are not too close, either, but we talk sometimes. She was here today with Ma."

"So now you have sworn off marriage, huh?"

"I just don't ever want to depend on anyone. Especially not a man."

She had a point, Unashe thought. How many happily married people had he ever come across? His own mother had hinted at unhappiness with his father, though of course they didn't discuss his father much. All he knew was that he was a soldier in the war of independence and when he came back, he was violent and chased his mother away when he was very young. Before Unashe could meet him again, he died in a bus accident. He was uncomfortable talking about it after how he treated his mother. The few married friends that he knew were always looking at other women while their wives were at home. To them, being married was like being chained. Surely, no man would feel like he was chained to Cilla. She was just incredible. He looked at her, the sunlight lying on her soft brown skin. Her lazy, dreamy eyes somehow told a woman's secrets. In her eyes, there was something deep, innocent and seductive all at the same time. There was a certain secret promise that drew him in even as he tried to fight it. Everything about her was sweet and inviting. He realized that he had to stay away from her.

She was special in more ways than just her sensuality. And he had no right to her. Not that she wanted him. Not that he wanted to settle down either, with all the complications a relationship with *her* would bring him. He had plans. His big plans that did not include anyone but himself.

"I don't want to get married, either. Not for many years to come," he said, as he leaned back on the uncomfortable chair.

"Why not?" she asked.

"Like I said, I want to go overseas. I want to study, get a job, a good job, make money—lots of it—and build a big house, drive a brand new car and just be able to go any where in the world I want."

"And when you have all that you will come and marry Chantel?" Priscilla asked.

He laughed. "What is it with you and Chantel?"

"Well, she was once the woman in your life, the only one I know about," she reminded him.

"That was once upon a time," he threw back.

They looked at each other for a while, and then Priscilla turned away from his gaze and looked out of the window.

"I can tell that we both have the same philosophies on life. That's good," Unashe said suddenly. She turned to him and smiled.

"Yep, we do. We have a lot to accomplish and don't want relationships stopping us."

"So when are we going to buy you a bed, and a radio and a TV?" he asked, and Priscilla laughed at the sudden change of subject. It made her relax, and she wanted to feel relaxed with Unashe and not be filled with butterflies as if she was riding a scary roller coaster. Lately, even as they laughed and talked, she could sense an undercurrent of something that seemed bigger than her plans for her life.

CHAPTER 10
Mutambo—Dance

A few weeks later Priscilla got a call from Unashe just as she was finishing work on Friday.

"What are you doing this weekend?" he asked.

"Nothing," Priscilla said.

"Not anymore. How about going to a soccer game?"

Priscilla agreed, and then sat staring into space. She was stunned.

"Who was that, Pri? You should see your face," Julie said. Priscilla had forgotten she was at the office and that her co-workers were in earshot.

"What?" Priscilla sat up straighter and punched the escape button on her computer.

"When you were talking you looked like, I don't know. Someone very much in love. Was that Mr. Chamu Tengani?"

"No. I'm done with his project. No. It wasn't him."

"Who then?"

"No one important. Listen, I have to finish this report."

Julie walked away and Priscilla wondered at Julie's words. Unashe was just a friend. Nothing more. And going with him to a soccer game was just for fun. Nothing more.

"That was a good game," Priscilla said as she picked up the ice-cream cups they had eaten during the game.

"I'm glad you liked it. Should we go out and eat?" Unashe asked her.

"I'm paying this time. Especially since Caps won."

They went out again that evening to the same restaurant, Vinola's. He told her about the job he had just started in the same bank in which her sister, Rutendo, worked. They would be celebrating two things – his new job and the game. He was finally doing what he really wanted to do: work in the financial world.

"Banking is where the money is," Unashe said after polishing off his steak and potatoes.

"You chose the right place." Priscilla lifted her glass of sweet wine to him. A thoughtful look flashed across his face. Priscilla stared wondering at the sudden change in his eyes.

"Do you want to go somewhere after dinner?" Unashe asked, a glint of excitement in his eyes.

"Where?" Priscilla eyed him suspiciously.

"Not home." There was mystery in his voice.

Priscilla looked at her watch doubtfully. It was almost 10 p.m. She wanted to go to her flat.

"It's late."

"Come on. It's your first month of freedom. No parents breathing down your neck. Nobody in charge of you. Don't you want to go somewhere you would never have gone before?"

"Coming here is new." Priscilla looked around the room, the empty tables, the few waiters waiting for them to leave. She smiled at him, eyes half closed dreamily. "Wearing jeans and trousers is new for me because *Baba* forbids us from wearing them. It's an adventure for me to be out at 10 p.m. eating dinner in a restaurant. I never did that before."

Unashe looked down and hit the table, like a judge announcing a verdict. "That's it, then. You need to try more new things. I think my job is to make sure you enjoy your freedom, because eating dinner in a restaurant can't be your only big adventure. Come on."

Unashe stood up and Priscilla got up slowly. They had paid their bill and had sat talking for over an hour. He waited for her to walk ahead and followed her to the car.

Unashe didn't have to convince her too much. She somehow knew that Unashe could ask her to do anything and she would say yes. They walked out of the restaurant and got into Unashe's car. It was amazing how quiet the streets were. Unashe was taking her somewhere. She wondered where it would be, but didn't ask again. The surprise would be fun.

They drove through Samora Machel Avenue, and, from a distance, she could see the lights from the city twinkling mischievously at her. The homes they passed were dark and she imagined all the families sleeping peacefully. Unashe drove into downtown and stopped his car by the Sheraton Hotel.

"What's going on, Unashe?" She shook her head. The thought of girls going to hotel rooms reminded her that Gilbert had taken Vimbai to a hotel, too, so long ago. She thought of sugar daddies and realized her opinion of hotels had been tainted by tales of old fat men taking young schoolgirls to such places to ruin their futures. "I'm not going to some hotel," she told Unashe.

"It's not that. There is a nice place inside where we can relax, meet up with friends and dance."

"Is this a club?"

"It's a nice, adult club. You'll like it. Come on." She remained seated, shaking her head. Unashe got out and walked to the passenger side. He opened her door.

"Come on. It'll be fine." He held out his hand to her and she looked into his eyes. They were warm, inviting, teasing but determined. His hand held out to her was calling to her and she reached for it and got out, holding on to his fingers tightly.

"Am I even dressed right?" She looked down at the black trousers and grey top she wore. Unashe glanced at her curly black hair and quickly down her slender body to her silver high heels.

"Of course. You always look great."

She looked around at the elegant people walking towards the hotel. Maybe some of them were not headed to the club, but some other event being held at the hotel, she guessed. Either way she felt unsure as she walked next to Unashe through the door. She felt odd entering the dark place with him as if people could tell she didn't belong there. The loud music and voices assaulted her senses immediately. At first glance, it seemed like an elegant place as she walked past tables and the bar and then to the dance floor.

Once they reached the dance floor, they stood side-by-side and watched people dance while the disco lights flashed on and off, on and off. Priscilla had to blink rapidly to adjust to the lights and the moving bodies. Unashe said something to her, but she didn't hear him over the strong bass of the popular local song playing. He leaned close to her ear and repeated his question.

"Do you want to dance?"

She shook her head, looking at him.

"Why?"

"I can't dance," she yelled above the noise.

"Everybody can dance," Unashe said. She shook her head again, her hair bouncing around her face. "Come, let's sit and I'll get you a drink."

When Unashe left, Priscilla sat at a table right next to the dance floor. She felt a little uncomfortable looking around at the constantly moving people, who all seemed to be enjoying themselves, dancing as if their life depended on it. A young man in a striped shirt and jeans walked towards her and tried to talk to her but Priscilla turned away from him. Just before she stood up Unashe arrived with their drinks. He gave the other man a look and he moved away, holding up his hands but still watching Priscilla.

Priscilla took the drink. She already wanted to leave, but Unashe seemed eager to stay as he nodded his head to the music and smiled at her. Priscilla nearly jumped when she heard someone scream Unashe's name.

"Unashe!"

"Chantel! Wow!"

Priscilla watched with surprise as Chantel threw herself at Unashe. "You have to dance with me."

Her voice was loud above the song "This Is How We Do It". A lot of the dancers were singing along waiving their hands in the air.

"Go ahead I'll follow," Unashe said. And Chantel was gyrating away from them, hands raised, dancing and singing along. Two other young women followed her. "This is our song!"

"Go ahead," Priscilla said and nodded towards the group.

"Nah, let me stay with you."

"No, don't be silly. Just go on! I need to find the restroom anyway." Priscilla looked around, trying to figure out where the signs were.

She stood up. "Go on," she said. He rubbed her shoulder and left her to join the dancers. He was not too energetic, but still he was enjoying the music as Chantel danced around him, saying something and laughing.

Priscilla couldn't understand how she felt. Bitterness filled her mouth like a rising volcano. The way he danced with Chantel and how she gazed at him made her head spin. He looked so relaxed while Chantel moved closer to him placing her hand on his arm, pouting, moving her hips this way and that.

Priscilla felt like a dud, like she was boring and hopelessly unsophisticated. Why was she sitting on the side while everyone else danced? Another song came and then she lost sight of Unashe as more people joined the throng. She tried to search for him, and then she stood up and started craning her head walking around the dance floor. By the third song and after five different guys had asked her to dance and she'd refused, she wasn't feeling angry. She was fuming!

She started looking for the exit as a very strong beat from Brenda Fasi filled the room and caused the walls to vibrate. The dancers responded positively.

Priscilla walked towards the door, fighting the crowds of people, but she kept looking back, hoping she would find Unashe and catch his eye. She concluded that he was probably too busy dancing, gyrating and rubbing his body against Chantel and her crazy wild friends.

Once outside, she took a deep breath of the fresh air, wishing she had never agreed to this adventure. She felt alone, confused and out of her depth, and it was getting cold. She rubbed her arms, wondering what to do, then as if by magic a taxi stopped right in front of her, letting out a smartly dressed couple.

"Need a taxi?" the driver asked, smiling. He was a friendly, bearded man. He had just dropped off this couple, so he had to be legitimate.

Just as she was about to get in she heard Unashe call her name. She completely ignored him and got in.

"Drive away fast," Priscilla ordered, glancing back to see Unashe stop by the door, staring after her. The driver seeming to sense her urgency and sped off, tires screeching. She settled back in her seat as the car drove off.

"Where to?"

"Eastlea." Priscilla gave him the directions then watched the meter with wide eyes. She just had twenty dollars.

As she sat back on the seat, she told herself that spending time with Unashe was probably not a good idea. They clearly didn't enjoy the same things, and as far as she was concerned he was not the safest person to spend time with. He was irresponsible, immature and certainly not someone to take seriously at all. She needed to cut him from her life without ruining their old friendship. Just get rid of him and let him spend time with Chantel and all those girls who went to private schools and had no worries and responsibilities. She knew that Chantel's parents were rich, gave her a car to drive and even took her on vacations to South Africa. She was his type of woman.

When she arrived home, she was surprised to see Unashe standing by his car waiting for her. He must have driven like a maniac through the streets of Harare to get to her flat before her. He walked towards the taxi driver and took out his wallet.

"How much?" he asked after a quick glance at Priscilla. He watched her walk towards the flat and disappear around the corner to the entrance. Unashe yelled to the driver to keep the change and ran after her.

"What are you doing?" he asked.

"Going home. Why don't you do the same?" She continued to walk, heels clicking on the cement.

Unashe followed her to her door, and when she was about to close the door in his face he blocked it with his hand.

"What's wrong with you?"

Priscilla just shook her head, walked into her lounge, and threw her purse on the floor. Surprised by what she was feeling and embarrassed to acknowledge it, she realized it was time she faced her feelings and Unashe. "I just wanted to go home, okay?"

Unashe shook off his jacket angrily. "So, you should have told me. Why didn't you just say so?"

"How was I supposed to find you? I looked for you!"

"I looked for you, too," Unashe said in a reasonable voice, trying to calm her down. He moved towards her, but she moved away from him. "What you did was dangerous. Going into that taxi alone."

"It's a cab," she said petulantly.

"I know, but you are a girl alone with some man you don't even know. Don't do that again."

"Don't tell me what to do!"

"I just don't want you to get hurt."

"I can take care of myself, Unashe. I don't need you or anybody else."

They stared at each other. Unashe was surprised at her anger, and she seemed shocked, too. He took a deep calming breath, then continued.

"I know you don't need anybody. You're still mad at me. What can I do? I'm sorry I took you to that place."

"And left me."

He was about to argue, she could tell, but he changed his mind. "Okay. I left you for a minute. Do you forgive me?"

She looked at him, his hands held closely together as in prayer. She had no right to be mad. She had told him to go and dance. Insisted that he do so. But she had been blazing with jealousy. She knew it now and it was ridiculous. He could be with whomever he wanted.

"Fine. I just don't think that's my kind of place."

"Because you don't dance? Why don't you dance?"

"I never have. I've never felt like there was a reason to."

"Let me teach you. It's easy." Unashe reached for her hands, but she laughed and shook her head.

"No, I can't. There's no music here."

"Just follow my lead. Step to the side like this," Unashe said and pulled her hands. He moved a little and she still shook her head, standing straight as a tree.

She remembered seeing him dance like that with Chantel, and finally followed his move to the right and then to the left.

"That's right," he said, but groaned when Priscilla shook her head again and then moved to lean against the wall.

"That's enough," she said.

"I'm sorry you were upset. I never want to hurt you. I really want to be here for you. I want to help you settle in."

"Thanks. It's nice." She swallowed hard. "I'm sorry I left."

"I'll make it up to you. I know a place where you'll like more than tonight."

"Really? I don't know if I want to go anywhere with you."

"Yeah, you do. It'll be good. I have to erase this whole mess from your mind."

Priscilla didn't say anything. Her anger was gone and now when she looked at him and he looked at her, his brown eyes looking dark and sincere, she felt her body react and she couldn't think of a thing to say. She noticed his face turn serious, too. Seconds that seemed like minutes went by. Finally, Priscilla looked down at her feet. Unashe remained standing where he was and now it seemed she couldn't look at him without noticing so many details about him. How he looked in his dark shirt unbuttoned at the top and dark jeans and shoes. His neck, his ears, the shape of his head and his slightly curly short dark hair. Everything seemed heightened, and her mouth dried up.

"I'm sorry again about the club," he said at last. "I don't want you to think I'm a bad person."

"Do you like it?"

"Sometimes. It's okay when you just want to get away from home and meet up with friends."

"I didn't know anyone there," Priscilla admitted. She walked to the window and glanced outside and then closed the curtain. She turned to him again.

"Sorry."

"It's okay. You were just trying to entertain me. It's very kind of you. I'm grateful."

He had that look again. And then Unashe let out a frustrated sound, as if he was trying to blow out a stubborn candle.

"I better go home soon," Unashe said with little enthusiasm. He was standing a few steps from her, hands in his pockets. "You can imagine Ma's lecture about getting home late. She said she didn't sleep. Said she wanted to call the police when I stayed here all night."

"Oh. She was worried. I feel badly. She really loves you. You are all she has," Priscilla said, twisting her fingers. She did remember Mukai also complaining to her about Unashe's absence, suspecting a young woman. She didn't want him to leave. It was so good when they talked and laughed together. It felt like a party to her, more than the club did. Now she realized why she hated the club. She didn't want to share him with anybody else. She wanted him all to herself, which was so stupid of her. But she realized that he was working his way into her mind, under her skin, and she didn't know how to shake him off.

"Cilla," he said in his deep, wonderful voice. Whenever he called her 'Cilla' it sounded so intimate. So different. Especially now. His voice touched her skin and made it tingle with heat.

'What?" The look in his eyes spoke to her. Did he have more secrets to reveal to her? Could she handle any more? Her heart was already racing.

"I think," he began, but stopped and shook his head before focusing his eyes on her again. "Something is happening between us. I've always loved you, like a friend."

He paused for a second then rushed in; his voice gruff and earnest. "It's the craziest thing, but it's different now."

Priscilla stared at him, stunned but knowing that her heart knew it. Her heart had been beating with those crazy feelings and she couldn't fight it anymore.

"I love you," she said simply, the heat turning into an inferno. She remembered seeing a fire on her way to the village near Mutare, the fire that ate up the whole countryside all the way up to the road. This feeling she had reminded her of that blaze, which was so strong and uncontrollable. She believed him, it was all over his face, his dark eyes had said it many times but she hadn't known what the powerful message was, the silent communication that turned her knees to water. He was a few feet from her but covered the gap in a few strides. It all seemed so simple. He reached for her, held her close to him, kissed her full lips, kissed her again until they were both breathless, their breathing loud and heavy in the small room.

"I better go," he said after moving back a bit, but he pulled her close again and they kissed deeply, sensuously. She had never felt like this in her life. No man had ever been that close and touched her in such a way. What wonder? She was drowning in his passion. She clung to him, all her independence was gone, her freedom tossed out the window. She felt irrevocably tied to him. Her words about not needing a boyfriend seemed like they were spoken by somebody else. Not needing anyone. Not needing this?

Unashe left her lips and their foreheads touched as he spoke with a voice that she didn't recognize but that sliced through her skin and touched her core. "I suppose it's okay for us, right. We're not related at all. If Uncle Oliver was never your father . . ."

"He's not," she finished for him. This time she kissed him, as if sealing the new knowledge. She drank from his lips as if they were the sweetest wine, eyes closed, lost. She loved feeling his body with her hands, each texture new and fiery. After a while, they broke apart.

"I better go," he managed to say, though he didn't move away from her arms. She smiled softly, trying to catch her breath. "I don't want to get carried away. Though, I already did."

"It's okay. Good night," she whispered and he held her tightly, molding her to him and she loved it all. Loved the feel of him, his scent, his voice, his kisses. All of it. What were they going to do?

CHAPTER 11
Rudo—Love

In high school Priscilla was never the smartest person in her class, but everybody knew she worked hard. She studied all night if she had to, and won top prizes for her effort. She never allowed fun to come between her and her books. At work, she was the same. Priscilla had always been a focused and dedicated worker who hardly took breaks and preferred to work during her lunch while others shopped around town. Unashe was changing her, and she both liked it and feared it. The fire he'd ignited within her continued to burn even when he was out of sight.

Now she would sit at her computer for minutes at a time staring at the wall with a silly smile on her face, recalling how he had made her laugh until her sides hurt, or simple things like buying boiled corn from a street vendor and eating it in the car during her lunch time.

Later, when Chamu Tengani asked her to lunch, she'd told him she was seeing somebody else for lunch. He didn't seem to mind and just said he would call her another day to discuss a client he could send their way. Priscilla was grateful for his kindness, but had little patience to talk to him about anything other than work.

She preferred to spend all her free time with Unashe. She met him at quiet places in town, and sometimes they would drive to a barbecue place outside of town to get *sadza* and meat freshly cooked in the open air.

Sometimes, though, she would lie in bed and decide that spending time with him was a terrible idea and that her family could never accept it. However, once he knocked on her door, her resolve would disappear, melting like frost at midday. She would fall into his arms and pull him into her flat.

Still, she remembered the day it all changed. A day that she decided that she never wanted to lose him, that she would give herself to him completely, no matter the consequences. It was the day she accepted that she was in love with him and there was nothing that could convince her to give him up.

The memory of that day filled her with intense pleasure that she had never felt in all her twenty-two years growing up in Glenview. It was the Saturday Unashe took her driving to the Mazoe Dam not far from the city. He told her that the trip was to make up for the club scene.

She enjoyed the meandering roads, the fields that went for kilometres planted with crops and cows grazing in the fields. It was a day with sunshine, and as they got to the water, she felt the breeze through the open car windows.

"I've never been here before," she said as Unashe drove down a dirt road. "Where are we going?"

"Wait and see." That was his response every time she asked. Finally, as he stopped the car close to a shed housing canoes, she got the idea.

"Are we going in there?"

"Yep. I hope you like it."

"I've never done this before, Unashe. Are we really going in?"

"Of course. Stay with me and I'll show you many things you've never done before," he said, holding his chest out proudly.

She squeaked when he threatened to push her in the water.

"Hey. I'm not even dressed right."

Unashe looked at her standing there in her long white dress. "You'll be fine," he said.

Unashe rented a canoe and then with the help of the man in charge he pushed it into the water.

"Come on." He encouraged her to get in.

"I don't know."

"You'll be fine. I promise."

Unashe guided her in, and, once she had settled down, rowed slowly across the clear water. When they got to the middle, he stopped and leaned back. There was no one on the water with them, just the sound of birds and the majestic mountains surrounding them. Finally, she could relax and look around at the glistening water. She looked at Unashe, who sat facing her.

"Come here," he said, a lopsided smile on his face. She shook her head.

"I'll fall in the water."

"No, you won't. The canoe is quite steady. Come on, Cilla."

"You come here," she challenged him, looking into the water fearfully. "I can't swim, and I don't want to get my dress wet."

"Do you trust me?" He held her gaze with his dark eyes, making her breath catch.

"I do," she responded automatically.

"So come." His voice was soft, but still demanded action. She couldn't say no to Unashe, just as she could not stop the wind from blowing gently on their skin.

Priscilla looked at him for several heartbeats. His gaze was patient and inviting. After a while Priscilla inched closer to Unashe, her eyes on him. The way he looked at her made her heart beat faster, and she squealed when the boat rocked and the wind flapped her skirt.

"It's fine. I'm here. I won't let anything happen to you."

His words filled her with boldness and she took the step to him. He reached out his arms. He had quiet confidence and strength that she responded to. And he was so sweet, making her feel valued, precious. Their fingers held and slowly she moved near him, giddy and pleased to be in his arms.

"This is where you belong," he said as she lay on his broad chest. His words seemed to go deep, to the very center of her being. She nodded, tightening her hold around his waist and sinking closer to him while he rested his hand on her back. She could hear his heartbeat and it made her feel safe, in love. They stayed like that for a long time, the canoe gently rocking, saying very little but accepting that something strong and powerful was happening between them. That day on the water, they both seemed to realize that there was no going back. When they arrived back at her flat and Unashe was about to leave, Priscilla held his hand, her eyes pleading with him to stay with her.

Shyly she reached for his shirt and opened one button, tentatively kissing his chest. She felt him take in his breath and looked in his eyes.

"You don't know what you are doing," he said.

"Show me," she said. Unashe hesitated for a long time. She took his hand and brought it the small of her back and leaned closer to him. If he had been fighting a battle, he lost it as he brought her close to him, kissing her gently until the dam broke loose and passion overtook them. When they lay on her new bed together, it seemed right and natural.

After that day at the dam and the night they gave in to the desire that had been building for months, they both decided to keep their relationship a secret. They didn't have to say anything, it was a silent agreement. She still hoped he would decide to tell his mother about the two of them even though she dreaded it, too. It would be ugly, and even though Oliver was not her father biologically, culturally everyone would still think of Unashe and her to be blood relatives. They would have to bring up all the issues with her father, and then questions would come up about her real father.

Yes, it was better for all concerned to keep everything quiet, Priscilla decided.

CHAPTER 12
Chokwadi—The Truth

Priscilla put the phone down, rubbing her head after a heated conversation with one of her clients. The fact that the data captures they had hired were not doing their job properly was not her fault, but she couldn't explain that to the client. The customer was always right, even when he or she was wrong.

She felt bruised emotionally. Being shouted at always upset her, made her tremble. Before she could go and talk to the manager, her extension rang again.

"May I speak to Priscilla, please," a woman's voice said.

"Speaking," she said, her brow furrowed. The voice didn't sound familiar at all.

"Hi. My name is Chantel Machipa. I'm a friend of your cousin Unashe," she said. It was a well-spoken and modulated voice. The private school voice. The expensive accent. It took Priscilla a second to remember the girl dancing at the club with Unashe.

"Chantel. I remember you," Priscilla said, still puzzled.

"I'm sure you are surprised to hear from me, but I really wanted to talk to you. Is it possible to come and see you at your home? Say, tomorrow after work."

"Okay. That's fine," Priscilla said and gave Chantel her address. After she hung up Priscilla wished she had asked more questions, like what she wanted to see her about. She had been too upset about the prior call to think clearly. Priscilla tried to rack her brain, but she couldn't come up with a possible reason why Chantel wanted to see her.

Chantel and Unashe are over, so why would she even want to talk to me?

Priscilla tried hard to forget about Chantel and her strange call, but an uneasy feeling stayed with her until it was time to go home. When she walked into the reception, she was surprised to see Monica sitting on one of the chairs waiting for her.

"Ma," she cried happily as Monica stood up with a small smile. She looked at the receptionist questioningly. Dadirai was new to the company.

"Your mother said not to disturb you. She got here a few minutes ago," Dadirai explained.

"Thanks," Priscilla said as she embraced her mother. It felt wonderful to hold her, to see her, though Monica did not like embraces. She missed her so much, and if Unashe hadn't been with her all the time she would have been miserable.

"It's good to see you," Priscilla said. "Where are you coming from?"

"I had to buy some fabric so I decided to wait until you were out of work. Your father is away with work. Do you want to come home with me?"

Just the thought of that house filled Priscilla with dread. Her answer came very quickly.

"No. No, thank you," Priscilla demurred. "Why don't we go and talk in a restaurant. I can buy you some supper since Ba—since you'll be alone at home."

"Are you sure you don't want to come home? I am all alone there," Monica persisted as they left the building.

They walked in silence for a while, but after a few meters on the busy sidewalk, Priscilla shook her head. Oliver might come back unexpectedly and Unashe might come to her place that night. She dreaded the one but couldn't do without the other.

"Let's go and eat somewhere," she said firmly.

They found a popular restaurant that was usually busy during lunch but had few diners at this time of evening. They sat opposite each other and Priscilla could sense the change in their relationship. She knew she was different. She wondered if Monica sensed a certain feeling of independence and maturity in her.

"I'm glad you came, actually," Priscilla began. Now that she had her mother all to herself, she decided it would be a good time to ask some questions that had been bothering her.

"I hope you are not thinking too much about what happened. You are not worrying, are you?"

"No. I've accepted the truth," she said.

"Which is?"

"You know what I mean. There isn't a good time to say this, but I found out at your wedding that *Baba* was not my real father," Priscilla said, trying to sound casual about it even though a lump clogged her throat like a huge egg.

"Oh." Monica spoke calmly, but Priscilla could tell from her eyes that her mother was not comfortable with the topic of discussion. But she never lost her cool. Monica was as cool as ice.

"It doesn't matter," Priscilla added.

"Who told you?" Monica demanded, now looking slightly ruffled. "I didn't want you to find out from strangers."

"When were you going to tell me?"

"I want to know who told you," Monica said.

"I overheard Aunty Mary and her friends talking, and then Aunt Mukai confirmed the whole story. I guess she filled me in on all the gory details."

"Don't say that," Monica said, and Priscilla could never ignore her mother's warning tone. They both ordered drinks and sipped them quietly for a while.

Monica looked upset now, and Priscilla felt bad. She never ever wanted to upset her mother. She had spent too much of her life distressed because of Oliver. She never wanted to add to her troubles. After a while, Monica started talking.

"I never wanted you to know. I just hoped we could carry on as normal and we could all be happy."

"Happy?" Priscilla exploded, unable to hide her resentment. "What was happy about our family? Tell me?"

"Priscilla," Monica whispered, her eyes darting to the few people in the restaurant who were beginning to stare.

"If you don't want me to tell you the truth, then we may as well not talk," Priscilla warned.

"Okay. Let's go." Monica stood up. Priscilla was too stunned to protest, but she stood up, too.

"Who is he?"

"What are you talking about?

"I want to know who my father is."

"Not now. Now is not the time."

"So when will be the time, Ma? When?"

"I'm not going to discuss this further in here," Monica said very quietly and walked out. Priscilla couldn't leave as she had to pay the bill, and after some moments she ran outside and found her mother standing on the pavement.

"You go home, my dear. Don't worry about anything," she said.

"How can I not worry? I worry about you and about my real father."

"I don't have anything more to say, my child. I will talk to you another time."

Monica patted Priscilla's arm and turned away. Priscilla stood on the pavement and watched her mother walking away, back straight and purse held by her side. Priscilla kept on watching until her mother had disappeared into the rush-hour crowd, and then she turned and walked in the opposite direction to go home.

In her flat, Priscilla regarded her reflection as she combed her salon-styled hair. Being in her flat and thinking about Unashe melted her unresolved conversation with Monica like ice in the sun. Thoughts of him filled her with joy and anticipation as she recalled the way he kissed her so tenderly and took his time removing her clothes, building the anticipation of getting lost in each other. She noted the sparkle in her eyes as she inspected the cream dress she had changed into, disappointed that she would have to cover most of it with a sweater. She could almost touch her excitement with her fingers as she saw her flushed face and felt heat invade her body as if her love was right there, looking at her.

Unashe didn't come that evening, and Priscilla was deeply disappointed, more than she would want to admit. As she sat on her bed wrapped in thick warm blankets, ridiculous thoughts came into her mind. Maybe he was already tired of her. It happened to many women.

She slept badly that night, and when he phoned her at work the next day she couldn't hide her frustration.

"Hi, darling," he said. "I missed you last night."

"Where were you?" She tried to keep her tone very light.

"Something came up. I have some great news. I think my UK thing is going to work out. The bank is willing to help me pay for my tuition in Manchester. Manchester, imagine. Right where my favorite team is. Can you believe it? I had to run around sorting out my papers and get contacts from Uncle Huggins. I finished very late."

"I wish I'd known," Priscilla complained.

"I'm sorry. I missed you, but this was important."

More important than me. She knew she was being unreasonable, but she had missed him. Something had to be done. She needed him every day. Staying apart just didn't work for her anymore. It was his fault. From the moment she left home, he had worked his way first into her apartment, then into her heart, with his sweetness, playfulness, deep conversations, and his touch. How amazing it was to be held in his strong arms.

"Really," she said. She didn't know what to say. UK. Uncle Huggins. She remembered their conversations about him leaving. It didn't seem like it would be so soon. It had seemed like a distant dream, far away.

"I'll come and see you tonight. I love you," Unashe said. "I have to rush to the British Embassy, get visa photos and many other places. It's amazing how much stuff I need to sort out. See you."

He was in such a hurry. She hated that other things got him so excited, especially things that would take him away from her, from the country. Priscilla worried the whole day until it was time to go home. As she rode on the bus, she remembered Chantel's phone call.

After the long, chilly journey home, Priscilla let herself in to her flat and turned on the heater to warm up the cold room. She heard a knock on the door.

Priscilla opened the door, and there stood Chantel. It could only be her.

"Hello," Chantel said, a speculative smile warming her face. Priscilla realized that she was taller than she remembered. She also took in Chantel's braids, tied in a neat ponytail, her make up, toffee-colored skin and her full lips painted a deep grape. Up close, Priscilla realized that Chantel was very attractive, though the makeup was too heavy for her taste. She looked mixed, and she knew that many young black boys liked girls who were half-white and half-black. Definitely a memorable face. Priscilla shook hands with her in greeting.

"Come in." Priscilla directed her guest inside her lounge, not sure how she was supposed to treat this intruder. They had never really spoken before, and she wondered what this whole visit entailed.

"I don't know if you remember me. I'm Chantel. Unashe's girlfriend."

Priscilla wanted to correct her and say ex-girlfriend, but she kept quiet. Chantel's words sent her mind spinning and her heart constricting painfully.

"I remember you. From a long time ago," Priscilla said, wondering if she should offer her tea, or the scones she had bought at the bakery. They both sat down diagonally to each other and Priscilla looked at her politely, hands folded by her knees.

"I didn't know who else to come and talk to. I understand you and Unashe are very close," she said, her bright brown eyes on Priscilla. Her voice sounded European, her words high and clear. She remembered how in high school they had felt jealous of girls who went to mostly European schools. Their parents drove Mercedes Benzes and lived in the suburbs or owned huge hectares of farms all over the country. Her friends would say they sounded like they had marbles in their mouth. Chantel sounded as if she had about a hundred of them in hers.

As Chantel talked, Priscilla was still puzzled.

"We are, I suppose. What's the problem?"

"I don't know how to say this," she said, smiling almost shyly. Priscilla felt warning bells, though she still had no idea what Chantel wanted. She couldn't even begin to guess, though she knew that she wasn't going to like whatever it was.

"Does this have anything to do with me?" Priscilla wondered if Chantel knew of her relationship with Unashe. Had people found out?

"Well," Chantel began tentatively, rubbing her hands together. "The problem is this . . ."

Priscilla listened with growing horror and shock as Chantel began to relate her story. She couldn't believe it, but was too shocked to utter a word.

". . . so I thought I would come to you," Chantel finished.

The story was unbelievable, yet had to be true. Unashe had been having an intimate relationship with Chantel, too, and now she was pregnant with his baby. He refused to acknowledge it. She had to be joking. Unashe would never have done anything like that.

You are lying! She screamed inside even as she believed what Chantel was saying.

"I love him," Chantel continued when she didn't get a response from Priscilla. "I thought we would get married if I got pregnant, but now he doesn't want to have anything to do with me." She was crying now. Tears trailed down her cheeks.

"What will I do? Can you talk to him?" Chantel begged. "I'm scared to tell my parents. They will kill me. I was supposed to leave for the UK, too, but Unashe doesn't want me to go with him. How could he do this to me?"

Priscilla was stunned. She wouldn't have been more shocked if Chantel had confessed that she was actually a pig.

How could Unashe refuse his own child after how his father rejected him? Did the apple not fall far from the tree? And when had he been seeing Chantel? He was probably with Chantel all the nights he didn't come and see her. Her mind flashed back to the club, when they had danced together so closely, and she felt her rage increase. All these thoughts went through her head in seconds, tumbling over each other as she stared at Chantel's tearful face.

After a while Priscilla spoke, her voice weak and pathetic to her own ears as she suggested, "I'm sorry I can't help you. I don't know him that well. Why don't you go and see his mother?"

Chantel nodded, but all Priscilla wanted was to be alone and figure out how she had finally given herself completely to someone, her body and soul, when he was seeing Chantel, too. Maybe he even took her to Mazoe Dam on the canoe and seduced her in the same way. What had been special and difficult for her to do had been cheap to him. She wanted to be alone to cry and give in to her anger.

CHAPTER 13
Chipengo—Madness

Priscilla's rage increased with each passing minute after Chantel left. When she closed her eyes, she saw red, bright colors of fire and fury.

Thinking of what to do to ease her boiling blood she stalked into the bedroom and pulled the few items that belonged to Unashe that were still in her wardrobe. They were contaminating her space. She found two shirts, the slippers she had bought him, a jersey and a cap. She threw them on the bed. She wanted to throw them out of the window, but restrained herself. Only just. She pulled two plastic bags from the kitchen and shoved all his clothes, cassettes and books into them, her breath coming out in murderous puffs.

There was a knock at the door. She froze in her tracks, her heart beating even faster than before. Still on the bed, she heard a second knock. She walked into the living room and stood there for a second. She didn't want to see him at all. She couldn't face him. She couldn't let him see how much she hurt. How humiliated she was by his behavior. But she had to.

Before he knocked a third time she opened the door. He smiled, holding a small package in his hand. He looked so good, so wonderful, and, at that moment, so deceitful.

"Cilla! Sweetheart." He hugged her to him but she pushed him away roughly, his scent making her weak. He always smelled so good.

"What's wrong?" he asked, closing the door and following her as she walked away from him. "I brought you this." He handed her a wrapped up parcel, which she took and roughly threw on the sofa. She avoided his eyes angrily, shaking her head, sniffing.

"Priscilla, what's going on? Why are you angry?"

"I don't want to talk to you about it. Why don't you just take your things and go? Just leave me alone," she yelled. She saw him flinch as if she had slapped him. Maybe she should slap him.

"Is it about me going? Come on. We can work it out . . ."

"Damn you! Just go. I have your nasty things all packed up," she said, and then marched into her bedroom and brought back the plastic bags with his belongings. He still stood where she had left him as if he was paralyzed.

"Here," she said and flung them at his feet. "Get out."

"What?" He was angry now. "You really are serious?"

"I am, Unashe. Just go."

Unashe felt panic rise in his chest, almost choking him. "Come on, Cilla. Let's talk about this," he said and reached for her. She jumped away from him.

"I don't believe this," he muttered, shock written all over his face. "Are you saying this is over? We are through?"

She nodded her head, throbbing with the effort of keeping her tears in check. "I can't stand you, Unashe. I don't ever want to see you again. You are the biggest mistake of my life!"

He glared at her for what seemed like a minute. She enjoyed it. He was feeling just as she was feeling.

"Mistake."

"Yes. I've come to my senses. You used my body and took advantage of me. So just go!"

"I—what? You were enjoying it just as much as I was!"

"That's where you're wrong. I should never have let you touch me. It was wrong! We were wrong. Just go!"

"So that's how we break up?"

"Unashe. That's how I do it, yes. If you don't leave now, I'm walking out of here. Just leave!"

"You are really something, you know. You should find out who your father is, because he could be crazy just like you."

"You bastard! I hate you!" Priscilla screamed and picked up the nearest thing, a vase with flowers, and threw it at him. He jumped out of the way and the glass shattered, hitting the wall. She stared at the flowers and water on the floor and glared at him.

They stood facing each other, her words forming a huge chasm between them. She couldn't tell him about Chantel. Her pride wouldn't let her tell him. A minute passed, and after that Unashe picked up the plastic bags and walked out and slammed the door. He didn't wait long enough outside her door to hear her sobbing as though her soul would break.

At work the next day, she was in a black mood. She sat at her desk and stared out the window.

"Julia, I'm sorry, but I can't talk to you at the moment," she said when Julia came to chat at lunchtime.

"What's wrong?" Julia asked, very concerned. "You look like someone died or something."

"I can't talk about it. Ever," Priscilla said, almost in tears. "I'd rather be left alone."

Mukai's phone call before lunch made matters worse.

"Pri. You've been so quiet. Is everything all right?"

"I'm fine," she croaked, trying to sound normal.

"Did Unashe tell you?" she asked, but obviously didn't wait for an answer. "He's going to the UK. Everything has worked out. I'm so relieved. He'll be going to study for a business and financial degree. He managed to organize a partial scholarship and accommodations through the bank. He's trying to finalize his papers now," she said and sighed. Priscilla assumed she was waiting for a response.

"That's wonderful," she said.

"You don't believe me, do you?" Mukai asked. "Between you and me I'm glad he's going to school. I think Chantel is the girl he was seeing, spending all those nights away from home. I think she wanted to get married to him. Imagine. He's only twenty-two. Some women. Bad news, though. I think she's also going overseas soon. I think even if they get together while they are studying it's better than to get too serious before they have a proper education and job, don't you agree?"

"I agree," Priscilla said.

"Anyway, I don't have much time. I need to go to the bank and then to Truworths to buy him some new clothes. I want to make sure he has warm clothes. It'll be cold there soon. You take care."

"I will," she said and hung up quickly as she began to sob. She ran to the ladies' room, cried and threw up.

When Priscilla came back to her office, she had another phone call. She picked it up and mumbled a hello. It was Unashe.

"Cilla, we need to talk," he said at once.

"I've nothing to say to you," she said, about to hang up.

"Listen. This is crazy. What's going on?"

"There's nothing more to say. It's over. Accept it. Goodbye," Priscilla said and hung up the phone. When he called again she put the phone down before he could even say anything, and when he came to the office she refused to see him. She felt that if she saw his face she would try and claw his eyes out. Anything to make him feel the pain she was experiencing.

At the end of the workday, she packed her bag and walked tiredly from her office. She gasped when she saw Unashe sitting at reception, head in his hands, elbows resting on his knees. Her heart skipped a beat, but she didn't approach him. She just stared at him for a while, and then walked back into her office. She knew other ways to leave the building without running into Unashe again.

Mukai phoned again on Friday morning. "Unashe's leaving tomorrow. Are you coming to the airport?"

"I'll try." Priscilla scratched her head as she tried to think of a very good excuse not to go.

"Good," Mukai said. "I'll come and pick you up."

Priscilla wanted to scream "no", but instead she said the first thing that came to her mind to get her aunt off her back. "Don't worry. I'll come over to your house and say goodbye properly."

"Are you sure? You have to take two buses."

"I can manage," she said, knowing that nothing would make her go to Mukai's house while her cheating and lying son was still there.

Chamu called and asked her to go to the races on Saturday at the Borrowdale Race Course. She agreed. That way she wouldn't be home if her aunt decided to check at her house. It was a desperate move, maybe one she would live to regret.

Chamu was very sweet, caring, and, in a way, that was a balm to her wounded and still bleeding heart. She even bet on a horse and found herself screaming for Beetle Ray to win. The excited crowd added to the frenzy as Beetle lost the race at the last minute. It came second, but even after such a close victory, she couldn't help checking her watch to see how long Unashe had before he left.

Chamu, dressed in a pair of dark blue corduroys and a shirt, was very attentive. He ordered drinks for her as they watched the races. Afterwards he drove her home in a new silver Mercedes.

"How about going for something to eat?" She looked at him and tried to smile. How bored he must be of her.

"I'm sorry for being so quiet. It's just somebody who is very important to me is leaving today."

"Anyone I know?"

"No."

I don't know him all that well either, she thought.

"So can I treat you to a nice steak dinner?" She had to stay away from her flat. If she went there then she would have some explaining to do to Mukai. She couldn't do that without breaking down and crying. She couldn't face Unashe's mother. Not yet.

"Okay," she replied.

She was very impressed when he took her to the Miekles. It was the best five-star hotel in the city.

"Is this where we are eating?" she asked, surprised as if she had just woken up from a dream.

"Yes," he said after parking in the basement. "Do you mind?"

"No. I'm just surprised, that's all," she said, taking off her seat belt.

It was hard for her to concentrate, even in those beautiful surroundings. A young man played the black grand piano and the diners spoke in muted voices. The food was like cardboard in her mouth, though she knew that under different circumstances she would have loved the tender steak and seasoned vegetables.

Chamu did most of the talking, while she nodded and agreed with him as he told her some of his business ideas. He didn't seem to notice her depression, but at the end of the meal he gave her a very penetrating look. Maybe he did suspect that something was wrong.

It was 9 p.m. Unashe would be getting ready to board his plane, and where was she? Sitting here with Chamu. Why was she here? She could at least go and see him off. Aunt Mukai would be very upset.

"I think I want to go home now," Priscilla said suddenly, looking at Chamu. "And I'm sorry I haven't been good company. You are a good friend and you deserve better than the way I've been acting."

"Don't worry. I enjoyed spending the day with you. I think every man in here envies me," he said, glancing at the other diners. Priscilla didn't even have the energy to glance around.

"Thank you for the day. I have to be home," she insisted, giving him a tremulous smile.

On the drive back Chamu talked about his business, but Priscilla's mind was miles away. He insisted on walking her to her door and made sure she was in safely.

"Will you be all right?" His tone was gentle and kind. She could tell he wanted to be invited in, but she would not do that.

"Yes," she answered.

"If you need to talk you can call me," he offered and touched her gently on the shoulder.

"Thank you," she said and closed the door, already feeling weak with the feelings she had been holding in check.

Oh, Unashe.

Priscilla looked at the clock in a panic. Maybe she could rush to the airport and at least see him for the last time. His flight was due to take off at 10 p.m. Priscilla picked up her phone and dialled the number for a cab. It would cost her a lot of money, but it would be worth it. Then she put the phone down after one ring.

No. She would not go after him after what he had done to her. She tried to ignore the wave of loneliness that engulfed her in an instant. Feeling pathetic, she fell on the sofa, willing her mind to forget him. Every corner of her apartment reminded her of him, and memories hit her one after the other.

She saw him walking out of the kitchen holding a bottle of beer, or a glass of Mazoe Orange diluted with a lot of water. She imagined the door opening; he would walk in as he always did, coming from soccer or the gym, wanting to talk to her, hold her . . .

"What have I done?" she said to the silent room.

Even as she sobbed those words, his plane took off into the night sky.

CHAPTER 14
Madiro—Choices

"You are pregnant," Dr. Mpinga said to an incredulous Priscilla. She had suspected it, but to have her fears confirmed was still a mind-blowing experience.

The moment she heard the news her mind flashed deeply personal images of her and Unashe, remembering the first time they had become intimate. Her face flashed with heat and humiliation. His voice came clearly to her as her mind went back to that time when she had found herself falling for him, jumping in with both feet without a thought about consequences. As much as she tried to push him out of her mind after the news, Unashe stayed with her as she left the doctor's office, remembering each detail like it was just yesterday.

Looking back, she realized one of the problems with her relationship with Unashe. She had needed him too much. She didn't have any other friends and spent all her spare time with him.

Now she remembered a saying her grandmother would mutter. "Pretty calabashes sour the beer." When she said that, Grandmother Pasipano had been talking about Monica right in front of her face. Talking about her beauty, hinting that it hid some inner flaws. Well, thinking back the same could have been said about Unashe. Being with him had been so beautiful, but his true nature was revealed with that horrible visit from Chantel. Now she was left holding the baby.

Unashe was gone and she had to deal with something she had always feared since Vimbai was chased out of her home at fifteen. She was pregnant, alone, and pathetic.

What will Mama think? What will Oliver say?

He would call her every bad name he could think of, plus many new ones. There was no way she could tell anybody who the father was. It was all so ironic. She didn't know who her father was, and here she was going to have a baby who was not allowed to know, either. After she left the doctor's office, she walked around town in a daze, her mind numb with terror.

Chamu was good about looking after her, though she wondered why she was letting another man into her life. She certainly wasn't in love with him, but he was a good friend. He listened as she told him about her broken heart without mentioning any names. He'd been kind and understanding.

"After this if you don't mind I don't ever want to talk about him again," she'd said to him.

"I don't mind," Chamu said.

That evening Chamu came by again after work, still in his expensive suit and tie. She let him in and couldn't help noticing the look he gave her. Could he tell she was pregnant?

"How are you today?" He sat down on the sofa close to her.

"I'm fine," she said. "How's business?"

"Going very well. I can't complain. Thanks to your programming and computerising all our departments we now are able to do things more efficiently, and I will be able to track all my accounts and catch anyone stealing."

"You don't have to thank me. A number of us worked on your account."

"I think you were the creative power," he said. "You are also the best person to deal with at CMS."

"You flatter me," she said, embarrassed.

"No. It's the truth. You are not just the most beautiful woman in the world. You are also intelligent, modest, kind . . ."

"Stop, Chamu," she cried. "I'm not intelligent. I'm so stupid."

"Don't say that about yourself. It's not true." She shook her head but said nothing.

"You are wonderful. And, Priscilla, I'm in love with you. Have been for so long," he added, serious now.

"Chamu," she said shocked at his words, trying to cut him off.

"I mean it. I love you very much. I hate seeing you this upset."

"You really mean that?" she asked, surprised at the ardor in his eyes.

"I do," he said. "And I have a question to ask you. Will you marry me?"

"You want to marry me?"

"Yes. I love you more than anything in this world. I know you loved the other man that left you, and maybe it will take you a while to love me, but I really want to spend the rest of my life with you. I need you."

Priscilla looked at his defined features and his small penetrating eyes. His attractiveness came from his confidence and charm. He always knew the right thing to say.

"You can't want to marry me," she said. "I have something to tell you, too. I just discovered today that I'm pregnant. With his baby."

Chamu was very still and quiet all of a sudden. It seemed he hadn't expected that. Who would have expected that? He quickly recovered.

"Are you going to tell him?"

Priscilla shook her head. "I haven't even thought about that, but I don't think so. What is the point? He doesn't love me, but loves somebody else. It's my problem. I'll take care of it."

"What do you mean by that?" Chamu asked suspiciously.

"I would never try to get rid of my baby," Priscilla said firmly. "I mean I will look after my baby on my own. I have my own place, I have a job. I won't be the first single mother in Harare."

"I'm not asking to judge you. I just want to help you."

"Thank you, Chamu," she said, lying back on her sofa and sighing. "Now you see why I'm not the marrying kind."

"You are to me. I still love you. I still want to marry you," he insisted. Priscilla sat up.

"Before you say no, just think about it," Chamu said, holding up his hand. "I want to be a father to your baby. Nobody needs to know that it's not my baby. I'll take responsibility. I love you. I will love your baby. Can you think about it please? I love you."

I love you. I love you. His words echoed in her mind that cold night and the others that followed as she sat alone by her tiny heater. Chamu came to see her every day, bringing her expensive gifts of perfume, jewellery, baskets of fruits, flowers and clothes.

"Please take it, Pri. It gives me pleasure just to see you wearing something I've given you. There is no obligation. I just love to make you happy. Give me that, at least."

"I'd like you to see my home," he said the following week when he went to pick her up at her office. She looked into his brown eyes that seemed to try and dig their way into her soul.

"Your home? With your parents?" she asked.

"No." He laughed. "I now live alone. I bought it last year and only now am I confident enough to show it to someone."

"When would you like me to come?" she asked.

"Now. We'll go there, you can tell me what you think, and then we can go for dinner," he cajoled. "I will take you anywhere you want after that, Beautiful."

Priscilla tried to smile. Instead she fought tears of despair.

CHAPTER 15
Kanganwa—Forget

Priscilla had once been told that being a fool was part of life, but experience would help her become wise. During the last few months she'd had a lot of experience, but was she any wiser? She didn't feel wise. She felt confused and lost.

Unashe had left without promising her anything. No marriage, no future, no love.

A month of misery had gone by, and she was determined to put him out of her mind. She did it in the most drastic way. She began to resent him, completely. Priscilla could get herself to do anything. Hating Unashe wasn't that difficult.

It was a windy day in August, the day before Priscilla was going to meet Chamu's family. She stood in the protective shelter of her bedroom and wiped the mirror with her damp hands. Standing naked, she gazed without expression at her reflection. Her mind was blank as she looked, and she refused to let any thoughts come into her head. Thinking had made her feel sick, and training her mind to be totally still had been essential.

With her pregnancy, her skin seemed to be glowing. It was as if a light had been switched on inside her and now blazed through her semi-translucent brown skin. When she had finished dressing, she heard a knock on the door.

"Who is it?"

"It's Aunty Mukai."

Priscilla ran to the door and flung it open. "Sorry to keep you waiting."

This was the first time she had seen her aunt since Unashe left. It was probably the longest time that they had not seen each other. Their recent phone conversations had been brief.

"Pri," she said. She wore a lovely deep maroon embroidered African outfit, complete with the headscarf. She made a disapproving sound as she sat down and pursed her lips in further dissatisfaction.

"How are you?" Priscilla asked, smiling as hard as she could.

"I don't know. You haven't even bothered to come and see me. Where have you been keeping yourself?"

"I've been here," she said feebly.

"Priscilla, I know you. I was very upset when you didn't come to see Unashe off. I really don't understand you. I thought you two were close. And all this lack of respect. I'm not supposed to be coming to your home, you should be visiting me. I am your aunt. I am older than you. More than that, I thought we were friends. I never expected such lack of respect from you. Not you, Priscilla."

"I'm sorry, Aunty," Priscilla said, wanting to be angry but feeling distressed instead.

"Come on, Priscilla." Mukai leaned closer to her and then changed her attitude completely. "What's wrong? Were you crying?"

"No."

"Yes, you were. Tell me what is bothering you," Mukai said, then looked at the flowers on the table by the window, a beautiful arrangement of red roses and white carnations.

"Have you got a boyfriend? Did he upset you?"

"No, Aunty."

"Are you missing home?"

"Yes," she replied. "I miss Mother the most. I always worry about her there at home. I'm okay here on my own."

"And this guy who sends you flowers. Is he serious about you? You should tell me these things."

Priscilla was always amazed. Her aunt could be angry one minute and comforting her the next. Her abruptness could be hurtful, but she should be used to her by now.

Priscilla smiled. "He's a very nice person."

"Where does he work?"

"In town. He's self-employed."

"That's good. You can't go out with a man who doesn't work. Believe me, I've been there before. Tell me more. Does he want to marry you?"

"Yes," Priscilla replied very quietly.

Mukai leaned even closer. "Well, that's good, isn't it?"

"It's perfect," Priscilla said.

"You don't sound too happy. Priscilla, what's going on with you?"

"Nothing. You are just imagining things."

"Well, I think I should meet this gentleman," she said. "Will I meet him?"

"Yes," Priscilla said and stood up. "Would you like a drink?"

"Thanks. That will be nice."

Priscilla went to the kitchen, curious what her aunt was thinking about all the news that she had just given her. It was also a relief to be away from her and all the emotions that she evoked. She took the orange juice from the refrigerator and filled two glasses. Then she walked back to her lounge and handed Mukai the drink.

"So what's he like?"

"He is a great person. You'll see when you meet him," Priscilla said. With her concerned expression, Mukai suddenly reminded her so much of Unashe it made her heart beat faster.

Dear God, she thought, *this is my child's grandmother.*

"You'll have to bring him to me. You know how these marriage things are. It's complicated."

"You mean the *lobola* stuff?" Priscilla asked, having witnessed her sister's traditional marriage years before. It had been a serious affair with her father demanding more and more money from the groom. The future husband had his own group of people to negotiate the deal. It had seemed rather emotionless to her, and her sister had been angered by the whole event. What obviously made it worse was the fact that she was pregnant and Gilbert was charged "damages" as a result. It was quite a considerable amount of money to pay, and Gilbert's family grumbled amongst themselves. Priscilla wondered if that was why both her sisters' husbands treated them so badly.

"I suppose *Baba* will have to get the money, even if he is not my real father," Priscilla said after taking a sip of her drink.

"It'll have to be decided. It's never that straightforward," Mukai disclosed, pursing her lips to show the seriousness of the situation. "You'll have to come and see me with this guy. What is his name, by the way?"

"Chamu. Chamunorwa Tengani," she said.

"Tengani. I know that name. Is he the one who owns stores in Highfields?"

"I really don't know," Priscilla said. "Maybe. Some of his uncles also own businesses."

Priscilla noticed the way Mukai studied her. Priscilla wondered if she smelled something fishy.

"Who will be there?" Priscilla asked Chamu as they drove through the sunny streets of Harare towards his parents' home in Avondale.

"My brothers and sisters and maybe a few other people. My mother will be there, of course," he said. Priscilla looked out of the car window, uneasy about what lay ahead. Not just that day, but also the rest of her life. She was going to meet the family of the man who she was going to marry. A wonderful man, but one she did not love but only respected. She had set traps in burnt grass and should no longer be afraid of her apron getting dirty. That's what her father had said when Vimbai got pregnant. She had been naughty, and now she had to accept the reward. Besides, Oliver had also said that a hard bed could not kill, and she was going to accept her situation with dignity.

She looked at her hands on her lap, folded nervously over her blue outfit. She had bought the suit especially for this meeting. It was a pale blue two piece, which wouldn't show the small bulging of her stomach. She appeared as flat as she did before, and sometimes wondered if she had imagined the doctor's words.

"Are you worried about meeting my family?"

"Not really," she said. "A little, maybe."

"It'll be fine," he assured her. "We are almost there."

They got to Avondale and were now driving in a rather secluded and peaceful area. The houses were high up on top of hills or hidden way down below so that she couldn't really see them. The roads wound up and down like a roller coaster. As the car inched up the driveway, it seemed like they were climbing a mountain. It led right up to the front of the house. With a thudding heart, Priscilla realized they had arrived.

"This is it," Chamu said, switching off the car engine and throwing a look Priscilla's way.

The house was white and built in a Spanish style. The land sloped down in a steep incline to the main road. There were also some flowers, but there wasn't much lawn. As she scanned the place, she caught a glimpse of a gated swimming pool. In the distance, she could hear a dog barking. While Priscilla sat in her seat with the safety belt still on, a chubby woman wearing an apron ran out to greet them, heavy breasts bouncing.

"Chamu," the lady cried happily as she ran towards the car.

"That's my aunt," he said, getting out of the car. Priscilla got out, too. "*Tete* Thembie!" He turned to the cheerful woman and held her hands firmly. "This is Priscilla."

Tete Tembie turned to Priscilla and looked at her from top to bottom, like an inspection at boarding school.

"Priscilla," Tembie said, making her name sound like a song before shaking her hands firmly. She smelled of washing soap and spices. Before Priscilla could recover, a line of people came to meet them. She stared, fighting down panic.

"Those are my brothers and sisters," Chamu said. He came over to her and put his arm around her.

"Is she scared?" *Tete* Thembie asked. Priscilla didn't appreciate the way she was being discussed as if she wasn't there.

She took a step forward and greeted the rest of the family. Chamu's younger brother Sidney was a lighter brown and thinner version of his older brother. Gwen followed, an unsmiling woman, who seemed to take her position as the eldest daughter very seriously. Priscilla smiled as she shook her hand but did not get a smile in return. She shook hands with two other young boys. The whole family looked at her curiously, but later on when she thought about it and really analysed that first meeting, she realized that their glances were more than interest. There had been something a bit more disturbing in their eyes. It would be a long time before she understood what those intent stares meant.

CHAPTER 16
Rusimbiriro—Determination

After the visit with his family, Chamu took her home and walked her into her flat. The visit had been awkward, and she wasn't sure if she had been welcome. Things seemed to go downhill from the moment Chamu's mother, Lina, asked Priscilla why she wanted to marry her son. The visit seemed to Priscilla as if it had been the longest day of her life. The meeting proceeded with questions, unusual conversation and plenty of food to eat. She had not completely relaxed as the talking went on around her.

The whole family seemed very close, but there was something queer that she just couldn't put her finger on. She sensed it when she looked up from her plate and caught Gwen, the eldest girl in the family, looking at her. Another time Lina stared at her strangely, as if she knew her whole life story.

Chamu's mother Lina kept intruding on her thoughts. Did she know about her and Unashe? Why was she so hostile one minute, and then trying to cover it with jokes the next?

While they ate the well-prepared food in the beautiful dining room, Priscilla had wondered about Lina's little comments. Something she said that stood out still made

Priscilla's blood boil. "So, which university did you go to?"

"I didn't go to university. I got my diploma at Universal Business College."

"Is that right?" Lina turned to Chamu. "I thought you wanted a wife with a degree, not the uneducated type."

"Ma, she's educated," Chamu said with a laugh. He seemed to find his mother's comment amusing.

"I'm just joking, Priscilla," Lina said and looked in her eyes, a devious smile on her face. "I'm sure you learned a lot at your little college."

Thinking back, Priscilla knew that Lina wanted to insult her and had succeeded. Priscilla had been so humiliated that she couldn't think of a smart response. She should have asked *her* what degree she had.

"Did you have a good time?" Chamu asked as he sat opposite her in the living room.

"It was all right. I need to get used to everybody."

"You will," he said. "When we start planning the wedding you will really get to know my whole family."

Priscilla nodded. She was not eager to discuss the wedding. She felt she needed to know more about his family, so she asked him more questions. Chamu answered her with detail.

"Well, all those kids are younger than me, but since my father passed away I have been the head of the house. Sidney works in the family company, Gwen is married with one child, Brian and Richard are both at the university studying medicine, Sekai and the youngest, Tawanda, are both still in school."

"I'm sure in time I'll know them more."

"How are you feeling?" he asked with concern when he saw her rub her back.

"I'm fine," she replied, sitting down opposite him. Her apartment was so different now; it seemed that with each gift Chamu brought her, he took away more of Unashe. It was now looking more like a home. Chamu had made sure she had even more than she needed. She tried to argue, saying she was happy with the way things were, but he insisted on buying her potted plants, paintings and every electrical gadget a person would need. He was very convincing. She could tell that he was not used to anybody telling him no.

"Can I come and sit next to you?" She thought about it for a second, and nodded her head. He walked to her and sat down next to her. He smelled of musky cologne, so different from Unashe's more subtle one. She didn't feel comfortable when he put his arm around her.

"I love you," he said, turning her to face him. She hoped he wasn't going to kiss her.

Not yet. Please.

"Even . . ."

"I don't care about anything else except to be with you. I don't expect you to say you love me yet, but I'm going to love you and give you everything you need. My love will be enough for both of us," he said, his voice filled with emotion.

"I don't deserve you," she said softly, meaning it.

"We were meant to be together," he said.

Priscilla looked down but didn't say anything.

CHAPTER 17
Kuenda Mberi—Moving Forward

Chamu Tengani was in a very good mood. He had completed a successful business deal, and it seemed like everything he had always wanted was within his grasp. Zimbabwe had been dominated by foreign companies and banks, and now it seemed like Africans were about to break into traditionally white-dominated industries. He couldn't be happier with his life. The woman of his dreams was about to become his wife, and he was going to get even richer. In his excitement, he picked up the phone on his desk and dialled her office number.

"Hi, darling," he said when her heard her voice.

"Hello, Chamu," Priscilla said.

"Can we meet for lunch?" he asked, trying to disguise the hope in his voice.

"Mmmh, I have a lot of work to do today. Let's meet after work instead," Priscilla said.

"That's fine. I'll have some lunch delivered to your office," Chamu said.

"I'm not very hungry," she insisted.

"You have to eat," Chamu said. "And I'll see you tonight."

He hid his disappointment as he hung up the phone and looked around his massive office. He had what many other people would only dream of in any country in the world. And now he had a beautiful fiancée. Life was good. He wasn't going to focus on the fear that she might change her mind, or that she didn't seem as impatient as he was to spend time together. That would all come in time.

But one thing was for sure. As soon as they got married, he would have to find a way to make her quit her job. That job took up too much of her time, and too many men were salivating for her. He would have to tread carefully. There was an air of independence about her. Though he found it endearing now, her independent streak could be a problem later on in life. A woman needed to feel pampered, and he wouldn't have any wife of his slaving at a desk when he made enough money to buy the company she worked for. No way.

Priscilla put the phone down at her desk, eating the lunch Chamu had sent to her office. She now wanted more than anything to find her real father. She felt the urgency growing inside just as her baby was being formed in her belly. Before it had been a nagging feeling, nudging at her. Now it was something she thought about each day.

Aunt Mukai was going to tell her parents about her intended marriage. They had discussed how they would do it at length, and Aunt Mukai advised her to just have the marriage ceremony through Oliver and not bring up anything about her real father. Mukai felt that opening up that hive of bees would just delay her marriage ceremony. The fact was that Priscilla had recently learned the name of her biological father.

Getting his name had not been easy. Monica refused to speak, but Mukai knew the place where she had worked when Oliver kicked her out. It was a grocery store in Chitungwiza. After finding that out, she had asked the employees to find out about Monica Pasipano. A call had come through that Monica had worked there twenty-three years before and was about to marry the owner's nephew, Robert. The owner remembered her very well.

Robert Chigoni. My father is Robert Chigoni.

After work, Chamu came to pick her up. For such a busy man he always had time for her. Priscilla got into his Mercedes and put her head back. She felt exhausted.

"Did you have a wonderful day?"

"It was nice, Chamu. I'm just tired," she said.

"We can go and have dinner somewhere," he suggested, putting his car in traffic.

"Something quick, like Nando's," she said, smiling.

"Nando's? That's fine, but I was thinking more of a fancy restaurant."

"You take me to too many of those," she said.

"I like to take my lady to the very best."

The Nando's line wasn't very long. They bought quarter chicken and chips. Priscilla ordered a very hot one. She had been craving spicy food lately, and Portuguese chicken fit the bill.

As they sat down to eat, Priscilla decided to tell Chamu about her father.

"I would like to find him," she said after her explanation.

"What's his name?" Chamu asked. He was still shocked at what she had told him, but was not going to show it and make her more upset.

"Robert Chigoni," Priscilla said.

"I know that man," Chamu said, surprising her.

"You know him?"

"Yes. He's very well known in the political field. He had a top position in government at one time and even served as ambassador to a few countries." Priscilla touched her neck and looked down. He knew her father. Her father was somewhere in this city.

"He owns a lot of buses now from what I have heard. He could even be my competitor," Chamu continued.

"Thank you for the information, Chamu," Priscilla said, wrapping her half-finished food in a bag.

"What are you going to do? Do you want to see him?"

"I don't know, Chamu. I'll have to sleep on it. I didn't think it would be so easy to find him. I thought I would have to hire a private detective."

"Well, I'm your man. I can arrange for you to meet him," Chamu said, taking a sip of his Coke.

"No. I think I want to do this alone," she said. Chamu looked disappointed. "Thank you, though," Priscilla added. She seemed to be always thanking him.

They talked about the wedding as they drove home.

"I can't wait for this arrangement to be over so I can take you to my house as my wife," Chamu said.

"It won't be long. Aunt Mukai is going to speak to my father and his uncle," Priscilla said, looking at the setting sun. Getting married was such a long process. Even though times had changed, some of the old traditions still remained in the people of Zimbabwe. Before a traditional marriage ceremony could be arranged, many people had to be notified. After telling aunts and uncles, the parents would be told. Chamu disliked the long and unnecessary process, but knew that there was no way to avoid it. The culture was in the people no matter how different they dressed or lived.

When they got to her apartment, Chamu insisted on walking her to her door. He followed her into the living room. Priscilla wanted to tell him to leave, but felt she would be going too far. She knew she was lukewarm to him most of the time. Being outright rude would be unfair.

He was such a sweet man. She wanted to be alone and think about what he had told her about her father, but she would have to do that later, after he was gone.

"I'll sit with you for a while," Chamu said, sitting down on the sofa. "What were you going to do tonight?"

"Watch some TV," Priscilla replied, sitting on a sofa opposite him. She turned on the TV with a remote. It was another gift from Chamu.

"What are you thinking?" Chamu asked looking at her. "You look serious and very beautiful." Priscilla didn't want to tell him exactly what had been on her mind, but there were many other things she could discuss with him.

"I was thinking of buying a car," Priscilla said.

Chamu raised an eyebrow. "A car? What do you need a car for?"

Priscilla felt her defences coming up. "What do *you* need a car for?" she challenged him, and Chamu laughed.

"You are right. I know you need a car, but I always have my drivers ready to come and pick you up. I even had a taxi from my company to be on the ready to pick you up any time, any place."

"I know, but I feel uncomfortable with drivers," Priscilla said. "I might be able to get a loan at work and buy a car. I just want to be independent. Come and go as I please."

There goes the word again, independence, Chamu thought, trying to curb the anger rising in his chest. He had to choose his words carefully with her. She would flee at the slightest sign of restriction. She had flown from her parents' home in the middle of the night.

"You want to buy a car? I want to buy you a nice car. One that is worthy of the loveliest woman in Zimbabwe. I don't want you driving any old car from the junkyards. You need a nice reliable car with an alarm."

"I just want something to get me around, and if I can afford it then why should you buy it for me?" Priscilla asked.

"Because I love you. I love to see you in nice things. When I spoil you, I feel happy. Is that so bad?"

"No. No. I won't buy the car. I'll start having lessons, at least," she said.

"I can teach you," he said.

"Thank you," she said, and then sat back and watched the news with Chamu. She fell asleep on the sofa and woke up as he carried her to bed. She gasped.

"What are you doing?"

"Putting you to bed," he responded, his face close to hers. She panicked when he kissed her lips and fought to get free.

"I'm not going to do anything," Chamu said, laying her on top of the bed. He looked down at her form, sprawled on the white duvet. It took all his strength not to drop down on top of her. He moved back and smiled at her. She looked at him, the fear slowly fading from her eyes.

"You are not ready to sleep with me yet?"

"After we get married. I should never have slept with anyone before marriage. That is how I ended up in this mess," Priscilla said, sitting up. "I'm sorry, Chamu."

"It's all right, my love. At least you know I'm not marrying you just for your body," he said with a chuckle. Priscilla smiled nervously.

"You are kind and wonderful. Why have I been so lucky?"

"I am the lucky one, Pri. You have made me the happiest man on Earth."

"I better sleep. I'm tired," Priscilla said. Chamu felt her dismissal like a slap, but straightened and walked to the door.

"I'll see you tomorrow," he said. "We can go and look at the venue for the wedding."

"Tomorrow then. Good night," she said.

After he was gone, Priscilla went to lock the door. She stood in the living room for a while, holding her belly, gently stroking it. She wasn't ready to make love to another man yet. How long would Chamu be patient with her?

CHAPTER 18
Hasha—Anger

"I don't want to see that girl in my house again," Oliver Pasipano shouted. Mukai breathed angrily but kept quiet. The visit was not going as planned. However, that's what they all expected from Oliver. Oliver was still angry with Priscilla. In fact, he had been angry with her since she was born.

"Who wants to marry her, anyway?" Oliver looked around like a quizmaster at the three people sitting in his living room—Mukai, Monica and his mother's brother, Farai. The whole purpose of the visit was to tell Oliver of Priscilla's intended marriage to Chamu. Oliver blew up the moment he heard the words.

"The young man's name is Chamu Tengani. He owns a lot of businesses," Farai explained.

"I don't care how much money he has. That girl has caused me nothing but trouble," he ranted.

Mukai bit her tongue hard. She had many words to say about how much trouble Oliver caused, but kept quiet. He made her so mad she wanted to force feed him a thousand needles! Of all the people Mukai knew, no one made her as angry as Oliver did. He was living up to his reputation of being a tyrant.

Mukai looked at Monica. She sat there, her lovely smooth face closed and unchanging. She was difficult to read. Mukai admired what Monica wore, a lovely African print dress with the headscarf tied carelessly on her head. Mukai could smell delicious food from the kitchen. She was the homemaker Mukai knew she could never be. Mukai never cooked, but instead had her maid cook all the meals. She had too much else to do to bother with cooking, but still envied Monica's skills. What was she now, almost fifty but didn't look a day over thirty.

"So what should we tell the young couple?" Mukai turned her eyes to Oliver. She wanted to say something stronger but had counted to twenty before speaking. The elders knew what they were talking about when they said "If a monkey reigns, prostrate thyself before him."

"I don't care what you tell them," Oliver said. "I just don't want them in this house."

"That's fine, then." Mukai nodded, looking at Farai with a frown. What she really wanted to tell Oliver was that nobody liked being in his home anyway, but she had to bite her tongue so hard that she tasted blood. She had to focus on Priscilla and her marriage.

"*Baba* Hope, may I talk to you alone?" Monica asked Oliver calmly. Mukai and Farai looked at each other and then both stood up, mumbling something about going to the store.

Mukai wished she could be a fly on the wall and hear what Monica had to say to her stupid husband.

"Why don't you want her to get married properly?"

"She has no respect. Running away from home and marrying the first man she finds," Oliver complained.

"Let's just do this and then forget about the whole Priscilla incident," Monica said.

"You just want me to do everything your child wants. I have given in too much," he shouted.

"No, Oliver. I want you to do what's right," Monica demanded, looking him in the eye.

"What's right?" His voice got louder now.

"Yes. I don't want to talk about how you have treated that child all these years, but enough is enough," Monica said calmly but firmly.

"What! She has caused me nothing but trouble," Oliver yelled.

"So you are going to deny her the right to get married? A man is willing to pay *lobola* for her and he is willing to love her and protect her without first getting her pregnant. Isn't that better than everybody we know?"

"You don't tell me what to do, woman." Oliver stood up with a finger pointed at her head.

"I have watched you ruin our children's lives for too long, Oliver," Monica said quietly. "I won't stand for it anymore."

They looked at each other, Monica calmly sitting down. Oliver stood up, breathing heavily.

"What are you going to do, huh? You are nothing without me. You don't work, and you are old now. What can you do to me?"

Monica swallowed deeply, letting his words sink in. This time his threats were not going to make her back down. No more!

"I have many options, Oliver. Many years ago, you kicked me out of my home as if I was an orphan. Right now, Oliver, I'm willing to leave this home of my own free will if you don't stop your actions against Priscilla. I have been quiet for so long and watched you drive all my children out of their home. Vimbai is living in hell with that man. Hope is lost to us, and Priscilla might be, too, but no more, Oliver. I can't watch you destroy Priscilla, too. My daughter will have her marriage without any problems."

Monica watched her husband deflate like a balloon.

"I always knew you could not be trusted, woman," Oliver said. Monica didn't respond.

"Now you talk to me like a donkey because of Priscilla. I always knew she would come between us. She has always come between us."

"She never did, Oliver. She has tried to please you all these years. I have watched her try, and each time she came to you with a plate full of love, you slapped her in the face."

"When she was born you could never have any more children," Oliver reminded her, his eyes big with conviction.

"I know you wanted a son, so did I, but that was not God's plan for us," Monica said.

"She . . . she—" Oliver said.

"Say it, *Baba* Hope. She's your child," Monica said.

141

He shook his head. "*Baba*, I am tired of having all these feelings hiding in us and we never say anything. What do you want to say? What do you really think?"

"Nothing, Monica. You will have what you want. You can have your daughter's marriage. You win."

"Oliver." Monica reached for his hand. He moved away from her.

"There is nothing to talk about. I don't want to talk about her anymore. You will have your way in this. I will accept that man's money and her marriage and be done with it, but let me tell you something. I won't be happy about it, and I will remember the way you were today because of Priscilla."

Everything was set. Chamu was going to marry Priscilla. He had his team of escorts ready to go to the Pasipano home. He wore a dark suit, shirt and tie, and so did all the six men who would be part of his marriage team.

"Brother, you look sharp," Sidney said to his older brother. He also wore a wonderful suit his brother had bought him. They stood next to each other and looked in the mirror. They were the same height, but Sidney was leaner. Chamu was stockier and stood more confidently.

"You need to start eating, Sidney," Chamu said, giving his younger brother a shove. Sidney moved a few meters, laughing.

"The girls still like me," Sidney said, fixing his jacket.

"Not girls like Priscilla," Chamu said.

"There is only one Priscilla," Sidney pointed out, fixing his tie.

"Let's go. I don't want to be late," Chamu said, taking one last look in the mirror then walked into the living room where the rest of the men sat around watching soccer on TV.

"Come on, guys, get up. Its time to go," he said, and they all stood up like soldiers in front of their commander.

"You look great," Vincent, Chamu's long-time friend, said. Everybody added his own flattery and Chamu grinned, soaking it all in.

"It's an important day. I hope you all won't embarrass me. I know I'm expected to be quiet so Vincent, you will do most of the talking and negotiating. You can't just agree to whatever payment they ask for. Hustle a little. You know how it's done."

"I do, Mr. Tengani. I escorted my little brother to his marriage last year," Vincent said.

"They cleaned you out, didn't they?" Chamu said and grinned.

"Left the poor guy penniless. I had to help him out," Vincent said, and all the men laughed, taking their cue from Chamu.

"Let's go, men. I want this over and done with," Chamu commanded and led the group of men in dark suits to the expensive cars parked outside in his driveway.

CHAPTER 19

Manyemwe—Excitement

Priscilla rarely took time off work, but weeks after her marriage ceremony, she woke up late and stared at the ceiling, different images playing in her head like a jumbled movie. There was her traditional marriage ceremony that had taken place at Oliver and Monica's house. She was surprised that it had happened without Oliver shouting at her. It's true what she'd heard, *money softens disputes as water softens clay.*

The marriage happened without her saying a word, and the money passed on to her family from Chamu's leather briefcase. She could tell that Oliver was softening as the plate filled with thousands of dollars tied with a rubber band.

Her family was excited, especially her sisters and aunts, who were impressed by Chamu's line of Mercedes Benzes taking over their tiny street. She still didn't feel married after the money was exchanged, the gifts given to her family and the food was served. Only one moment filled her with hope. She saw Monica laughing at something Chamu had said.

It had been two weeks since her marriage ceremony. She listened to the morning sounds outside her window, glad that winter was over and September was warm and dry. The morning rush hour rumbled on and children in school uniforms filled the streets. There was a school a few streets from her apartment.

Now that she was a married woman, she set her mind on the next goal. She had decided to go and meet her father. Nobody knew, not her mother, not Chamu, and not even Aunt Mukai. This was something she wanted to do alone, and do quickly.

Her outfit hung on a coat hanger in front of her wardrobe, already pressed and ready to wear, as usual.

Robert Chigoni. Priscilla tested his name on her lips as she got out of bed. A nice long soak in the tub calmed her nerves, and she put on the striped black suit and red blouse. With her pumps on, she liked what she saw in the mirror and wondered what her father looked like again. She had dreamed of him, a man without a face. In her dream, he was kind and loved her. In her heart, she believed that meeting her father would make her world all right. He was the hole in her heart and he could fill it. He would make all the pain of living with Oliver disappear.

Priscilla left her flat around 10 a.m. and walked to the bus stop. She didn't want to ask for Chamu's car this time around. She couldn't wait to get her own car and drive herself whenever and wherever she wanted.

She stepped into the mini bus, paid her fare, and stared out the window away from the man in overalls who sat in the seat beside her.

Finally, the bus reached her stop. The First Mutual building stood high in the middle of the city center.

Priscilla looked up at its tall pillars that almost reached the sky. It looked menacing as it swallowed people up when they reached its stairs.

"This is it," Priscilla mumbled to herself as she started climbing the concrete steps. She didn't know what she was going to say to this man she had never met. She kept telling herself that when she met him she would know what to say. It would all depend on how friendly he was or how he would receive her news.

When she reached the sixth floor, she walked towards a young and pretty receptionist. The young woman was busy operating the phones as if she was doing a very complicated science experiment, and from the way she talked Priscilla could tell she felt very important.

Priscilla walked up to her but she held up a finger with a long, red nail. Priscilla looked at the nail then took herself to the nearest seat. She didn't mind waiting at all. What she was about to do was not very pleasant anyway.

"Can I help you?"

The young receptionist didn't seem very friendly, as if she knew what Priscilla was up to. Did her face give her away? Did she look like she was about to let the big family secret out of the bag?

"I'm here to see Mr. Chigoni," Priscilla said, trying to keep her face as expressionless as possible.

"You are?"

"Priscilla. Priscilla Tengani," she said, deciding to use her soon-to-be-new married name. If she used her real name, Robert might run scared and refuse to see her.

"What business do you have with him, and which company are you from?" The woman was pursing her lips and looking Priscilla up and down. Priscilla wanted to tell her that it was none of her business, but she knew that would just make her chances of seeing her biological father even smaller. Another man came in and the receptionist gave him such a big smile it took Priscilla by a surprise. So, she did have a smile after all.

"Mr. Kumene. How are you?"

"Fine, Chengeto. You look lovely, as usual," he said.

"Thank you. Mr. Chogoni is not here right now. He's at a seminar at the Miekles Hotel. He decided to go just this morning," Chengeto said, now totally ignoring Priscilla.

The man looked disappointed, but he smiled when he looked at Priscilla.

"And who are you, my dear?" he asked her, eyes bright with interest.

"I was also looking for Mr. Chigoni, but I'll have to come back later," Priscilla said, putting her purse over her shoulder and turning to leave.

"Miss. I don't know when he's going to be back. In future you should make an appointment," Chengeto said, her smile now replaced by her earlier pursing of lips. Priscilla nodded and walked out of the building.

Disappointment and relief fought for control in her heart as she stepped down the stairs and joined the crowds of people hurrying along the streets. In her way of thinking, if a cow can't find meat it will eat grass. She had to think of another plan because her first one hadn't worked.

Deep in thought, she walked past street vendors, and a man preaching next to the water fountain. She listened for a few minutes while the wind flapped her jacket around her body. Her curled hair played around her face.

"Jesus is coming soon," the man preached in a loud, hoarse voice, theatrical in his presentation. "You have to ask for forgiveness. He will wash away all your sins. He will make you as clean as snow. Confess. Confess. Confess."

Priscilla felt guilt as she thought of what her life was fast becoming. Secrets on top of secrets and shame. She appeared perfect on the outside, but inside she felt like she was the biggest liar of them all.

She walked away from the man's accusing voice as it brought memories of her days in the church with her mother, hearing God's word and finding solace in it. When was the last time she had been to church? She couldn't remember. Her life was now lost. She hadn't even asked God if what she was doing was right. She just went on and married Chamu anyway.

Priscilla kept on walking, not seeing the women who stared or the men who whistled. She walked past the street vendors who sold magazines right outside a top bookstore. She followed the crowds of people who crossed the busy streets and walked past fast food restaurants and designer boutiques. When she looked around, she realized she was across the street from Meikles Hotel.

This is where the man who was a part of me is, she thought. She crossed the street and walked around the hotel to the imposing entrance. There were quite a few people gathered in the lobby checking in or checking out.

Some were just using the hotel as an entrance for the stores inside it that sold African artifacts and clothes.

Priscilla asked the concierge if there were any business seminars going on at the hotel.

"Yes," the young woman answered warmly. "There is one in the Steward Room. I think they are on a tea break now."

"Thank you," Priscilla said, and looked around. So, he could be any one of the men sitting in the dining room. She walked towards the bar and looked inside.

There were very few people in there. It was only 11 a.m. He could be one of the men in there. She had no idea what Robert Chigoni liked to do when he had time to kill. Priscilla made her way towards the Steward Room by following the gold lettering on the elevator. The sign said that the Indigenous Business Consortium was on the first floor. In the elevator, Priscilla tried to rein in her thoughts.

She got to the conference room and looked inside. There were many people just milling around talking. Refreshments were placed all around the room, and the men filled their plates with tiny sandwiches and jam tarts. From the looks of most of the men, they had tons of money. Their huge bellies strained out of expensive suits. Priscilla stared, wondering if she fitted in this exquisite environment. There were very few women around. A young man in a flashy suit holding a glass of orange juice walked towards her.

"Good morning, miss. Are you looking for someone?" he asked.

"I'm looking for Mr. . . . Robert Chigoni," Priscilla said, not wanting to encourage any conversation with the man. He was staring at her as if she was meat on a stick.

"There he is on the cell phone," the young man said and pointed towards the side of the room. Priscilla moved her gaze slowly towards the direction the man pointed. There was a man sitting alone, smiling at something somebody said on the phone. She stared, taking in his suit, his cleanly shaved face and neatly combed black hair. She couldn't see his eyes because his head was bent but he seemed calm, happy and not knowing that the world as he knew it was about to change.

Before Priscilla could decide what to do the man on the phone looked up. He stared at her and something seemed to shift in his eyes. Their eyes locked for a couple of seconds; he talked a little longer on his phone and hung it up. Priscilla felt panic rise up inside of her as the man stood up and walked towards her. She couldn't move, but inside she wanted to run away.

He held out his hand and reached for a handshake as he got to her. Priscilla shook his hand.

"Do I know you?" Robert Chigoni had a questioning look in his eyes. His smile was there, straight white teeth, eyes warm and kind. He looked so young. His brown skin didn't have any lines and his black hair was cut short.

"Are you Mr. Chigoni? Robert Chigoni?" Priscilla asked, letting go of his hand and gripping her purse strap.

"Yes. You do look very familiar, but I do not remember your name," Robert said.

"Priscilla. Priscilla Tengani," she said in a croaky voice. She cleared her throat and swallowed hard. She tried to remember when she had been this nervous, but couldn't recall as the buzzing in her ears continued.

This is my father. Can he tell I'm his daughter?

"Doesn't ring a bell," Robert said, scratching his head.

"May I talk to you in private? I have some questions to ask you," Priscilla said, looking around for a private space. She couldn't break the news in front of all these people. Robert Chigoni looked suspicious, but was curious.

"Let's go on the terrace," he said and led the way out the door. After passing a few more doors they found one that led to the terrace. Outside there were tables and chairs that overlooked the city. She could barely take in the view of the city park that was filled with vendors who sold different wares, from beautiful stone sculptures and bouquets of flowers. Priscilla sat down on a chair and Robert sat down opposite her. She found it hard to look at him.

How shifty I must look, she thought.

"What is this about? I'm surprised you even know my name," he said, looking straight at her.

"Do you know Monica Pasipano?" She watched his face as a light seemed to be turned on in his eyes.

"Of course. You do look like her. Is she all right? Are you her daughter?" Robert asked. She saw something flash across his eyes.

"She's my mother."

"It's amazing how much you look so much like her, or like she did," Robert said, shaking his head. "Is she doing well? I haven't seen her in many, many years."

"She's always fine. Nothing ever seems to affect her," Priscilla said, then decided to add. "I suppose you didn't know she had your child?"

The words dropped from her mouth like bricks from the rooftop. She felt their force in Robert's reaction. He looked at her puzzled, and then shock filled his face. She had come this far. She couldn't give up now.

"What? You must be joking."

"That's why I'm here. I wanted to find my real father." This time her words seemed to land on the coffee table, because that was where Robert was looking. He gave a nervous laugh.

"What?"

"You are my father," she said.

"I don't think so, young lady. I have my own daughters. I was speaking to her just as you arrived and stared at me like a ghost. I'm a happy, family man."

"I'm sure," Priscilla said, her heart breaking.

"What do you want, anyway? You want a job? You want money?"

Priscilla stood up in the middle of his questions and unappealing scowl. The big white smile was gone.

"I just wanted to find out who you were," she said, her voice heavy with unshed tears.

"I don't believe that. You come here in the middle of an important event and just expect me to believe that you are my child? Do you think I was born yesterday?"

Robert gave a harsh laugh. "I would appreciate it if you never say that I am your father to anybody. I don't need such rumors going around the city about me."

Priscilla looked at him, his scowling face that had been friendly a few minutes before. He seemed angry, and she tried to shield her heart from the pain that was threatening to engulf her. She put her bag over her shoulder and stood up straight and proud.

She took one final look at him then walked away. By the time she reached the bathroom, her face was drenched with tears.

CHAPTER 20

Kuziva—Knowing

After nine holes of disastrous golf, Chamu went home to visit his mother. Lina was one person who always told him the truth. He was surrounded by people who always wanted to please him because of his wealth and status. Even Vincent, though they had been friends for a long time, hardly questioned him. His mother, on the other hand, always spoke her mind and could still speak to him as if he was twelve.

When he got to the house that he grew up in his younger brother, who was the only one home, came to greet him. His mother was in the kitchen helping the maid with the evening meal.

"Chamu! What a surprise!" She greeted him with a smile as she continued to stir the pot.

"Don't make it too thick," Lina Tengani told Ruchiva as she passed the spoon to the young girl in a maid's uniform. Ruchiva was new. Her employees never lasted. Not many could keep up with her strict instructions or meet her high standards of morality and cleanliness. This young girl didn't look like she would last very long. Lina gave the already confused girl instructions to boil and serve *nyimo* and *mbambaira*. The round nuts and sweet potatoes were Chamu's favorites.

"Come and sit. You look very tired. Were you working?" Lina led the way into the living room.

"I'm coming from golf," Chamu said.

"Golf. That is a white man's sport. What happened to playing soccer?" Lina asked. "I can come and watch you play soccer. Your father liked watching soccer."

"I know, but these days in business you have to play golf. That's how you make business contacts, and you can still look smart as you play."

Lina clicked her tongue. "My son the businessman. Your father never had to play golf, and look at the businesses he built."

"I know, *Amai,* but I'm not in the same business he was in any more," Chamu said.

"Those businesses helped you all go to school and afford the things many children couldn't afford," Lina said. "I don't want you to ever look down on what your father did."

"Ma! I never said I looked down on it. *Baba's* business helped me get where I am, but I want to do more. I have big dreams."

Lina smiled. "You have done well, Chamu. And your brothers and sisters are doing well at school also. You are sending them all to the best schools."

"The main reason I worked hard was for them," Chamu said, calming down. His mother had a way of pushing his buttons.

"I hope nothing will change now that Priscilla is in your life," Lina said. The same look that always came to her eyes when she mentioned Priscilla was there again.

"What do you mean?" Chamu's calm fled like the wind.

"Some women change men. As it is you didn't come and visit last weekend," Lina complained. Ruchiva brought in a plate of sweet potatoes and water.

"Don't spill," Lina told her, and that's when Ruchiva's hands started shaking.

"Last weekend I was getting married, *Amai*. I went to pay *lobola*," Chamu said, peeling the sweet potatoes.

"I think they charged you too much. That girl hasn't even been to university. I really didn't want you to marry her, and I'm annoyed that even though you have paid for her she's still living in that flat until the wedding," Lina said.

"That is what she wanted, and, *Amai*, that is one subject that you cannot talk about that way. As it is I don't know if she still wants to have a wedding," Chamu said.

"What do you mean? She doesn't want to marry you?"

"She's not sure, I can tell," Chamu said, wondering why he always ended up telling his mother everything.

"I knew that girl was a mistake from the moment I met her. You can do better. She grew up in that horrible neighborhood where young girls walk the streets with nothing to do. Why won't you listen to me? She's wrong for you, Chamu. You men can be fooled by beauty. A *roro* fruit may be red on the outside, yet inside it has been eaten by worms. You can still change your mind about her."

"She's all that I want. I don't want to talk about it anymore. Nothing you say can change my mind,"

Chamu said firmly, drinking the juice the timid Ruchiva placed before him.

"Sometimes I think she has bewitched you," Lina added.

"I have loved Priscilla since we were in high school. She didn't make me love her. She has done nothing to encourage our relationship. It has all been me," Chamu said. He threw the half-eaten sweet potato onto the plate.

"I don't understand that. Many women are after you, and you have to make a fool of yourself to get her. What is it with her? Just the pretty face?"

"It's everything about her." He decided to change the subject. "Where's Tawanda, anyway?"

"I told him to feed the chickens. I'm going to sell most of them at the end of the month," Lina said. Chamu shook his head. His mother continued to work even though he gave her money each month and she wanted for nothing. They were the same. They both had to be working at something, creating something. His mother was just as tough a businessperson as his father ever was. She had been right beside him as they built their businesses from the ground up. She had encouraged him to expand when he was happy with just one shop, and she had brought technology to their operations. She was a smart woman, and sometimes her intuition about people scared him. She always hit a nerve when she talked about Priscilla and made him notice things he would rather ignore. If she knew that Priscilla was pregnant, not by him but somebody else, then Lina would definitely fight him at every turn. Better to keep that bit of news to himself.

CHAPTER 21
Yeuko—Memories

"That dress is gorgeous," Mukai said, lifting up the silky white dress in a clear plastic covering. The wedding was a week away, and Priscilla took her dress to Mukai's huge bedroom for safekeeping. Her apartment had no space to hold any more clothes, especially not her wedding dress with its full skirt and wide petticoat. Mukai had invited Priscilla to use her house to get ready for the wedding, and she had accepted the offer. It was all working out well.

"Don't you think my stomach will show?" Priscilla asked, looking down at herself.

"I don't see anything," Mukai said and laughed. "But give yourself a couple of weeks and you will be as big as an elephant. I remember when I was pregnant with Unashe. I didn't show until almost my sixth month. I was so skinny then it was hard to believe a baby came out of me. But the following month I just blew up."

"I don't want to look like an elephant," Priscilla said as she sat on her aunt's bed. She watched her aunt admire the wedding dress. Many times, she wanted to tell Mukai about her and Unashe. Many times, she wanted to ask her for his phone number so she could tell him. Maybe he would say that he loved her and wanted to marry her. She knew if she told her aunt, Mukai would stop her from marrying somebody she didn't really love. If Mukai knew that she loved Unashe and loved his baby she would help her make the right decision. Maybe Mukai would even insist that she fight for him and take him away from Chantel.

I should tell her the truth, Priscilla thought.

"I'm so glad you could leave from here, my child. I didn't want you all by yourself at your flat."

"Thank you for letting me prepare here." *Now, Priscilla. Tell her now.*

"I wish Unashe could be here. He would be so happy for you," Mukai said. "Have I shown you some of his pictures from England?"

Priscilla froze. This could be the best time to tell her. What would she say?

I don't want to see his pictures.

"No. I haven't seen his pictures," Priscilla said, trying to think of a way out of seeing them. Hunger came to mind. "Why don't we go and eat something. I'm starving. I can cook the food."

"Now you want to be as big as two elephants," Mukai said, taking a white envelope from her dresser. Priscilla stared at Unashe's unmistakable handwriting scrawled across the envelope and saw the British stamp of the queen stuck in the corner. With a dry mouth, she watched her aunt take pictures from the envelope.

"Here." Mukai tossed them to her and sat next to Priscilla. Hands trembling, she looked at the first one and felt her heart beat wildly. Her eyes connected with his even on that paper. It was hard to move to the next picture; there he was again, dressed in jeans and a white t-shirt, sitting with his strong arms behind his back. How she remembered his hands with their long, strong fingers and his amazing eyes. He looked so good in that picture she wanted to trace his smile, but fought hard to be still.

"Isn't he handsome? He's at a wonderful university and loving every minute of it." Mukai kept on telling her things she definitely didn't want to hear, about how hot the summer was and about the friends he had made. The last picture made her blood freeze. It was of Unashe and Chantel dressed for a function with their arms around each other. They were both smiling in the picture, mocking her.

"They are nice," Priscilla mumbled and threw the pictures on the bed as if they burned her. She stood up holding her back.

"What's wrong?" Mukai asked standing up and picking up the photos. She put them back in the envelope.

"I'm fine." Priscilla walked away. "Pregnant women always need the bathroom." Priscilla walked into Mukai's bathroom and closed the door. She turned on the water, feeling rage like a boiling volcano.

"That bastard. I hate him! I hate him! Damn him," she whispered viciously into the mirror. Tears filled her eyes and made her angrier. If she had any doubts about marrying Chamu, that horrible photo had erased them all. Unashe seemed to be getting on with his life, and she would now get on with hers. A small voice seemed to tell her to be calm, but her anger banished any other words from her mind. She had one more week and then she would be Mrs. Chamu Tengani.

The afternoon of her wedding day, her sisters surrounded Priscilla in Mukai's huge bedroom. Rutendo was the expert with the makeup brushes and curling irons.

"You don't need too much makeup. Your skin is glowing," Rutendo said as she outlined Priscilla's eyes with dark eyeliner.

After the makeup Vimbai carefully placed the veil she had made on her head. Priscilla smiled at her sister in the mirror, admiring the lovely two-piece suit that she had made herself.

The color theme was peach, and it seemed to have exploded in Mukai's bedroom.

"You look so beautiful," Vimbai said, admiring Priscilla's white satin and organza dress with tiny peach flowers splashed all over it. Vimbai hadn't had a wedding, and was enjoying herself immensely.

"Thank you."

"I've never been to an evening wedding," Vimbai said. "Wasn't it hard to organize? You never asked for help."

"I'll be honest with you. I didn't do much except choose my dress. Chamu did everything else. He would tell me his plans and I could either agree or disagree. Mostly I agreed because he hired a great wedding coordinator. She did most of the planning."

"You have a wonderful husband, Pri. God be praised," Vimbai said. Priscilla just smiled.

Priscilla knew that this wasn't how weddings were done in Zimbabwe. She should be at her home with her mother and her mother's family, but because of Oliver she was at Mukai's house choking with memories of Unashe, whose pictures were now framed and scattered around Mukai's bedroom and hallway. She wanted to pull down the one with Chantel, but never had the opportunity. Priscilla turned away from the photographs and watched her aunt suspiciously as she dialled the phone.

She better not be calling Unashe.

"Hello, Unashe. You won't believe what's happening today. It's Priscilla's wedding day. She's here getting dressed," Mukai said in her loudest voice. Mukai was quiet for a while, listening to Unashe with a smile on her face.

"Unashe," Rutendo said, smiling. "He left for England just last month, right?"

"I think we should get going," Priscilla said. She tried to stand, but with her dress, she could barely get up on her own. Nobody paid any attention to her suggestion, but continued to do the final touches to her hair and makeup.

"You should talk to her," Mukai said, looking in Priscilla's direction. Priscilla knew she looked like a rabbit caught in the headlights of a truck.

"No," she murmured. "I'll call him afterwards."

"Just say hi," Mukai insisted and thrust the phone into her hand.

"Your phone bill," Priscilla muttered, taking the phone in her sweaty hand. She put the cold phone to her ears.

"Hello," she said, trying to smile. She was sure everybody could hear her heart beating and see the sweat sprout on her forehead.

"Hi, Priscilla," Unashe said.

Oh, my God. His voice. Oh, Unashe, I miss you. I hate you.

"How are you?" She finally managed to control her voice.

"I'm fine," he said. "It's your wedding?"

"Yes," Priscilla breathed into the phone. It was hard to speak with everybody looking on. "I'm getting married."

"That was quick," Unashe said.

"Thank you," she spoke quickly. "I can't talk for long. Your mother's phone bill will be too high."

"Well, good luck with your future. I have to run," he said and the phone went dead.

She was breathing hard as she put the phone back besides her aunt's bed. She was fighting the tears even as they pooled in her eyes, but somehow she blinked them back.

No more, she told herself firmly. *No more tears for that boy. This is the beginning of a new and exciting life without him. It's finally time for goodbye Unashe, and good riddance.*

Chamu and Priscilla's wedding was flawless. Later, as couples danced, Priscilla sat on the silken covered chair alone for the first time in hours, still feeling like she was dreaming.

Is this really my wedding?

She was still lost in thought when she glanced to her right beyond the candlelight and saw someone she didn't know looking at her. A woman dressed in a blue suit and matching hat approached her. She had greeted hundreds of people she didn't know, but somehow this woman looked familiar. She sat in Chamu's seat.

"Congratulations, Priscilla," the woman said, almost reverently, her voice smooth and confident.

"Thank you," Priscilla said. There was something about her eyes that seemed memorable. She seemed like she was someone who meant so much from her past. She seemed genuinely happy, unlike most of the people at the wedding. Who was she? Priscilla wondered.

"You don't know me, but I'm so happy to meet you. I'm Vera Sibanda. I am Robert Chigoni's sister." Priscilla's heart started racing at the mention of her real father's name. She suddenly felt hot in her wedding dress, mixed emotions fighting for dominance in her heart. They did look alike. The eyes, the gentle manner.

"What are you doing here?" Priscilla looked around, wondering if her mother would recognize her or if Oliver would also catch her talking to her.

"He asked me to give you this. I wrote the check, but the gift is from Robert for your wedding. He's sorry for the way he reacted when you first met him, but it was because of shock and other circumstances."

Priscilla felt tears in her eyes.

"I thought he hated me," she said softly.

"No. He's happy for you today. I'm so happy to meet you. It's not your fault or his fault that you didn't know each other. If you look at the door, you'll see him. He'll not come in, and I have to leave anyway as the guard at the door is watching me."

Vera looked behind her at the line of people waiting to congratulate Priscilla. She pressed the envelope in her hand, stood up, gave her a kiss and a hug and then left.

Priscilla looked at the door and, in the distance, she saw him, a man standing against the wall arms folded, watching. Robert Chigoni. The man who had insulted her. Her anger towards him melted away, flowing away like water in a river. No matter what he had said to her, no matter his doubt, he had come to her wedding, and that meant he acknowledged her as his daughter. Vera walked up to him and they both walked out the door and disappeared. Now her day was almost perfect.

Part II

Paidamoyo—Heart's Desire

CHAPTER 22
Pamusha—Home

Priscilla opened her eyes long before the sun came out. She stared at the ceiling, excited and nervous about the day ahead. She couldn't believe how time had flown. Smiling, she turned and looked at Chamu, who snored lightly beside her. He slept so soundly because he worked so hard during the day. Lately he seemed busier than usual. As she closed her eyes again she heard tiny feet running towards the bedroom. A bigger smile filled her face, and before she could get out of bed a little girl in a long pink nightdress flung her bedroom door open.

"Mummy. Mummy. Wake up," Rudo said. "Daddy. Daddy."

Chamu woke up and immediately smiled. She walked up to his side of the bed, and he picked her up and put her on the bed. Rudo put her arms around him.

"Do you know what today is?" Rudo looked at Chamu. Her eyes were wide and questioning. Priscilla watched her adorable face, warmed by the love on Chamu's face. Rudo always made him smile no matter what time of day it was.

"Sunday?"

"No," the child said.

They played the game for a few minutes then Rudo started tickling Chamu.

"It's my first day of school," she cried. He tickled her ribs and she fell back in fits of laughter.

"All right, you two, enough playing around," Priscilla said, getting out of bed. "You have to take a bath."

"Me?" Chamu asked.

"You, too, sir, but mainly the little lady. She thinks she can go to school without bathing," Priscilla said.

"I bathed yesterday," Rudo quipped. Priscilla loved her voice. It was a younger version of Aunt Mukai's, so husky and sweet for such a little girl. She called it a honey and Sprite voice; it was sweet, but with the fizz that tickled her heart every time she heard it.

"I know you did, but today is the first day. You have to smell nice. Come, I'll use bubble bath in our Jacuzzi tub."

"Yeah!" Rudo excitedly jumped into Priscilla's arms. While Priscilla ran the water in the huge tub, she could hear Chamu's cell phone ringing. She swirled the bubbles around with her hand, one ear intent on the bedroom.

"Why are you calling me so early? I told you not to call me at home." Chamu's accusing voice carried clearly to her suspicious ears. Priscilla realized she wasn't supposed to be hearing the conversation.

When she left the bathroom to get Rudo's towels Chamu immediately stopped talking. He looked warily at her first and then gave her an uneasy smile, phone still pressed to his ear. Priscilla walked out of the bedroom, anxiety filling her heart.

Rudo was ready and dressed in thirty minutes. Priscilla couldn't get enough of looking at her baby in the green school uniform, long brown socks and brown shoes. Her hair was neatly braided in cornrows at Mukai's salon and she wore silver studs in her ears.

"You are the most beautiful first-grader in the country," Priscilla said, holding back tears. Her little girl was going to school.

"Thanks, Mummy. But can we go now?" Rudo said.

They walked into the kitchen. The maid, Maidei, had made a full breakfast, and also a lunch for Rudo. She was a young woman that Chamu's mother had found for them and trained before Rudo was born. She had been with them for six years. Priscilla treated her like family, paying her more than the going rate and training her with cooking and sewing courses. Maidei loved Priscilla like a big sister.

Her daughter was going to those schools she had only dreamed about. Rudo had the world before her, and Chamu was seeing to it that she got the best of everything.

After eating breakfast, they all stepped out into the warm sunshine. The gardener, Lovemore, busily wiped down the silver Mercedes, making it shiny and spotless. Priscilla watched him jump around like a puppy trying to please Chamu and make sure that everything was perfect. Lovemore adored Chamu since he moved into their servant quarters three years ago. He had been selling wares on his bicycle when he accidentally swerved in Chamu's way. After talking to him and hearing his struggles to sell fruits and vegetables around the city and failing to support his three children, Chamu had given him a job. Lovemore was delighted. At first he brought his wife to live with them, but after a few months he had decided to send her to a village somewhere close to Rusape to live with his family. When Chamu explained it, Priscilla was not impressed but had no choice but to accept it. How did Lovemore manage, only seeing his three children once or twice a year?

The early morning sun sparkled on the windows, sending shards of rays out to greet the family. Their sleepy dog lay on the corner of the wall, gazing at them lazily.

"Bye, Bruno! I'm going to school," Rudo called to the sleeping mixed breed. Bruno just twitched his ears and burrowed further into the wall. Priscilla giggled. That dog was the laziest animal she had ever seen. He was supposed to guard them at night, but she was sure he would do nothing if intruders came.

"The car looks great, Lovemore," Chamu commented, inspecting it.

"I'm glad you like it. I'll take care of yours, madam. It's not looking bad, but I can polish it up." The last was directed to Priscilla, and she thanked him. It had taken her a while to get used to having people doing everything for her, cooking, cleaning and washing cars. If her mother could see this, she would not be amused. Monica believed in hard work more than breathing.

They drove to school and dropped off Rudo together. Priscilla tried to hide her tears as Rudo walked into the classroom confidently. The teacher, Miss Bradwell, was a tiny woman with short blonde hair and pale blue eyes. She looked kind, and that was very important to Priscilla. Her only concern was she hardly saw any other black children as she scanned the class. She felt better when another little black girl arrived just as the bell rang.

She looked at Chamu, who held a video camera. Rudo looked comfortable, happy, and even waved goodbye to them as they left. Rudo was doing better than the other children, who cried and clung to their parents.

"She's going to be all right," Chamu said as he opened the car door for her. "She's a strong girl."

"I know." Priscilla wiped her tears and put her head back in the car.

"I won't be able to meet you for lunch today," Chamu said.

"Oh. I thought we could celebrate her first day together with a nice lunch," Priscilla said.

"Why not dinner?" Chamu asked. "We can book a table at the Miekles."

"No, dinner would keep us out late and I'd like to be home early tonight. This is such a big day for Rudo, she'll probably go to sleep early," Priscilla said. "I'd like to be home to hear all about her day and to tuck her in."

"I'll make it up to you," Chamu said.

Priscilla didn't comment. Lately something had been preoccupying him. Somebody kept calling the house and speaking to him even late at night, but he would never tell her who it was.

Priscilla was still unsettled that weekend when Chamu left the house very early and didn't call her the whole day. He had always been so attentive, so romantic, and Saturdays were usually reserved for their fun outings or dinners at fancy restaurants. Even Rudo was puzzled.

"Where are we going today?"

"I don't know, my dear. What would you like to do? You and I can go and visit *gogo*."

"Can Daddy come?" Rudo asked.

"He's not here right now, and I can't reach him on his cell phone. Let me call *gogo* and then we can go and visit her," Priscilla said.

She called her mother, but when Monica finally picked up she seemed to be in a hurry. "I have to go to a meeting at church. I'll talk to you tonight, my dear. Bye."

She really didn't want to spend time with Chamu's mother. That woman still acted strange around her, but Priscilla couldn't put a finger on the cause. Priscilla felt that Lina didn't like her at all. Lina hadn't warmed up to Rudo, either. It didn't make sense. It was almost as if she knew about Rudo, but surely Chamu would not have said anything. She would go and see her out of duty and because it made Chamu happy. Lina always had something to complain about when they visited. She was abrupt with Rudo and didn't like the way Priscilla cooked or washed dishes.

"When you cook sadza you need to make sure that it has the right texture. Yours is either too hard or too soft," Lina had said the last time she visited.

When they finished eating the sadza, which was too hard this time, Priscilla walked to the kitchen to wash the dishes. Lina didn't want her servant to do anything when

Priscilla was there. The maid could take a break or even go and watch television with the kids while Priscilla worked alone in the kitchen.

"I can see a streak in my special pot. You need to let it soak for a few minutes before washing, or use this to get rid of the marks," Lina said, taking a tub of sand and giving it to her. "Don't put those glasses there. Glasses need to be dried immediately or they'll have marks on them."

By the time she left the house, Priscilla felt horrible, as if she had no brain and couldn't do anything right. Her head ached and her manicured nails had lost their gloss. Her feet hurt from standing and walking from the kitchen to the dining room.

Remembering the negative emotions she got when at Lina's house, Priscilla still reached for her cell phone to call Lina, but it rang before she could dial her mother in-law's number. It was Chamu.

"Hi, Mai Rudo. How about I come home and pick you up and visit some friends who are having a house-warming party?"

"Who are they?" Priscilla glanced at her daughter, who was playing with her dolls on the living room floor. The house was all Chamu. He had decorated most of it before she even moved in. Nothing much had changed since her visit. It was the same house he lived in when they met; Priscilla had tried to add some touches, but it was hard. Lina had chosen most of the furniture, and it was all her taste of laces and frills and flowery curtains. Priscilla was still waiting to get the energy to redo the whole house.

"Can Rudo come? Will there be children there?"

"Yes, of course she can come. I'll be there soon," he said and rang off.

Priscilla dressed in a cream cotton flared skirt and a long red and cream top that she bought when they were in Paris. She was finishing the final touches on her simple makeup when she heard Chamu drive in. She quickly smoothed Rudo's hair, which was in cornrows, and dressed her in jeans and a flowery pink top. When they left the bedroom, Chamu was just getting into the living room.

"You look beautiful," Chamu said, giving her one long look.

"Thank you," she replied, trying to see something in his eyes. He did look different somehow. There was a light of excitement in his eyes that Priscilla couldn't place, and he seemed harried. He was always busy, but lately he seemed even more preoccupied.

"Well, let's go," Chamu said.

About twenty minutes later, they arrived at the gated community where she could glimpse a few huge residences above in the hills. There was a security guard at the gate.

"Wow. Who lives here? Government ministers?" Priscilla asked as she looked around. One house they passed was so big it looked like a hotel. It even had a lake and a lake house, and really only people in government or with connections in government could live like that.

"No. Just wealthy people with good taste," Chamu said with a grin.

"Daddy, look at that house," Rudo cried, pointing to her right.

"You like it?" Chamu asked her.

"Yes. It's nice," Rudo said, her eyes wide with wonder. They had visited people with lovely homes before, but none as big and ostentatious as those. After winding up the road a little there came into view an incredible cream house with palm trees lining up the driveway all the way up to the mansion, a hundred meters away.

Priscilla gasped as she stared at it. It was like arriving at a tropical island.

"Wow. This is some kind of heaven," she said. Chamu grinned.

He rang the intercom.

"Who is it?" a male voice asked.

"Chamu," he said and watched as the gates yawned open. There were a few cars parked in the driveway, and more in front of the three-car garage.

"It must be a very small party," Priscilla said. She looked at the surrounding lush green grass and pond with white ducks. She particularly loved the stone Shona sculptures. She remembered how she had always wanted a garden with a few Shona sculptures, and was annoyed that somebody else had copied her idea.

While she was looking around Chamu came to her side of the car and opened her door. Priscilla and Rudo stepped out, both staring at the house and surrounding gardens.

"What do these people do?" Priscilla asked, walking with Chamu towards the door. "I'm guessing government. They are the only people who seem to have such money."

"Not government, but they are into many things," Chamu said. He knocked on the front door and a waiter in white and black clothes and a bow tie opened the door.

She stepped into the darkened room. Just then the lights in the room came on.

"Surprise!" Priscilla's jaw dropped in shock and Rudo jumped behind Chamu, stunned. They were surrounded by about twenty people.

Priscilla saw her mother and Oliver were there, and, at closer assessment, she saw that she knew everybody gathered in the barely furnished room. There were tall tables and stools covered in white tablecloths and a bouquet of flowers on each one.

"What's going on?" Priscilla asked, looking at Chamu with tears of shock. "It's not my birthday."

"I know. This is your new home," Chamu said, spreading his arms to encompass the marble floors and crystal chandeliers.

"What?" Priscilla gasped, and tears of shock tumbled from her eyes.

"It's your new home," Rutendo said. Even her sister knew about it. "Chamu has been working on this for over a year. He didn't want you to know."

"He what?" Priscilla cried and laughed at the same time. Chamu drew her to him in a hug, and her mother walked towards her and embraced her.

"It's a beautiful house," Monica said, smiling. There seemed to be genuine joy in her mother's eyes, and it made Priscilla feel even happier.

Aunt Mukai came forward, too. "Congratulations, my dear. You have an incredible husband."

After the initial shock, and after everybody finished congratulating her, the party began and Priscilla was able to enjoy herself. Priscilla still could not believe it all as Chamu took her on a tour of the house. It was completed, he told her, but the furnishings would be up to her. They went up the winding staircase to the bedrooms that all had attached bathrooms; two of them had a Jacuzzi tub and huge separate shower. Their bedroom took her breath away with its lush white carpet, sunken tiny lounge and the most incredible gold and cream bathroom with brown and gold tiles, a shower that looked like a tropical rain forest with a skylight and a huge bathtub that looked like a swimming pool.

"What do you think?" Chamu's voice was close to her ear.

"Wow! It's-it's amazing," Priscilla whispered, running her hands over the marble sink. She touched his cheek as she marvelled at the beauty surrounding her and tried to contain it all inside. She remembered her friend Julia's words just after she got married to Chamu.

"Chamu is nice now, but wait until a year. Then he will show his true colors. My mother always tells me that he who is courting bows down, he raises his head when married."

Priscilla shook her head at the memory, glad that Julia had been so wrong. Chamu was in a class all his own: a husband who grew more devoted with time.

The kitchen had light tile with brown flecks, and the cabinets were a deep solid oak with stainless steel appliances. The three living rooms were all different but all beautifully finished in deep lush carpet. Priscilla took in the fireplaces, the sliding French doors that overlooked the garden and felt like she was dreaming.

After the tour, Priscilla ate with her family and Chamu gave everybody the details of how he tried to conceal the house from her.

"The last few days were the hardest because there was so much to be done to finish off, and finally I left the planning of the party to my secretary, who kept calling me day and night with questions and problems. I was beginning to feel that she was getting suspicious. Many times, I nearly gave up and just wished I could tell her what I was up to, but I think it was worth waiting to see the look on your face today, Pri. It was worth it."

"I think I only suspected something this week. Before that I never imagined anything."

"I used to take her around to look at houses and see what she liked. I knew you liked palm trees and Shona sculptures," Chamu said, putting his arm around her. Priscilla smiled, nodding her head.

"This home is more beautiful than I would have imagined. Thank you," Priscilla said sincerely and put her arm around him.

Chamu continued to relate how he had master-minded and visualized that very day and all the problems he had encountered, making everybody laugh with joy.

Priscilla laughed, remembering how suspicious she had been. Rudo, after the initial shock, was running up and down the stairs and had already claimed her room. Priscilla looked around at her smiling sisters talking to her beaming mother. Vimbai was without Gilbert, of course.

Mukai sat chatting to Oliver, but they were both smiling and Mukai was nodding to something Oliver was saying. Priscilla held her glass of sparkling champagne and then met Sidney's eyes. Chamu's younger brother seemed pleased also. Finally, Priscilla locked eyes with Lina. The look in her mother-in-law's eyes made the blood in her veins freeze. Lina stared at her with unmistakeable anger and hatred. Priscilla tried to shake off her stare and bring a smile to her face, but Lina's eyes continued to be hard and unfriendly.

Priscilla rubbed her arms, suddenly feeling chilled, and turned and walked away.

CHAPTER 23
Hupenyu Hwakanaka—The Good Life

The business climate continued to change in Zimbabwe in a way that pleased Chamu. There were many opportunities for enterprising black men and women. For many years after Zimbabwe won its independence from the British, the white minority still owned the land. It staggered Chamu that only five percent of the country owned ninety-five percent of all the land. The whites owned all the farms, tourism, businesses, and real estate. Where he lived, he was one of the few black people, just like his daughter's school had a handful of black children. However, things were changing. Indigenous black people could now own land by buying it, not stealing it as the British had done.

Chamu was just the man to take advantage of situations and prosper beyond many other people's imaginations. He was always ahead of the curve when it came to business opportunities, just as his father had been. Jonathan Tengani had been one of the first people to open a grocery store in the city. Most blacks tended to have businesses where they lived, but Jonathan had broken from the mold when he opened a grocery store in town in the area that had mostly Indian establishments. If they could do it, so could he.

"Chamu, don't let anyone tell you that you can't change your circumstances. If you think it, then go for it. I did it, and so can you."

Chamu remembered his father's words as he began to dream about opening a bank. He wished he could talk to his father about his desires, but he knew that his father was smiling down at him and encouraging him to follow his dreams.

Chamu saw how incredibly all his plans fell into place. Three years before he had told Priscilla to give up her job and promised her a position in his bank once it was established. For the past three years, she had been waiting for that moment to use her programming skills, and it seemed the time had finally come. She had spent the three years focusing her time on Rudo and helping and volunteering in her pre-school and attending long distance classes. He knew that he didn't want her to work, but he could tell that she was restless. At the bank he could monitor what she did and who she spent time with. Yes, having her help at the bank was the best plan.

Chamu was about to take his corporation to the next level, and he wanted to see his businesses grow to be respected all over Africa and make his way into Europe and America. The world was his to take. He talked to Priscilla about it at great length.

"I know it's going to work. I may not have a banking background, but I have the drive and ambition to make it work, especially with you by my side."

Priscilla smiled at Chamu's enthusiasm. When he first brought up his desire to start a bank they'd been in Cape

Town on holiday. Every year they travelled to different countries for shopping and relaxation. Often after a trip, Chamu would come up with a brilliant idea to grow his existing businesses or start new ones.

"A bank. I never knew it was that easy to open a bank," she said.

"It's not easy as such. Everything is hard work."

"I know, but you make it sound so easy. You are doing so well, while many others are leaving the country."

"I don't understand people who leave Zimbabwe. Right now there are so many opportunities to make money, but I think those who leave the country don't have the vision to start something. They just want to go to England and work in homes, looking after sick people."

Priscilla would have argued that some people who went to England were able to buy homes and help struggling families, but she kept quiet.

"All you need is to get people with the knowledge, someone who knows more than me, and then in a few years we will have our bank," Chamu said.

Now, three years later, Chamu remembered the conversation they had had. Chamu had identified a struggling bank that would do well with the capital he would bring. After months of negotiations the final plan had been drafted by the country's top lawyers, and Chamu now owned the bank. He could find ways to make Priscilla happy according to his plans.

He would never want to lose Priscilla. He would rather lose all his fortune first.

"How is my little angel?" Mukai took Rudo by the hand and led her into her living room.

"I'm fine and how are you?" Priscilla watched her aunt's eyes widen.

"I'm fine," Mukai answered, and then looked at Priscilla. "You've raised her well. She's well spoken." Priscilla nodded, but sighed when she heard what Mukai had to say next. "So you two have finally decided to visit me?"

"Has it been that long?" Priscilla asked. Rudo settled down on the chair and took out a book from her bag. Mukai watched, impressed.

"I haven't seen you since your surprise house party," Mukai said.

"Oh."

"You know that's true, Pri. I was beginning to feel rejected. I was afraid you would change, become too good for the rest of us."

"How can you say that?"

"It's true. Your mother says you never go to visit her that much," Mukai continued. "I've lived a long time. I've seen people be changed by money."

Priscilla felt tears fill her eyes. "I want to visit. I just don't feel like dealing with *Baba*."

"I know, but she's your mother. You should still go there sometimes."

Priscilla put her head down. She felt like a little child. She looked at Rudo reading her book, not even paying attention to them.

"I want to visit all of you more."

"All I can say is, what gives away is the hand. The mouth does not give away. I go by your actions, not what you say."

Priscilla was speechless. So according to Mukai nothing she could say could change the reality of her actions.

"Shall we have some juice?" Priscilla asked instead, getting ready to get up.

"You remember where the fridge is?"

Priscilla got up, looking around the living room, fighting the pain in her heart. Pictures of Unashe gleamed from every corner from the time he was a baby to manhood. He was Mukai's dearly loved son; if pictures around the room meant how much she loved him, then Unashe was truly precious. Oh, goodness, he looked just like Rudo did when she was a baby. Rudo had Unashe's eyes.

Priscilla almost ran to the kitchen, breathing hard after glancing back and seeing Mukai start to read Rudo's book to her. There was a good reason not to visit Mukai.

Being with Mukai was too dangerous. She always feared that Mukai would see something in Rudo, like the way her right cheek dimpled just like Unashe's, or how her eyes could melt even the coldest day. Maybe she was too paranoid. Still, being in Mukai's house had a way of taking away from her marriage. It always brought back memories that she preferred locked away forever. When she opened the refrigerator, she was plunged back to the times she spent in this kitchen, joking around with Unashe. At that moment, the memories were so powerful she could almost feel his presence, see his smiling face behind the kitchen counter while they talked for hours.

Priscilla poured the orange juice, added ice and water and slowly stirred. Was her memory of her love for Unashe greater than it really had been?

Maybe time has made me blow things out of proportion. Maybe he didn't make me laugh that hard or make my heart go that fast.

Priscilla shook her head and went to the lounge. Rudo had disappeared.

"Where did she go?" Priscilla asked. Mukai seemed to watch her carefully. Priscilla felt guilty, wondering if her thoughts of Unashe were all over her face.

"I told her to go play with Unashe's old toys. I have kept some of his things for his children," Mukai said. Priscilla almost spilt the drink.

"Are you all right?" Mukai asked.

"Fine." Priscilla's voice croaked. She could see that Mukai wasn't convinced, but made the decision not to pursue it any further.

"I kept all his favorite books. Of course some of them were torn. Can you believe his fire truck is still there on the shelf?"

"You keep that room very intact," Priscilla said.

"He's my only child. I'm waiting for the time he gets married and gives me grandchildren. He's almost twenty-eight now. Don't you think it's time he finds a nice girl and settles down?"

"I don't know. I think he wants to get some things in order first, like his career, before getting married."

"I wouldn't mind Chantel as a daughter-in-law. They have been together since he was in high school."

"Really," Priscilla said, feeling her heart beat faster.

"Oh yes. I always thought she loved him more than he loved her, but now it seems like things may be getting serious," Mukai said. "So how are you and Chamu doing?"

Priscilla took a sip of her drink. "We are fine. He's a wonderful father and husband."

"He is. I sometimes think he would do anything for you," Mukai said.

"Meaning?"

"I think he's different from most men I know. He knows how to treat a woman. Buying that house, taking you on holidays overseas. You have been all over the world."

"I really can't complain."

Rudo walked back into the living room with a fire truck in her hand. Mukai laughed, but Priscilla had a sense of foreboding.

"You are just like Unashe, aren't you? He loved that truck when he was your age, too," Mukai said.

Priscilla felt heat invade her body. "I think all children love fire trucks."

"There's something about Rudo that reminds me of Unashe," Mukai said, watching her drive the wretched thing on the carpet. Priscilla jumped up nervously.

Don't say that! Don't look too closely.

"Let's go, Rudo. Please put the truck back where you got it."

"No. Let her keep it. She can have it," Mukai said.

Priscilla stared at Mukai, wondering how she could refuse.

As she drove away, Priscilla turned to look in the back seat as her daughter somehow bonded with her real father through that fire truck.

CHAPTER 24
Vamwene—Mother-in-Law

"Where's Priscilla?" Lina and Chamu were sitting in the living room at "Pamusha", which was the name they had given to the new house. The room was decorated in white leather sofas that complimented the tropical theme. The palm trees added to the restful, calming atmosphere. Lina thought the rooms were too bare and needed more ornaments and flowers. She would tell Priscilla her ideas the next time she saw her.

"She went to visit her sister's husband. She might come back today. He's not feeling well. I would have gone, but with the new bank . . ."

"How's the bank?"

"Getting there," Chamu said and smiled at his mother. "The amount of work is staggering. Priscilla has actually been a great help. She's smart. She has more aptitude than some of my executives."

Lina pursed her lips. She wasn't going to agree with Chamu. Saying anything positive about Priscilla actually made her ulcers act up. "Do you think you'll be able to launch the whole thing as planned?"

"I have to. I've found two young men to run the corporate banking division. I want to invite them over here for a final interview. One is from South Africa, and the other is coming from the United Kingdom."

"You couldn't find someone from here?"

"I like these young men's credentials. I think they will make a nice fit in the bank."

"But does Priscilla have to work there? Don't you want her staying at home and running this house for you?"

Chamu laughed. "Priscilla is ready to jump out of her skin. She wants to work."

Lina stood up and took some peanuts from the plate. She took her time thinking of a way to broach what had been bothering her for years. She had to say something or she would choke with it. "Don't you think you give her everything she wants? Even more than she needs."

"She's my wife," Chamu said in a way that Lina couldn't argue with.

The maid, Maidei, came in with a dish of water for the two to wash their hands. Lina watched the young woman in an immaculate maid uniform. She didn't look into their eyes as she held the dish for them.

"I know but people are talking," Lina said as she wiped her hands on the soft white towel Maidei had handed to her.

"Talking about what?" Chamu asked. Lina could tell he was trying to hide his impatience, but she had to get this out. He was her son and had to respect what she had to say. She was only looking out for him.

"Well. The way you are raising Rudo, for instance. I have often complained to Priscilla about the way that girl speaks only English. She is black and she speaks as if she has stones in her mouth, like a white person. I haven't heard her speak a word in Shona."

"It's her school, Ma. If she is not confident in English, she doesn't do well. Whether we like it or not, English is the international language, and my daughter will speak it better than the English people."

"Still teach her some Shona, Chamunorwa! I like English, too, but our children are losing their culture and Priscilla acts all English when she grew up in Glenview."

"There's nothing wrong with Glenview, *Amai*. Not everybody lives in one room, and it is not their fault they can't afford more."

"Fine. Do what you want with Rudo. Now this house, for instance. The way you presented it to her in front of everybody makes me worry about you. I thought you were going to have a heart attack the way you were working so hard to build it in one year and to keep it a secret from her. And then the way you presented it to her in front of everybody, like she deserves it."

"I wanted people to see how much I love her and make sure everybody knows that she's mine," Chamu explained, perplexed by his mother's comments.

"We all already know that. Why do you still treat her as if you haven't paid for her already? She belongs to you."

"I know, *Amai*. She belongs to me on paper, but I still want to win her more. I always feel there is a part of her that I can't reach." Chamu looked on the wall where their wedding portrait stood between the two palm trees.

Lina's eyes followed. She felt for her son. He was going to die of stress trying to please that woman.

"She should be grateful for all you've done. You should show her who is boss. Your father never did what you are doing for this woman."

Chamu smiled, shaking his head. He was not going to talk to his mother about how he should treat his wife. Times were different. Women were no longer to be treated like objects, and he certainly enjoyed the challenge of winning his wife's heart. She kept him on his toes and he would not jeopardize his relationship so soon by making her feel like a prisoner.

Chamu called for the maid and Maidei came to the door waiting for instructions.

"Can you bring us dinner," Chamu said. Maidei nodded and scurried out.

"The girl has no manners. She's supposed to kneel when talking to you," Lina said. This time Chamu decided not to reply.

"The way your maid treats you is a reflection of how your wife treats you."

"*Amai.* Do you honestly want Priscilla to kneel all over the place like I'm some kind of king?"

"That is how women are supposed to behave. Not dress in men's clothes and show no respect. I think a woman has to know her place. I always knew my place with your father."

"I'll talk to her." Chamu was willing to say anything to end the conversation, but it seemed that his mother was not done yet.

"Even the way she is raising Rudo. That little girl shouldn't be lying all over the chairs, sitting with you while you eat. A young girl should be learning to help in the kitchen, kneeling when greeting adults and not always getting anything she wants."

"What has Rudo done to show disrespect?"

"She doesn't kneel when she greets me. She barely talks to me."

"Don't you think she's too young, Amai? She's only six."

Lina sighed, leaning back. "I'll talk to Priscilla. I blame most things on her because you are busy running the bank while she is supposed to be running a smooth home, teaching your child and maid manners and not trying to act like she's white."

Chamu was relieved when Maidei brought in the food and cut off the hopeless discussion. His mother didn't have one nice thing to say about Priscilla, he decided. He knew that his wife did her best to please her, buying her gifts, going to visit her often, wearing dresses, but nothing seemed to work.

Lina wanted to say more but decided not to at that time. She feared that Priscilla was going to hurt her son, and she just didn't want to stand by and watch.

Lina took a walk around her son's home after eating while Chamu went into his office with his cell phone. The flowers bloomed in different sections bordering the bright green grass. She got off the bricked driveway and walked on the lawn past the tennis court. She glanced at the huge pond a few meters away and decided to head in that direction. The wooden bridge had rails, and she stood there for a while and looked back at the incredible house.

"That woman doesn't deserve this house," she muttered under her breath. The windows gleamed in the sunlight and the palm trees in the middle of the circular driveway made it look like an exotic holiday resort.

Lina walked towards the lake gazebo and sat on the wooden chairs. The goldfish in the pond danced around, mesmerizing her.

Did her son have time to look at all the beauty surrounding his home? Did he get moments to admire the incredible stone sculptures that were randomly placed around the property? He was busy making money for his wife and child.

Just then, Lina's attention was drawn to the gate.

Speak of the devil, she thought. She saw Priscilla's car drive in smoothly and stood up to wave. Priscilla waved but continued to drive in. Lina was not going to follow her into the house.

Lina felt satisfied when she saw Priscilla leave her car and walk towards her.

"Hello, Mama," Priscilla said and smiled as she got closer.

Lina was disturbed at how Priscilla seemed more beautiful every time she saw her. Priscilla had to have some hidden darkness behind her smile. She wore a fancy cream suit that moved in the breeze as she walked, and it took all Lina's willpower not to click her tongue with disgust.

Oh, she could see why her son couldn't resist this woman. Why he couldn't think straight until he got her, and why he was willing to take all those drastic measures to keep her. Lina resented the power this woman had over her son. Her smile was unique and dazzling. Her hair black curls on her collar. Too perfect.

"How are you, Priscilla?"

Priscilla hugged her. Lina inhaled her expensive perfume.

"I'm fine." She sat down next to Lina on the chairs facing the water. "How are you?"

"Just enjoying the view of this beautiful house," Lina said. "Where were you?"

"I just got back from Gweru today, and I did a little bit of shopping on my way home. Rudo has grown so fast. I got her some new shoes," Priscilla said.

"She's growing fast, isn't she?" Lina said. "Didn't she turn six in April?"

"Yes," Priscilla said. "When did you come?"

"This morning. I was spending some time with my son. He hardly comes to visit. Neither do you."

"I'm sorry. I've been visiting my sister's husband. Gilbert's very sick," Priscilla said.

"What's wrong with him?"

"I don't know yet. The doctors are doing tests."

"Which sister is this?"

"Vimbai. She lives in Gweru," Priscilla said. "I'm worried about him."

"I'm sure," Lina said.

"So how is the family?"

"They are all fine." Lina told her stories about Chamu's brothers and sisters. Chamu's sister had just been promoted. She'd been given a company car.

"Your children are all doing well," Priscilla said. "You must be proud."

"So when are you going to have more children?" Lina's question took Priscilla by surprise.

"More children?"

"Yes. I've kept quiet all this time."

Priscilla felt the heat rise into her face.

"Rudo is only six," Priscilla said.

"I'm sure Chamu wants a son. He has always wanted a son to name after his father," Lina said.

"I didn't know that."

"I don't think he likes to put pressure on you," Lina said, feeling bolder as she talked.

Priscilla looked at Lina, totally at a loss for words.

"So when are you planning on giving Chamu a son?" Lina asked, irritated by Priscilla's silence.

"It's not up to me," Priscilla said, showing the strain from the conversation.

"What do you mean?"

"Haven't you talked to Chamu about it?"

"No. That's why I'm asking you. I know you modern girls don't want a lot of children, but I know what Chamu wants. It's unfair to refuse, and Chamu is just too nice to pressure you."

"I had a miscarriage," Priscilla whispered, tears filling her eyes. She stood up wiping her cheeks.

"Why didn't you tell us?"

"I really don't want to talk about it," Priscilla said. Lina looked shocked.

"I understand. Chamu must have been devastated," Lina said. She got up and started to walk away, not offering any comfort to Priscilla. Priscilla reached for her hand.

"We will try again soon, but Ma, please don't talk about it with Chamu. He also doesn't like to talk about it."

Lina looked coldly at her. "I can talk to my son about anything I want."

With those words she walked away and left Priscilla sitting by the pond, alone.

That evening Priscilla sat reading a banking book while Rudo did her homework. The gate bell rang. Chamu had gone with his mother to see another relative. He always opened the gate with his remote control. She walked to the intercom and asked who it was.

"It's Sidney."

Priscilla opened the gate, wondering why Chamu's brother was visiting so late. Sidney was a nice young man and Priscilla didn't mind seeing him. It was Lina who made her uncomfortable. She opened the door for him with a smile.

"Sidney. What a surprise," Priscilla said.

"How are you? Hey, Rudo." Sidney picked her up and held her in his arms. Rudo enjoyed the attention and gave him a hug back.

"What did you bring me, Uncle Sidney?" Rudo asked. It was Sidney's fault. He always brought her something when he came to visit, and now she expected it.

He handed her a bag of her favorite chicken flings. "Here you go, pretty lady."

"Thank you! Can I go eat them, Mummy?"

"Sure, baby. Go ahead."

"Where's Chamu?" Sidney asked, setting Rudo down.

"He went with *Amai* to visit one of your uncles who wants help with his business. I was glad I didn't have to go along."

"He didn't tell you where?"

"No. I was too tired to ask for details. I just got back from Gweru today."

"I see."

Rudo walked towards her dolls and the red truck that they sat in.

"I'm going to play school," Rudo said and left the two adults standing facing each other.

"Wow, this house is quiet," Sidney said, sitting down in the family living room.

Priscilla looked around at the beautiful decorations and nodded her head.

"It is, especially when it's just us two at home. I usually like to leave the TV and radio on."

"How does it feel living in the most expensive and gorgeous house?" Sidney asked with a smile. Priscilla could see why many women at Chamu's company liked him.

Priscilla realized that Sidney had had quite a few relationships, but they never went beyond dating. He didn't seem to be in a rush to settle down. There was no rush. She turned to him now, remembering his question about the house.

"I'm getting used to it. I don't really mind where I live as long as it is safe and clean," she said.

"This takes the cup." Sidney looked around. "Chamu is one lucky guy. He has it all."

"I'm the lucky one. He is so generous."

"My brother is used to getting what he wants out of life."

"He works hard for everything he gets, Sidney."

"You think you know him so well, don't you?"

Priscilla wondered what Sidney was driving at. She had no idea there was any bad blood between them. What a day this was turning out to be. First she had to deal with seeing her sister's husband looking hopeless and gaunt, then listen to Lina ask her about children, and now Sidney was implying there was something wrong with Chamu. He was not perfect, but he was close enough to it. Was Sidney jealous of his brother?

"I've been married to Chamu for six years. I think I know him pretty well."

"I knew him for over twenty years before that," Sidney said, his charming smile still intact.

"So you drove all the way out here just to talk about Chamu?"

"No. I was hoping he was home. I wanted to talk to him. He's a hard man to pin down. He told me to come here tonight, but I think he forgot."

Priscilla nodded, but became further astonished at Sidney's next question.

"Doesn't it bother you that he stays away a lot?"

"He doesn't stay away that much. When he's at work I'm also doing some work at home, or he works from here."

"He's lucky to have you. I don't think he deserves you."

Priscilla shook her head making a face. "I don't even know what you are talking about."

"When I met you the first time I didn't think you would marry him. I was hoping you wouldn't."

"Why?"

"I thought you were more my type than his. No, I am more your type than him."

Priscilla laughed. "You are joking, right?"

"A little bit."

"I can't talk to you if you joke about things like that. It's not even funny."

"One day you will know what I mean," Sidney said. His tone, the look in his eyes, disturbed her.

"Why don't you tell me what you mean exactly? If you have something to tell me, just tell me."

"Why don't you pour me a beer? Then we can talk," Sidney said, sitting back comfortably. Priscilla stared at him for a moment, strange sensations going up and down her spine, then stood up and went to the kitchen. She nearly jumped when she heard the kitchen door open. It was Chamu. His car had driven in so quietly that she had not heard it. She was relieved to see him.

Priscilla decided to take Sidney's statements as ridiculous jokes with terrible punch lines that she was glad she had missed. She couldn't take him seriously at all. She wouldn't know how to deal with that.

CHAPTER 25
Rufu—Death

The following night the phone rang. Chamu picked it up after glancing at the clock. It was 2:15 a.m. He listened to the message while Priscilla sat up groggily next to him. He put the phone down and turned on the light.

"Who was that?"

"Vimbai's husband is dead. Gilbert died a few hours ago," Chamu said.

Priscilla whimpered and started crying.

Chamu took her into his arms, rocking her as she sobbed. She had just seen him and even though he had been a mean bastard, the news still hurt.

"It was AIDS, Priscilla," Vimbai said a few weeks after Gilbert's funeral in Gokwe. The village where Gilbert was buried was far from civilization and Priscilla had spent three difficult days living in a hut, bathing in the river and cooking food by fire. On top of that, the nights were dedicated to singing so Gilbert's spirit could go away cheerfully. Her head throbbed most of the time from the constant drumbeat and the loud mourning of

Gilbert's family. Gilbert was still very young, and, though mean to Vimbai, was dearly loved by many.

"What?" Priscilla felt the world spin right before her eyes at the deadly word. AIDS.

"I was tested, and I'm HIV positive, too," Vimbai added.

Priscilla stared at her sister as if she was already dead, wanting her to take back the words she had just uttered. Priscilla started weeping, hiding her face in her hands as if she could run away from Vimbai's deadly words.

After what seemed like hours, they talked, sitting in the bedroom that Vimbai once shared with Gilbert and his girlfriends. Priscilla had come to Gweru to talk to Vimbai about her children and her future, but it seemed like her sister didn't have much of a future anymore. Life was so unfair!

"I've been going for counselling. I have to eat healthy. There are drugs I can take and ways I can make sure I have a longer life."

"I just don't believe it. That bastard gave it to you," Priscilla said.

"He was a fool. Men always tell each other that they can't get it."

"Why didn't he tell you?" Priscilla's voice shook with anger. She wanted to ask Vimbai why she had stayed with him for so long, but didn't. She recalled Vimbai telling her that Gilbert had not wanted to marry her, but in the beginning it wasn't so bad. When they lost their first child to malaria, it had brought them closer together. They had grieved together, but by the death of the second child he began to change. He blamed her for losing their children. As the years went on, he got worse and worse.

"I don't think he ever got tested until the very end. I'm telling you this because you never know who has it. I'm going to let the family know, but I wanted to tell you first, baby sister."

"I don't want to believe it. You must get a second opinion, get another test," Priscilla insisted.

"It's true," Vimbai said, blinking back tears. "I have accepted it. I now have to make plans for my children."

"You'll live long. They don't have it, do they?"

Vimbai took Priscilla's hands into her own and squeezed them.

"No. Thank God. Thank God."

AIDS. It was something that had crept onto the nation's radar. First, it had been smoke in the distance. Now it was a blazing fire threatening to destroy all that were dear to her.

CHAPTER 26
Tsakatika—Lost

Chamu found that keeping his wife busy meant that she wasn't spending all her time grieving and worrying about Vimbai, who wasn't responding well to the drugs they were ordering from overseas. Priscilla took her sister to Victoria Falls and took her to see doctors in South Africa, but being busy with Vimbai wasn't the solution.

Several months after her trip to Victoria Falls with Vimbai, Chamu asked Priscilla to host an important dinner in their home. He knew she wasn't comfortable acting as hostess, but she had impressed Chamu the few times she had done it.

For days before Priscilla worked hard to plan and organize the event. She was happy that everything was in order when the big day arrived. After Priscilla supervised the dinner making, she went upstairs to take a bath. She was confident that the two chefs who worked at the new Mukadota Hotel and the maid helping with the chopping and dicing had all made a feast worthy for a king.

The bathtub was full of hot water and bubbles and she sank in with a sigh. Yes, it was nice to close her eyes and not think for a few minutes of pure heaven. The vanilla scent, mixed with other exotic, relaxing oils, made her feel lightheaded, warm and at peace.

Priscilla opened her eyes quickly with irritation when the bedroom door opened.

"Pri, are you here?" It was Chamu.

"In here," Priscilla said. She was annoyed. She had wanted to spend more time alone.

He knocked gently and opened the door, letting out some of the steam from her foggy bathroom. He had loosened his tie, but was still wearing his dark blue suit.

"The food smells good downstairs," Chamu said, looking down at her.

She sat up and reached for the towel on the rack close to the tub. He grabbed it and held it for her. His eyes roamed her body as she stepped out of the tub covered with soapy bubbles. He watched her for a while, and she could see the desire in his eyes.

She reached again and he passed the towel around her back and kissed her shoulders. She smiled weakly, then moved away.

"I have to get dressed," she said.

"I know. I also need to get ready. I will have a quick shower."

"What time are the guests coming?" Priscilla asked as she tied a knot in the towel above her breasts. She sat on the edge of the tub and released the water.

"In about an hour," Chamu said, pulling his tie off completely, his eyes on her exposed legs. "Thanks for doing the dinner and the flowers. The house looks great."

"I don't mind. I had better hurry. I want to make sure everything is perfect."

Priscilla walked out of the bathroom and walked into her huge dressing room. She sat down on the chair and started to apply lotion and perfume. Her hair had been done that morning in an up-do, so all she had to do was smooth it. She had chosen an ivory designer dress for the evening. It had discreet embroidery that gave it an ethnic feel that she liked in almost all her clothes lately. A top Ghanaian dressmaker who sold her clothes out of a posh store in Borrowdale had designed this particular dress.

She was standing before the mirror admiring the magnificent dress when she heard Chamu leave the bathroom and enter his dressing room.

The delicious smells reached her as she made her way down the curving staircase. She liked the way the dining room was set with candles and her best dinner set. The formal lounge was clean, as usual. They hardly used the formal room, but today it would be put to use. She had placed bouquets of flowers around the room and would have liked to light a fire, but the night was too warm.

Chamu came down and met her.

"There will be one extra person tonight, by the way," Chamu said, walking over to the bar and pouring a glass of juice.

"So it's not just eight of us?"

"Nine or ten. I've hired another young man who has just come from England," Chamu said, looking at her. "You look amazing."

"Thank you," she replied, and then touched the lapels of his jacket. "You look great, as usual."

Chamu laughed. "I think you will like the group of people I've invited. You can also tell me if anyone doesn't appeal to you in some way. I think you have good instincts."

"All right. I'll do that," she said, then startled when she heard the gate bell.

"I'll get it," Chamu said, going to answer the intercom and press the open button. Chamu came back and surveyed the formal living room with appreciation.

"We really went to a lot of trouble for these executives. I'm sure they will be impressed."

"They better be. I want them to have confidence in Primehouse Bank. They should know that they will be working for the best bank in the country. Image is everything."

While he was speaking, the doorbell rang and Chamu went to open it. In came two lovely women and two men about the same age as Chamu.

Chamu shook hands with them.

"Joe, Tapiwa," Chamu said.

"Good evening, Mr. Tengani. This is my wife Nyasha," Joe Kame said. He was intelligent looking, with thin-rimmed glasses and a clean-shaven face. Priscilla stood aside, watching Joe greet Chamu. He had a sweet smile. His wife Nyasha was dressed in a stylish two-piece suit and her pretty face was framed by micro-braids.

"Nice to meet you Nyasha. This is my wife Priscilla," Chamu said, putting his hands possessively around her waist and drawing her into the circle.

"And this is Tapiwa Ngoni and his wife Caroline. She's a doctor at Parirenyatwa Hospital."

"Hello," Priscilla said.

"Tapiwa will be the operations manager for the bank. He has already started working there," Chamu said. Before Priscilla could respond, the bell rang again. While Chamu answered, she took the other couples into the formal living room and had them seated on the black leather sofas with cold drinks in hand. Her maid and the hired cook were quick to serve appetizers on plates.

Priscilla was talking to Caroline and Nyasha when she heard Chamu walk in with a booming laugh. The voice she heard sounded so familiar it took her from that moment into another distant time when she was somebody else. It brought sensations familiar yet forbidden in their flavor.

Her panicking mind worked overtime as she listened to the two women with one ear and strained to hear the conversation happening away from view. Chamu walked in with a tall man and a young, light-skinned woman holding his hand. It took her a shocking second to realize that Unashe stood right in front of her. His smile died as his eyes caught hers.

CHAPTER 27
Kudzikama—Calm

"Everybody, I would like you to meet our young banking operations director, Unashe Made," Chamu said with a big smile.

Joe and Tapiwa stood up to shake his hand. Priscilla stood up as well as everybody shook hands with excitement and enthusiasm. Then it was her turn.

"Unashe," she said.

"Hello, Priscilla," he said.

"This is a surprise. Does Aunt Mukai know you are here?" Priscilla was trying hard to avoid asking any other questions. *What are you doing here? How did you and Chamu get to know each other?*

Her heart was beating so hard she wondered if the guests could hear it as loudly as she could hear the noise in her ears. She had learned to hide her feelings, but she wasn't sure how well she was doing with this particular shock.

"Of course. I forgot you two may know each other," Chamu said, looking at Priscilla.

"I'm very close to his mother," Priscilla said, looking at Joe and Tapiwa. "It's good to see you."

"This is my wife," Chamu said and walked over to hold Priscilla again. It took all of Priscilla's strength not to step out of his arms; his grip felt too tight, and Unashe was watching his hands in a way that disturbed her equilibrium. "I didn't know she was married to you," Unashe said as he brought his companion forward.

"This is Dora. Dora, meet Priscilla." Priscilla shook the hand of the smiling, gorgeous woman.

"Everybody enjoy the hors d'oeuvres. I'll check on dinner. I'll be right back," Priscilla said to the room in general, and then walked to the kitchen and out the laundry to the back garden. She really had to be alone to clear her head. She had to get herself together before she made a fool of herself.

She needed more time to cool her heated skin, but she knew it would seem unusual if she stayed out any longer. The evening was warm with a gentle breeze, and she had a good mind to walk and sit by the pool all evening. She couldn't face him. Or could she?

After taking several deep breaths of the cool evening air, she walked into the kitchen. Her panic had subsided but her heart hadn't slowed. She was as terrified of going back to her guests as she had been as a child facing Oliver after she had done something wrong.

"How is the food coming along?"

The two men dressed in white chef uniforms turned away from the stove and looked at her.

"It's done, madam. We can serve as soon as you are ready."

"You can bring it in now," Priscilla said and walked back into the living room.

Another couple had arrived, so that meant ten people for dinner. Chamu was talking to the men and the women, as usual, were talking in a group on their own. She glanced at Unashe very quickly and looked away. He was busy listening to the other men talk, a glass of wine in one hand and the other in his pocket.

She walked over to the women and introduced herself to the newcomer, a mother of four and business owner, Faith Sekeranai. Faith was very warm and friendly. Priscilla gravitated toward her. She liked her independence and the way she had started her catering and wedding planning business. Listening to her talk was calming. At last Priscilla was finally able to get her mind off the huge distraction in the room.

"My next venture is to move in another direction. I want to buy land and develop a wedding venue. There is a lot of money in that also. I know a couple that had to pay thousands of dollars for a piece of grassy land to have their wedding. I can do better than that, and create a beautiful garden with water features and exotic flowers."

Priscilla paid attention to the conversation, but her whole being was alert, completely aware of when Unashe took a drink or laughed or said a word. As they were getting ready to go to the dining room, Rudo came down the stairs. Priscilla laughed when Rudo walked in and saw everybody. The child's eyes went round with surprise. Priscilla's smile froze when she caught Unashe looking at Rudo.

"Say hello to everyone, Rudo," Priscilla said. Rudo walked around giving everybody a handshake, the way they had taught her after Lina's lecture. The last person she greeted was Unashe. He seemed enthralled by Rudo.

"I knew you had a daughter, but I didn't know she was this big," Unashe said, looking at Priscilla.

"Time flies," Priscilla said.

"Rudo, you can go to the kitchen and Sisi Maidei will give you your dinner. We can't eat together tonight," Priscilla said.

"Because of the people?" Rudo asked, looking around.

Everybody smiled or giggled at her comment and the way Rudo asked the question.

"I'll take you," Priscilla said and walked with Rudo to the kitchen. She was aware of everybody's eyes on her, but only one set made her tremble.

Dinner was a mixture of traditional and Western food. The rice mixed with peanut butter was a family favorite, and there were two kinds of meat, oxtail stew and roasted chicken. The coleslaw salad was always there, and Priscilla had asked for some mushroom sauce on the side.

Priscilla sat down opposite Chamu on the long glass and oak table while the other couples all sat opposite each other on either side. Unashe was separated from her by one other person. She could see everything he did in the corner of her eye.

If asked, Priscilla couldn't tell anyone how the food tasted. Her mind kept racing throughout the meal. Unashe was so close, and she couldn't even have the luxury of yelling at him or slapping him or holding him.

"That was an excellent dinner," Chamu said as they got ready for bed. Priscilla removed her earrings in front of the dressing table. Her mind worked at high speed as she tried to think of the appropriate things to say.

"It was good. How on Earth did you get hold of Unashe?" Priscilla looked at Chamu in the mirror. She hoped her voice sounded neutral.

"I had a talk with his mother," Chamu replied.

"Auntie Mukai?"

"Yes. She knew that he would be coming back, so we decided to get him the job. He has been working in Standard Chartered in England, and I figured he would be an asset with his international exposure and banking certifications." Priscilla nodded slowly. Chamu undressed and went to stand behind her.

"Come to bed," he whispered in her ear.

Priscilla wiggled out of his arms and walked into her closet. She took off her dress and put on a long night-dress. She started tidying up her closet, but, after a while, she knew she had to go bed. Chamu sat on top of the gold bedding looking at the newspaper.

"I'm really tired," Priscilla said, getting under the sheets. Chamu folded up his newspaper and joined her under the satin sheets. He reached for her.

"Come on, Pri," Chamu said, pulling her resisting body to his. She stiffened and curled her legs up to her chest.

"I'm exhausted. I can't do that tonight," Priscilla whined.

"You are always tired. I'm a very understanding husband, but I think it's time to try for our next child."

"I know," Priscilla said with little enthusiasm. She was tired, yes, but more importantly, her mind could not calm down. She had just said good-bye to Unashe at the door.

Unashe.

CHAPTER 28

Nakai—Be Beautiful

A week had gone by since the dinner and Priscilla was going out of her mind. She had tried to guess what Unashe might be feeling. All she had managed to accomplish was to give herself a major headache and a minor heart attack every time she recalled the moment she'd looked up and saw him at the dinner party.

She tried to figure out how he had just walked into her house and announced that he would be working in Chamu's bank. When did Chamu hire him? Why did Unashe accept? She couldn't get any answers to her questions because she completely avoided having any Unashe-related discussions with Chamu. The only way she could get some answers was to visit Mukai.

She greeted Mukai with a hug. They walked out to the other side of the garden by the swimming pool, which was drained of all water.

"Why didn't you tell me Unashe was back?" Priscilla asked. "And working for Chamu?"

"My son didn't tell me everything until just a week ago," Mukai said. "I didn't know what day he was coming until the day before he came. That was two weeks ago."

"Oh."

"He should be back soon so you can shout at him," Mukai said. Priscilla's heart thudded at that. He was coming here? This was ridiculous. Seeing him again was probably a good idea, because then she would reduce the effects of the minor heart attack she experienced every time she heard his name.

"He's staying here?" She didn't want to sound too eager to know all about Unashe's business.

"He's here until he furnishes his new townhouse. Chamu is very good to his employees. He gave them loans and company cars."

"I know you must be so happy to have seen him after all these years," Priscilla said. She sat down on a garden chair and turned her face towards the sweetness of the sun. She tried not to worry about Chamu giving Unashe a job and loans. What if he found out the truth?

Before they could discuss more, they heard a car honk and the gardener ran to open the gate, his black boots throwing gravel into the air. Priscilla felt her heart stop in her chest. That had to be Unashe.

"That's him now," Mukai said.

Priscilla unconsciously smoothed her hair. She hadn't seen him or talked to him since the dinner at her house, and that seemed like a lifetime ago. She realized that not seeing him didn't stop her from thinking about him daily.

"We are here," Mukai called out as Unashe walked towards them. He wore dark baggy jeans and a loose-fitting cotton shirt. The shirt wasn't buttoned all the way to the top, showing the skin above his collarbone. Priscilla's eyes travelled to his face, but with the dark glasses it was difficult to tell what he was thinking. He looked so handsome, so confident, so unreachable.

"Good afternoon, Mum." Unashe greeted his mother by putting his hand on her shoulder. He turned to Priscilla. "Hello, Priscilla."

"Hi, Unashe," Priscilla said, working very hard to keep her voice calm. She cleared her throat.

"Did you get the furniture you wanted?" Mukai asked.

"I got the bed. It'll be delivered on Monday. I don't like any of the sofas I saw so far. I wish I had shipped mine from the UK," Unashe said and looked at Priscilla.

"Why don't you sit down?" Mukai said. "What's wrong with our own country's furniture?"

Unashe sat down opposite Priscilla, stretching his long legs out in front of him.

"I'm not being snobbish, Ma. It's just that all the furniture here is all the same. I'll see it at everybody's house when I visit. There is no variety. Now in Priscilla's house they have real Italian sofas that nobody else owns in this city."

Priscilla sensed the mockery in his voice. "Chamu ordered it."

"How is it being married to money?" Unashe asked.

"Being married is fine," Priscilla said, widening her eyes at him.

"I hardly see her anymore," Mukai complained again. "I guess we are too poor to spend time with."

"That is very hurtful," Priscilla said. "I always come and see you."

"It's a joke, my dear. You seem to have lost your sense of humor. I know you have a lot on your plate. Let me leave you to simmer down," Mukai said, standing up. She looked irritated, but she gave Priscilla a smile.

"What do you want to eat, Unashe?" Mukai directed her question to her son.

"I'll have whatever you want," Unashe said. "Preferably *sadza*."

"That's my boy," Mukai said and walked towards the house. Priscilla continued to look down, stung by what Mukai had said.

"Why are you being mean to my mother?" Unashe said, shocking her even more.

"What? She's the one saying I'm now showing off because I have money," Priscilla said. "That's very hurtful."

"She was joking," Unashe said. He looked angry, and it upset her so much more than anything Mukai could say to her.

She wiped the tears from her eyes and glared at Unashe. He stared back at her. Even angry he looked as amazingly handsome as he always had. The glasses were off, and the dark brown eyes pierced her and silenced her. What could she say to him now?

"It's been a long time. Let's not fight," Priscilla said at last.

"You are the one good at starting fights," Unashe said.

"What on Earth are you talking about?"

"Is there any point in talking about the past? You have done very nicely for yourself. You have proved what I always thought."

"What?" Priscilla put her hands on the chair's arms, ready to spring at him, but she didn't understand anything he was saying. Was that disgust on his face?

"I would like us to forget the past. We were very good friends once," Unashe said instead.

Priscilla took deep breaths. The hem of her soft cream dress and the scarf around her neck danced in the wind.

"You don't have anything to explain to me?" Priscilla asked.

"No. I think everything that happened was meant to be. I was angry at you for a long time," Unashe said.

"You? Angry!" Priscilla's eyes flashed at him. She was so upset she hadn't even seen Mukai coming.

"Don't tell me you two are fighting," Mukai said, shaking her head.

"No," Priscilla said trying to calm down. There was still fire coming from her eyes. At that moment, Priscilla wished she could burn Unashe into tiny little pieces of ash. He just looked at her steadily.

"Come on. Are you angry at Unashe for not telling you he was coming home?" Mukai asked Priscilla.

"Yes," Priscilla said. Among other things, she added silently.

"You have to make up. Priscilla is going through a lot with her sister's illness," Mukai said to Unashe, and then turned to Priscilla. "And Unashe's going through a lot because of my illness."

"What?" Priscilla cried.

"It's not that bad. I'm still having tests to find out what's wrong," Mukai said.

Priscilla stood up and went to hug Mukai. "I'm so sorry. I didn't know anything was wrong. I'm sorry."

Mukai put her arms around Priscilla. "It's fine, my dear. I'll be fine. I didn't want to burden you, what with Vimbai and her husband's funeral."

"It's not a burden to be there for you. You have been there for me all my life. I want to be there for you, too."

Priscilla stood up straight and walked to Unashe.

"Come here," she said. Unashe stood up and Priscilla held out her arms to him.

"I'm sorry for yelling at you. I'm there for you, too," Priscilla said. When she felt his arms go around her waist, she held her breath. She wanted to be lost in his embrace, to be swept away to some faraway place where only the two of them existed. Her breath practically caught in her throat.

"Now come on, you two. Let's go in the house before we turn as black as my pots," Mukai said. Priscilla laughed as they walked into the house.

"I need a nap just for a few minutes before lunch. You two can keep each other company," Mukai said, walking into her bedroom and leaving Unashe and Priscilla standing alone in the hallway.

"She gets tired easily," Unashe said.

"Do you know what she's suffering from?"

"They suspect she might have stones or some growths around her stomach area, which they hope are not cancerous. The doctors think she might need surgery just to find out. We are still waiting to find out exactly what the problem is and doing more tests."

They walked into the living room, their feet silent on the carpet. It was strange being alone with Unashe. Priscilla had conflicting emotions. Unashe sat on one sofa and turned on the TV but did not put up the volume. Priscilla sat on the same sofa but left enough room for two people to fit between them.

"Your daughter is pretty. She's very clever, too," Unashe said, surprising Priscilla. He kept flipping the channels, and there were over two hundred of them.

"Thank you," Priscilla said, her eyes on the TV.

"What's her name again?" Unashe asked and they looked at each other.

"Rudo."

"Love."

"Yes," Priscilla said. She looked at the pictures on the walls. Mukai was always adding new photographs, and the most recent one was of Unashe's graduation.

"I didn't know what seeing you again was going to be like," Priscilla said and turned to look at him.

"Same. The last time we were together, we were just kids. We made kids' mistakes."

"What do you mean?"

"I mean the whole situation. That was a huge mistake. Us. We should never have done that. I'm sorry for my part."

Priscilla couldn't believe what she was hearing. But he had to be right. It had to have been a mistake, but her daughter was not a mistake. If he looked at their relationship that way then he had no right knowing about Rudo. He would just dismiss her as a mistake.

Her eyes filled with tears, but she would not let them come out. She blinked them away rapidly and, remembering Chantel, her eternal rage returned to take away the soft, silly girl who still longed for her lost first love.

"You are right," she said, dismissing all her obsession as a silly childhood mistake. "I'm sorry, too."

Unashe stopped flipping the channels when he found a soccer game and looked at her with a smile.

"So tell me about your life. What have you been up to?"

So that was it then. The whole time they were together was nothing. It was almost like a dream. How shameful. Priscilla wanted to smash his face in, but she was no longer a child. It was time to grow up and accept reality. Unashe didn't look at her the same anymore. She was just like some distant friend who he had made a mistake with and now all was forgotten and they could move on with their lives.

"I'm married to the most wonderful man," Priscilla began in her dreamiest voice. She conjured up all the sweet things Chamu did for her and their child. "Did I tell you how he bought me that house? Just handed it to me like a cake."

Priscilla laughed, enjoying how Unashe's smile faded. The afternoon wasn't going to be bad after all. She had a lot to tell Unashe. So much for wanting to grow up. Acting childish was just the way to get through the time with him.

CHAPTER 29
Zvichabuda Pachena—Out in the Open

Since her wedding to Chamu, Priscilla had talked to her real father a few times on the phone and only seen him three times at restaurants, like a secret lover. Another secret in her life of eternal secrets.

Priscilla wondered how many more secrets she would have to keep, and how many more were being kept from her?

Robert said it was hard to see her because he didn't want to explain her to his family. Not yet. It was now six years later, and she had not met her brother or two sisters.

Robert Chigoni claimed his wife was crazy and would probably kill them both if he knew Priscilla existed. She asked Chamu if he could visit her at her home.

Robert agreed to visit their house two Saturdays after she had visited Mukai and Unashe. Priscilla could barely sleep the night before. She really wanted to have a relationship with him and have him play a role in her daughter's life. The visit ended up making her greatest fear come true. The horns she had been hiding poked out of the paper.

"You have a beautiful house," Robert Chigoni exclaimed as she showed him around the gardens. Like many people who saw the house for the first time, Robert was impressed. It felt good to show him that she didn't need him, that she had wealth and money and he was just in her life for what he was meant to be: to love and be her father.

Chamu was sitting in the living room watching BBC News when they came back from the tour.

"So what do you think of the house?" Chamu asked Robert.

"It's great. I thought I had seen the biggest and best homes in Harare, but yours surely takes the trophy as being number one!"

"Why has it taken you so long to come and visit?" Chamu asked.

"I'm sure you understand the situation I'm in. I can't see Priscilla as much as I would like to. I have my family to consider."

Priscilla heard his words, the way he spoke so formally, like a diplomat, as she brought in the dish to wash hands for lunch.

"How are your real kids?" Priscilla asked holding out the dish while he washed his hands. Robert Chigoni looked at her with a raised brow.

"They are fine. Steve's almost graduating from Cape Town and the girls are all doing very well in the States."

"So it seems I'll never meet them. They are all far away now. And your wife?"

"She's fine. She's doing a lot of work for the AIDS council. She's helping getting funds for the orphans, especially in this region. It's astounding how many children have no parents."

"It is, isn't it," Priscilla said as she sat down with them. The food was always well prepared by servants, but that day Priscilla had made a special effort to cook all the dishes herself.

"How is Rudo?" Robert asked.

"She doesn't know you are her grandfather," Priscilla said.

"But she knows I love her. I brought her a gift today," Robert said.

Priscilla scowled. "Sometimes, Robert, for such an educated man you act like a child. You should know that things don't mean anything."

"Since I came here you have been nothing but rude to me," Robert complained. He didn't raise his voice, but he seemed angry. "Why should I stay here and be insulted by my own child?"

"I apologize," Priscilla said quickly, looking down at her lap.

"It's fine." Robert waved his fork in the air.

"Priscilla, are you all right," Chamu asked.

"I'm fine. I seem to be upsetting everybody wherever I go," Priscilla said. "I think I'm just tired of the secrets."

"What are you talking about?" Chamu said.

"I haven't told Ma and *Baba* that I've met my real father. I have kept that from them. How different am I from them? I'm keeping my relationship with Robert a secret."

"It's fine, Priscilla. Sometimes you hurt people more by telling them the truth," Chamu said.

Priscilla stared at Chamu. "Or, you set them free," she said.

There was silence as the words she had uttered sank in everybody's heart. After a while, Chamu started chewing his food.

Robert shrugged his shoulders. "The best time will present itself."

Robert nodded and turned to Chamu. "So, Chamu, I hear you will be opening Primehouse Bank soon. When is the big launch event?"

Before Chamu could answer, Priscilla was surprised when she heard their intercom ring. She wasn't expecting any other visitors, and because they lived so far out not many people just dropped by without first checking if they were home. She was surprised when she heard her sister Rutendo's voice. She walked back into the dining room and told Chamu and Robert.

"Rutendo? Your sister?" Robert asked.

"Yes. I'll just tell her you are Chamu's friend," Priscilla said when she saw the question in his eyes.

He could see that she wasn't very happy about having to lie to her sister.

"I don't like it, either, Priscilla, but now is not the time to tell your family about me. I wish there was another way, but I must insist." Priscilla nodded and took a sip of her drink. She heard Rutendo's car in the driveway.

"I better go and see Rutendo in," Priscilla stood up and walked towards the door. She opened it and nearly screamed when she saw Rutendo with her mother and father right behind her.

"Ma . . ." Priscilla said.

"We wanted to surprise you," Rutendo said and breezed past Priscilla in her usual forceful way. Priscilla hugged Monica and shook hands with Oliver. After she closed the door, she turned and felt like she was watching cars drive towards a head-on collision. She watched Oliver and Monica walk in and crash right into Robert Chigoni.

Monica visibly froze as she and Robert saw each other. There was a moment of disturbing silence that Priscilla found herself unable to break.

Finally, noticing the disaster about to happen, Chamu stood up to shake hands with Oliver.

"Oh, *Baba*," Chamu said with a wide smile. Oliver smiled and shook hands with him and Priscilla felt momentarily relieved. "This is my friend, Robert Chigoni."

Priscilla watched Chamu but couldn't help biting her bottom lip.

Oliver looked at Robert, and Priscilla saw his eyes turn cold.

"I know you," Oliver said.

Robert held out his hand to greet Oliver, but Oliver did not extend his hand. He looked instead at Monica; her face was calm, but he had read something when she walked in and he could see the way Robert had looked at her. Robert dropped his hand by his side, distress on his face. He sat down again.

"What is going on here, Priscilla?"

Priscilla felt the cold dread go up her spine as it used to when she lived in Oliver's house. She felt like a little girl again, forgetting that this was her home and she was married and no longer had to put up with Oliver's meanness.

"What?" Priscilla tried to speak, but her voice trembled. Why had she ever wanted the truth to come out? It's as if she had brought this disaster upon herself by insisting that Robert acknowledge her. But this wasn't how she had envisioned it at all.

"Monica. Is this your boyfriend?"

Priscilla watched her mother shake her head, looking distressed. "Don't say that to her," Priscilla said.

"Shut up," Oliver yelled at Priscilla, and she flinched as if he had slapped her.

Chamu stood up, holding out his hand to protect his wife.

"This is the man you had your filthy spawn with. This is the man that brought disgrace into my family, and Priscilla is seeing him behind my back? This disgusting man, this imbecile!"

"Don't talk about my father like that," Priscilla yelled, not caring that Rutendo was staring at her with shock. Oliver had a list of words she remembered from before. Words for stupid, dumb, whore . . . he had them all up his sleeve.

"Your father? Your father? Who raised you? Whose name did you hold for twenty-three years? Who paid for your school that you might even meet and marry this man who deserves way better than you? I swear by all the ancestors, you will pay for this."

Priscilla's bottom lip trembled. She had never been as humiliated in her life as she listened to him call her and her mother names, cursing them and wishing them dead.

"I think you should leave," Chamu said calmly, reaching out to touch Oliver's shoulder. Oliver flinched away. Priscilla admired Chamu's composure, though she could tell that he was furious.

"I will leave, but you, Robert, and your filthy child will pay for making me a fool. Nobody does that to me and gets away with it. And like I said to you, Priscilla, you are no child of mine and I wish I had never taken you in!"

Oliver turned, his anger still making him tremble. "Rutendo, take me away from here," he said sharply and walked out the door. He came back a second later and pointed at Monica, who stood still as a pole in the middle of the living room. "And Monica, you should find your-self another home."

"That was unacceptable behavior. I won't be surprised if your father, Robert, never wants to see you again," Chamu said.

"That will be just fine," Priscilla said, turning on the TV. Chamu walked to her and switched it off.

"I don't want to fight with you, too," Chamu said.

"That was the worst thing I've ever seen. I'm so embarrassed . . ."

"Why should you be embarrassed? Oliver had no right to say what he did to your mother or to you."

"I hurt him. I know he was a horrible man to me growing up, but I still wished he hadn't met up with Robert that way. I wish he wouldn't take it out on my mother."

"Your mother refused to stay here. She wanted to go home," Chamu said. He watched Priscilla stand up from their bed and pull her purse from the floor. She took her phone out and looked at it. He knew she was checking to see if her mother had called.

"Why? Why does she do it? Why does she go and stay with him when he is so angry?" Priscilla said and looked at Chamu beseechingly, as if he had the answers. He shook his head.

"There is nothing you can do, Pri. I'm sure your father will calm down and everything will be all right."

"If he hurts her, if he so much as touches her I will go and kill him myself . . ."

Chamu pulled her into his arms, but she remained stiff, refusing his comfort.

"Your father loves your mother. He would not hurt her."

Love? What kind of love was that? All he did was cause her pain.

Priscilla could not shake the fear in her heart as her mind took her back to the afternoon.

After Oliver and Rutendo drove away, her mother had walked into the kitchen without even looking at Robert. Robert remained seated, seemingly stunned by his meeting with Oliver. Priscilla followed Monica into the kitchen in time to hear her call a cab.

"Ma. What are you doing?" Monica still held the phone as she turned to her daughter, her eyes determined but soft.

"I'm going home," Monica replied.

"No. Don't go there."

"Priscilla, I swore on my mother's grave that man would not kick me out of my home again like a dog that stole the meat. I will leave when I want to. We are going home to talk. I'll talk to you about your actions later."

Priscilla jumped back, surprised at her mother's anger that seemed to appear out of nowhere.

"I told you to leave everything alone, but you had to go and find Robert. He's a weak man. He didn't even stand up for you, and he certainly didn't stand up for me when I was pregnant."

Priscilla gasped with shock at her mother's words.

She didn't even want to think of what happened next. Reliving the events filled her stomach with pain. Now, hours later, as she turned her thoughts away from the afternoon, she worried about her mother's future. What if Oliver refused to let her in? Where would she go? Would she call her? Would she just wander around alone at night?

She moved away from Chamu and walked onto their balcony. She looked out at the view of the evening. There were houses in the valley beyond her vision. The sound of the night and the smell of the roses in pots nearby did little to soothe her. Still, her mind went back to the afternoon and her mother's voice.

"He didn't stand up for you and he certainly didn't stand up for me when I was pregnant."

Robert walked in and had overheard her words, making an already horrible situation worse.

"What did you want me to do, Monica?" Robert asked, his voice clipped and his eyes filled with sorrow. Priscilla moved to the corner of the kitchen as her mother replaced the phone and looked at Robert with barely disguised distaste.

"Nothing," Monica said with an attitude Priscilla had never seen before.

"So don't say untrue things to Priscilla. She deserves to know the truth."

"I have nothing to say to you, Robert. You should stay away from Priscilla. She's not your child."

"What are you saying?"

Priscilla's heart froze at her words. What did she mean? Her mother had not raised her voice, but her words could have been the loudest thunder.

"You may have made her, but you had nothing to do with her upbringing. She's very much Oliver's daughter and not yours."

"How can you say that like it was my fault?"

"I want you to stay away from her. You will cause her nothing but grief."

"Ma, don't say that," Priscilla cried, tears pouring down her cheeks. They didn't even turn to look at her. Her parents were staring at each other as if she didn't exist.

"I wanted to marry you," Robert claimed, his voice filled with anguish. "I begged you to marry me, but you went back to him. You left me."

"You don't know anything, Robert."

"I know I wanted to be with you for the rest of my life. I would have done anything to have you."

"But you did nothing," Monica hissed, glaring at him. "You are all words, Robert, but no backbone."

"How dare you?" Robert shouted so angrily that Chamu came into the room to make sure everything was all right.

"I'm going. I don't want to talk to you about this. You should have stayed in the past where you belonged," Monica said and walked out the kitchen door.

Priscilla stood against the kitchen counter crying. She had never seen such emotion in her mother or Robert before. His face was lined with distress and she hurt thinking she was in the middle of the mess that was their lives. Robert shook his head, eyes on the door that Monica had just walked through.

"I knew I should have stayed away from you. I should never have come here," Robert said, his voice filled with regret, and something else. Was it sadness? Despair? It was hard to tell, but all Priscilla knew was that she hated him at that moment. The feelings came swift and certain.

Priscilla looked at him, biting her lip. His words cut deeply, and when she spoke, she put all her anger into her next words. Her eyes regarded him with scorn.

"You can go, Robert. My mother was right. You are a coward."

But now what about Rudo? How could she have made exactly the same mistake as her mother?

Priscilla jumped when she felt Chamu touch her on the shoulder, bringing her back to the present. He stood next to her, watching the view and rubbing her shoulder as if that could rub away her memory of the events that had taken place.

"Chamu. Do you think we did the right thing by not telling Rudo?" Priscilla broke the silence.

"What?" Chamu bellowed. "I can't believe you are bringing that up now."

"Don't you want to know who her father is?" Priscilla asked.

"No! That is all in the past. Let it go!"

Priscilla had never seen Chamu this angry. She wanted to hide from his anger, but still insisted on talking about it.

"What if somebody tells her and she finds out like I did?"

"Nobody but you and I know the truth. Oh, my Priscilla, I never thought we would have to talk about this again. I really thought we were a family."

"After today I'm so confused. Ma left without really explaining things between her and Robert. There seems to be more than I know. I wonder if he knew about me. Ma said he abandoned her when she was pregnant."

"That stuff happened a long time ago, and we are different from them. We love each other. Oliver never treated your mother with respect."

"The truth always has a way of coming out, Chamu." Priscilla turned and looked at him.

Chamu didn't say anything for a while, and then he spoke in a tone that chilled Priscilla. "The only way our 'truths' will come out is if you tell somebody, because I'm not going to tell anybody."

They stood in silence for a long time, the sound of the crickets becoming louder. Priscilla turned and faced him again her face serious and tense.

"The worst thing about today is that I'm facing the possibility that both my fathers probably didn't want me. It shouldn't hurt, but it does. I've been forcing my relationship with Robert, and Oliver hated me from the day I was born. Why? Why couldn't they love me? Is there something in me that is unlovable?"

"No. No. You are the most beautiful woman I have ever known, both inside and out. I love you. I'll love you for everybody who should have loved you."

When Priscilla went to bed she was counting all the people who had let her down. Unashe and his apology for loving her. Robert Chigoni, for keeping her his secret dirty child. Oliver Pasipano, for her nightmare growing up. Her mother for keeping secrets as she suffered.

Only Chamu had kept his promises. He was the only one who cared for her. She realized she had to set her life on the right path. Be a good wife to Chamu, have more of his children and live a happy, peaceful life.

CHAPTER 30
Kuwomesa Musoro—Headstrong

The launch party for Primehouse Bank helped Priscilla forget all about her problems with her family. Chamu spared no expense for the big opening taking place in the Miekles Hotel.

Priscilla had ordered a stunning black and white dress from South Africa. Chamu had emphasized how important it was that she be like an African queen, and had not minded the cost of the outfit. When she walked in heads did turn.

Priscilla was impressed by the African theme Chamu had incorporated in the decor. The room looked like an African safari, with life-size animal statues placed dramatically around the room. She took in the stone carvings of lions, zebras and giraffes. She glanced around slowly, taking in the crowd, and, when she saw Unashe talking to a lovely, slim woman dressed in black, her heart froze. Priscilla tried to suppress the sting of jealousy and longing that invaded her, but it was hard. Would she ever be able to look at Unashe without some sort of wild emotion invading her whole being? The few times she had seen him had been as devastating as an earthquake.

Later in the evening, Chamu gave a speech to a group of five hundred people eating steak and potatoes and having a decadent creamy dessert created just for the occasion. Everything displayed loudly proclaimed that this party was the biggest launch in the history of Zimbabwe.

Priscilla turned her eyes away from Unashe and his date and focused on her husband as he concluded his speech.

"We are moving Zimbabwe's banking into the future. With this bank, we hope to be able to launch a credit card system that is used in many countries and that will make it easier for our customers to buy goods and services. It will be a huge undertaking, but with all the people in this room on our side we can only be a success." As cameras from the news teams flashed, Chamu turned to face Priscilla.

"I would also like to thank my lovely wife. You know that behind every successful man is a beautiful, hardworking wife."

People clapped and Priscilla didn't know what to do with the attention as all eyes in the room swivelled to her.

Across the room, Unashe clapped along with everyone else. When the speeches were done, he turned back and smiled at his date for the evening, Vivian Matendeko.

"Priscilla is something, isn't she?" Vivian said.

"She is."

"I think she looks too good to be true. How can anybody look so perfect all the time? She's always dressed like she just stepped out of a fashion magazine."

"She's the most real person you'll ever meet. She's kind and warm. Don't be fooled by the perfect image. That's just money. Expensive clothes don't really change the person inside," Unashe said, his eyes on Priscilla who was smiling at her husband, his boss.

After dinner Unashe watched a lot of people walk over to Chamu and his wife. They were one of the wealthiest couples in the country. If all went well with the bank then Chamu was on his way to having enough money to buy even more banks and become more powerful. No wonder Priscilla had been so eager to marry the man. He could give her whatever she wanted, and he was already doing that.

A lively dance performance by a famous traditional dance troupe preceded the live band. The group began playing upbeat songs that were the popular hits that year. The young and hip guests were making their way to the dance floor. With the cold beer and expensive spirits flowing freely, the crowd was already feeling relaxed and adventurous. Later, Tuku opened up with his old popular hit, "Perekedza Mwana", and his hit song about a young man who should escort his girlfriend home as it was getting dark. The crowd went wild in their suits and sparkling dresses. For a song that that had been released years before, it got people moving.

"Would you like to meet Priscilla?" Unashe asked Vivian. He liked what his date wore, a sophisticated dress that skimmed over her curves. Her neatly braided hair hung down to her shoulders. When she moved her gold and diamond earrings sparkled. She was a very lovely woman. Vivian was the new brand of independent Zimbabwean women. She had her own three-bedroom townhouse and drove a twin cab. She was fiercely self-sufficient and let Unashe know that at every opportunity. She would not let him pick her up and she paid for her own meals. In some ways, she reminded him of the Priscilla of years before. What had happened to that girl, Unashe wondered.

"We can meet her, but I don't admire women who just marry men for money," Vivian said.

"I think you will find Priscilla to be just as independent as you. You remind me of her," Unashe said.

"Oh please. I'm not living in some mansion in the hills and spending my day doing nothing," Vivian said as she walked with Unashe towards a group that surrounded Priscilla.

"Hello," Priscilla said when she saw them approach. She left the group she had been talking to, and all the men stared at her with open admiration.

That must keep Chamu up at night, Unashe thought.

"Priscilla, I would like you to meet Vivian," Unashe said, introducing the two women.

"You look familiar," Priscilla said warmly.

"I was working on the ad campaign for Primehouse Bank. We might have walked by each other at the offices."

"You are right. You look amazing," Priscilla said. The compliment seemed to take Vivian off guard.

"Thank you. So do you," she responded. Priscilla's outfit was very regal, and she stood out by the uniqueness of it and the way she held herself. The A-line skirt reached her ankles, and only the tips of her silver shoes appeared beneath it. Over her arms, she held a scarf. Her long fingers clutched her purse.

"Thank you," Priscilla said, pushing back her curled, jet black hair. "You did a great job on the ad campaign. Your talents made Primehouse Bank almost a household name. Everybody is excited about it."

"Thank you, Mrs. Tengani," Vivian said, smiling broadly. Unashe watched as Priscilla charmed Vivian, her previous icy opinions melting like butter in the sun.

"Oh, I see a friend from work. I'll be right back," Vivian said, leaving Unashe and Priscilla standing alone. They watched in silence the people dancing to another of Tuku's classics.

"I haven't seen much of you," Unashe said, breaking the silence between them.

"I know. Every time I went to the hospital, you were not there. We kept missing each other. It's good to see your mum doing so much better."

"It's great. Thanks for being there for her," Unashe said.

"So where is Chantel?"

Unashe was so caught by surprise that he burst out laughing. "What is it with you and Chantel? You always used to ask about her," he said.

"I saw the picture of you two together at graduation. I always thought she was your girlfriend," Priscilla said.

"That was over seven years ago," Unashe said.

"Come on, don't lie. She's the reason . . ." Priscilla paused, and Unashe wondered what she was about to say. *The reason what?*

"She told me she was pregnant with your baby," Priscilla said. At that moment the music stopped. Unashe stared at her as if she had grown another head.

"You are joking, right? Priscilla, of all the lies to say . . ."

Priscilla stared at him, realising he was shocked by the news. She didn't say anything as Tuku started playing another song, this time a slow acoustic guitar song that tugged at her heart.

"Good evening, Mr. Made." Melody, Chamu's secretary, came to her side. "Mrs. Tengani. Your husband was looking for you." Unashe watched her turn, but he was still puzzled by what she had told him. He had no choice but to watch her excuse herself and walk towards his boss.

Priscilla left before the party ended, telling Chamu she had a headache. Chamu had to remain until the end. Though he let her go without an argument, she could tell he was disappointed.

When she got home she wanted to jump in bed immediately, but could not shake off what Unashe had said. She remembered clearly the day Chantel had walked into her apartment. Chantel had cried and said she was Unashe's girlfriend. She'd said she was carrying his baby. Why would she lie like that? Why would Unashe deny it if it was true? Was he lying?

After checking on Rudo, who was sleeping peacefully, Priscilla took off her outfit and silky stockings and wrapped her self in a long, soft robe. The maid slept in the room next to Rudo, as she often did when they were out late.

Priscilla went to the kitchen and boiled water for tea. The house was beautiful and silent.

While she made her tea, she picked up her phone and called Unashe's cell phone.

"Unashe here," he answered. She hadn't heard his voice on the phone for several years. Her heart beat even faster. It was as if he was right next to her, whispering in her ear. She could hear other voices and music in the background.

"It's Priscilla. Where are you?"

"I'm still at the Miekles. Are you all right?"

"I need to talk to you."

Unashe walked away from the other men from the bank and sat at an isolated table. Vivian was on the dance floor with a few of her friends from work.

"What is it?"

"It's about Chantel," Priscilla said.

"Come on. I told you she wasn't my girlfriend. Not that it's any of your business," Unashe said in an incredulous tone.

"Don't worry, I'm not after you any more, hot stuff," Priscilla retorted angrily.

Unashe laughed. "Is this about that crazy story about her having my baby?"

"Yes. That's what she told me. She didn't tell you?"

"No. And when she came to England she wasn't pregnant, either," Unashe said.

"Perhaps she lost your baby," Priscilla said.

"What baby? Damn it, Priscilla, I never touched that woman. From the moment that you . . . to the day I came back here I never had anything to do with her in that way. I never touched her," Unashe insisted.

"Can anybody hear you?"

"No."

"I'm surprised. You are shouting like a lunatic," Priscilla said, wondering why she chose such a day to ask him.

"I'm trying to get it through your thick head that she's not my girlfriend, and I don't have a baby with her," Unashe hissed deep into her ears.

"Go to hell!"

Priscilla cut the phone and wanted to hurl it against the wall. It rang again within a second.

"Hello," Priscilla said, her breathing still heavy.

"Don't you ever accuse me of things and then hang up on me again." Unashe's scolding tone set Priscilla on the verge of hysteria. Who did he think he was?

Priscilla sniffed. "You were calling me thick headed."

"You called me a lunatic."

Both of them were quiet for a while. Unashe had now walked outside the ballroom and sat in the reception area.

"Anyway, when did she say that to you?"

"The week you left for the UK," Priscilla said. The words hung between them for a while, heavy with implications.

"Before I left?"

"Yes."

"That was a lie," Unashe protested, his voice quieter than before.

"I believed her. Why would she lie to me?"

Priscilla could hear Unashe breathing on the other end of the line. His deep breathing matched her troubled voice.

"I was so angry with you," Priscilla said.

"I know. You wanted to flatten me with a vase," Unashe said, and Priscilla laughed nervously. They were quiet for a while.

"Why didn't you tell me what she said?"

"I was angry and disappointed. I felt used and stupid. I painted you with the same brush as all the men I hated, like Vimbai's husband. I have hated you all these years," Priscilla said.

"That's harsh. I never knew," Unashe said. "I thought you were mean and cruel. I actually thought you had gone crazy."

"Thanks," Priscilla said.

"Well, you put me in the same group as your father and Gilbert," Unashe said.

They were both silent, as if the phone line was dead, but they both knew the other was there, thinking, remembering. She couldn't deny how she had felt.

"I have to go, Unashe. This doesn't make any sense to me at all," Priscilla said.

"I need to see you," Unashe said. "I mean, I want to talk to you in person about this. Somebody was playing with our lives."

"Maybe it was for the best. You got to go overseas and study and now you are a top banking executive, making lots of money."

"And you gave up your career to marry the richest man in the country. Is that what you mean?"

"No, don't put words in my mouth. . ."

"You just put words in my mouth."

"I just meant that there is nothing we can do about it now."

"I'm going to get to the bottom of this. I have Chantel's number. I'll find out why she said that."

"What's the point? If she knew about us, then she wanted us apart. It was meant to be that way," Priscilla said. "Good night, Unashe."

There was silence for a few seconds, and then Unashe finally spoke. "Good night."

Priscilla felt pain in every part of the body as she hung up the phone. Her tea was cold in its teacup and she tossed it into the sink. Somehow, she felt afraid. She wondered how such a lie could have changed the course of her life. Still, would Unashe have stayed if he knew she was pregnant? He had his own ambitions, and not once had he really talked about marrying her.

She didn't want to be alone. She walked into Rudo's room and slipped into bed with her baby. Rudo mumbled something and put her arms around her neck.

At that moment Rudo was the only person who felt real to her. Everybody else, everything else, was not what it seemed but her child snuggled close to her and the world was all right.

"Oh, God, I have messed up. Show me the way to go. I want to be like Vimbai, so sure about everything even as her life is falling apart. Even as she's slowly dying, she's so sure of you."

A few hours later Chamu found Priscilla sleeping in Rudo's room. He watched them for a full minute, and then closed the door and went to their bedroom.

CHAPTER 31
Dudza—Reveal

Vimbai was joking about her doctor as they left the doctor's office.

"He couldn't stop staring at you, Pri. You had him tongue tied, my pretty little sister."

Priscilla couldn't understand her sister's optimism. Her heart felt heavy with fear, but Vimbai smiled peacefully, lifting her face to the sky once they were out of the stuffy brick building. Priscilla hated going to the doctor, and Dr. Patel was not giving her many reasons to smile. Dr. Patel had said that AIDS itself didn't kill; instead, Vimbai had to fear other diseases that her immune system could no longer handle. Where had that horrible disease come from? How could there not be a cure?

Her sister was dying. Would she make it to the New Year?

Outside, the sun was warm and the old trees sent their shadows sprawling on the red soil and fading green grass.

They walked towards the car without saying much. Once settled in, Priscilla glanced at Vimbai for a second and then adjusted her rear-view mirror.

"Where would you like to eat? I want to take you for lunch," Priscilla said, starting the engine.

"You know the best places. I'll trust you, little sister," Vimbai said.

"Do you want to sit inside or outside?" Priscilla asked as she drove her car efficiently into the flow of traffic.

"The sun feels good. Let's sit outside."

"I know just the place."

Priscilla drove to Kensington shopping center to a restaurant called Mateo's. They specialized in freshly baked pizza, but they also served chicken, steak and fish. It wasn't that far from the doctor's office. They got their table on the sidewalk, right next to a pharmacy and a children's bookshop.

"This sun tempts me to take a nap," Priscilla said.

"Don't fall asleep on me. People will think I'm boring," Vimbai said, looking around at the mostly white patrons. A waiter came and gave them the menus.

Priscilla already knew what she wanted but waited for Vimbai to choose. It was hard not to notice how thin her sister had become. Her usually full cheeks were slightly sunken, and it made her brown eyes look bigger. Even her dress hung on her.

"Stop staring at me, Priscilla. I'm fine," Vimbai said, her eyes on the menu. Priscilla turned her gaze to the menu.

"I'm sorry. I'm not making it easy for you. I know I can't be as casual as you are about your illness," Priscilla said.

"I'm not casual, Pri. I have given it up to God. He's carrying my burdens. I've done all I can, and now I let God do the rest."

"You mean you have given up?"

"No. I have surrendered. It's different," Vimbai said.

"What do you mean by that? Surrendered?"

"I'm not fighting with life anymore. I know who is in control, and it's not me. I know I made my own wrong choice when I was a little girl, but now that I've given my life to Jesus, He takes care of me and will take care of my children," Vimbai said with a small smile.

"I don't know how you can just surrender," Priscilla insisted, her eyes filling with tears that she fought hard to stop.

"It's not in my power. It's God's power. Think about it, Priscilla. He made the universe. He let Rudo grow in your stomach without any help from you. He has so much power that you can't do anything that he doesn't let you do. I guess in the end I had a choice. I could live mad with the world, my disease, or accept that I can't control some things but I can always control my attitude."

Priscilla nodded but didn't respond as the waiter finally came and took their order.

"He took his sweet time coming to us," Priscilla said.

"See? You are letting the slow waiter control your attitude. You should be relaxed. Don't let him spoil your day."

Priscilla sighed but could still not relax like Vimbai. She felt anger stirring in her, wild and volcanic. "It's easier to say than to do, Vimbai. The waiters here serve white people first, and they do it with a smile. They still see them as their owners. That annoys me. Not only that, how could I have changed my attitude as a little girl after Oliver messed up my childhood? All I knew was misery!"

Priscilla's rage spilled on to the table and Vimbai stared at it as if she could see it, ugly and toxic.

"I know. But you are older now, you can choose to let it go or let it get to you," Vimbai said, her eyes beseeching her sister. "You are so angry."

Priscilla just stared at Vimbai. Her softly spoken truths hurt. She felt her anger rise, but she let it deflate slowly, like a balloon.

Priscilla closed the menu, a lid on her temper. "I am, aren't I?"

"I don't want to leave you here on this Earth bitter," Vimbai said. Priscilla didn't even want to imagine life without Vimbai. She tried to shake it off but it hung between them, the finality of it scaring her. She wanted to change the subject but found she had more questions.

"Aren't you mad at Gilbert?"

"No. He was just a child himself who took the wrong turns in his life. He paid the price."

"But do you have to pay, too?"

"Yes. I made the choice."

"I feel like I'm going round and round in circles with you," Priscilla said.

"I never want to live like a victim," Vimbai said and pointed at the waiter. "Here come our drinks at last. It looks like we will be here for a long time."

"Are you complaining?" Priscilla teased.

"No. I'm thinking it gives us more time together."

Priscilla smiled and took Vimbai's hand. Yes, she thought, it was good to stay and talk to her sister. She was her best friend, the one person she knew she could trust.

They could talk about so much. There was more to share without talking about death, illness, or terror. Suddenly she wanted to share some of her secrets with her, get them off her chest. How would Vimbai react? Would she still look at her the same?

"I have something to tell you," Priscilla said suddenly, then took a sip of her ice-cold drink.

Vimbai regarded her seriously, searching for clues in her eyes.

"I have been meaning to tell you for all these years. I'm tired of keeping this secret."

"What is it, Priscilla?"

"It's a huge secret."

"Can it be worse than the one of you growing up thinking Baba was your father?

"It's just as bad." Priscilla took a deep breath, ready to dive in. "Unashe is Rudo's father."

"What? Don't joke, Pri," Vimbai said, her mouth open wide in shock. She shook her head, but when she looked in Priscilla's eyes, she saw the truth.

"I'm serious. Nobody else knows," Priscilla said.

"Not even Chamu?"

"Chamu knows it's not his baby, but he doesn't know who the father is and doesn't want to know."

Vimbai was quiet for a while looking at her lap with her mouth still open wide.

"How did you and Unashe . . . ? Isn't that taboo?"

"He always knew we were not related. When I found out, something just happened. But still. It was wrong."

"Tell me. What happened?" Vimbai asked. *There. No judgements.*

Priscilla told Vimbai the story as briefly as she could, beginning with the day she left home and ending up at Mukai's house. She remembered it like it had just happened.

"The minute we knew we were not related, something just grew between us. I had always loved him, always felt a special closeness with him, but when everything happened with *Baba* and he was just there for me, there was no turning back. It's as if the climate was just ripe for us to fall in love."

"So why didn't you just get together? You loved him."

"I did. I do. But one day a woman called Chantel who he used to date came and told me she was pregnant with his baby. I was so angry with him I wanted to kill him."

"He was seeing somebody else while he was with you? He doesn't seem like the type. Unashe just seems so honest, easygoing . . ."

"That's what I thought. But I was wrong. I just found out yesterday that he didn't know anything about Chantel being pregnant, and that it was impossible she would have been carrying his child because he never slept with her."

"You believe him," Vimbai said.

Priscilla nodded. "The crazy thing is why did she lie? Why would she lie to me?"

"Harare is very small, so she might have heard something and she was jealous and wanted Unashe to herself,"

Vimbai said. "Though I'm still finding it hard to believe that he is Rudo's father and you two . . ."

"Stop imagining that," Priscilla cried, embarrassed.

"Unashe and you?"

"Stop it." Priscilla laughed, throwing her head back. She noticed the other diners looking at them with interest, and then leaned towards Vimbai, her dangling gold earrings swooping forward.

"The thing that's keeping me awake this whole week is this. How did she know I was even seeing Unashe? Nobody knew except the two of us. We were so careful. We hardly held hands in public or went to clubs."

"Why were you being secretive? You could have just come out and told everybody you were in love."

"You think so? Imagine the outrage. We were just falling in love, and at that time it would have meant explaining that I knew *Baba* wasn't my real father and telling Aunt Mukai, who was dead set against Unashe getting into any relationship."

"She loves you."

"I know. But I don't know how she would have reacted if I had delayed her precious son from going to college in the heavenly UK, where everybody wants to end up. I know I was just nervous and still trying to understand what was happening between us. It was all new to me, and, at the same time, I was so insecure. I didn't want to believe anybody could care for me that much."

"Priscilla, you are beautiful both inside and out. He must have been hopelessly in love with you."

"I had no one to talk to, to share my feelings. It was just me and my thoughts, making my own decisions alone."

"Wow. And you have kept this all to yourself," Vimbai said. "Why didn't you come to me?"

"You had a lot on your plate," Priscilla said. "And now you still do, but we now have more time together."

Vimbai stared into the distance, not seeing the people walking around and cars coming in and out of the busy shopping center. "It's very strange. So did you speak to Chantel to ask her?"

"I don't know where she is. Unashe said he would call her," Priscilla explained.

Vimbai smiled. "I heard he is back in town and working for Chamu. Isn't that a little complicated?"

Priscilla smiled. Her sister was enjoying all these juicy stories. It was quite unreal. "No. I think Unashe has already put our relationship behind him. He has moved on."

"And you?"

"I have moved on, too."

Vimbai rolled her eyes. "Priscilla, you have just started telling me the truth, so don't lie to me."

"I can't go back there, Vimbai. I closed that door when I married Chamu."

"Does Chamu know Unashe . . ."

"No way. I kept that to myself. He didn't want to know anyway and just wanted to take Rudo as his daughter. She *is* his daughter."

"Are you going to tell Unashe the truth?"

Priscilla grew quiet. Vimbai looked at her sister's downcast head. She looked vulnerable and confused.

"Do you want to tell him?" Vimbai gently asked again.

"I don't think I can. It would just make life difficult for my baby, for Chamu. Unashe doesn't need that in his life. He has a girlfriend now and is starting a new career."

"Doesn't need his daughter?"

Vimbai's words had Priscilla quiet. She took a sip of her drink and looked at the passing traffic a few meters away and the pedestrians that continued to walk by them. She finally turned and looked at Vimbai's pleading face and sighed.

"I don't know, Vimbai. When I met my real father, he hurt me with his initial rejection. Even now, he doesn't really want me in his life. I wonder if I would have been better off not having met him. I really wonder about that."

Vimbai knew exactly where Priscilla's mind was. She decided not to say anything. Just then, their food arrived.

They each cut into the succulent chicken and took a bite. They ate in silence for a while, thinking deeply of what they had just talked about.

"Do you love Chamu?"

Priscilla looked at her, surprised. "He has been a good husband and father."

"That answers my question. You could have done a lot worse."

"I can't even complain about him. He always takes care of me and Rudo. We are his priority, no matter how busy he gets."

"So you trust him?"

"Chamu?"

"Yes."

Priscilla smiled. "What's there not to trust? He is kind, honest and faithful. He is generous to my family."

"I know all that. I just think most people don't take this AIDS thing seriously. You should still both get tested."

"I think he would be offended. He loves us. He works hard each day and comes home to us. He doesn't drink that much or go out, and I've never heard any rumours about him or had any reason to ever suspect anything."

"I don't want to say he does anything. I just want you to be careful, that's all. At least talk about it with him. I'm feeling overprotective, even in places where there's no need."

"I'll try and talk to him about it. It's worth talking about." She looked at Vimbai and smiled, surprised at how well Vimbai understood her situation. Could she really trust Chamu completely?

"Can I ask you something?" Vimbai asked. Priscilla nodded. "I know you had miscarriages. But do you want more children?"

"Of course I do! I seem to have inherited our mother's problems with pregnancies. She had many miscarriages, too."

"I'm sure Chamu would love that."

Priscilla nodded. She knew how much, though he never came right out and said it.

After their lunch, they went to the flea market. The Avondale flea market was their favorite to visit together. Vimbai was selling some of her tablemats and bathroom sets there. Priscilla had helped her set it up and hired girls to do the selling.

Priscilla bought Chipo and Rudo some crocheted tops and bought some of Vimbai's mats for her dining room. Vimbai scolded her as she watched her sister count the wads of money.

"I can make you a set for free. You don't have to buy them. They are so expensive!"

"What kind of businesswoman are you? You should charge everybody. Especially wealthy people like me."

Vimbai laughed, then started coughing, her slight body doubling over. They sat down while Vimbai caught her breath and Priscilla rubbed her back, willing healing into her sister's body with her touch. Tears pooled in her eyes.

"I'm fine," she croaked. Priscilla nodded and willed her heart to stop beating so fast.

CHAPTER 32

Kuzvinyepera—Lying to Yourself

"So you'll come to the party later?" Priscilla asked Chamu for the second time in two weeks after her lunch with her sister. Mukai was throwing a surprise graduation and welcome home party for Unashe. Priscilla wondered why she had taken so long to have the party. It had been almost six months since Unashe returned home.

"I'll be there late. I have shooting practice," he said as he took a bag from their safe.

Priscilla paused from pulling up her stockings. She remembered that Chamu had bought a gun. She didn't know how she felt about having a gun in the house, but after she heard about all the car-jacking incidents close to their neighborhood she understood his concerns. Chamu was a well-known, wealthy man who could easily be a victim. He had asked her to go to the range with him too, but she didn't yet feel comfortable shooting. He left for his practice before Priscilla finished dressing.

Mukai was already panicking when Priscilla arrived.

"What took you so long?" Priscilla just hugged her and walked into Mukai's home. She couldn't understand people's obsessions with surprise parties. They were stressful to plan.

"He's not here yet, is he?"

"No. I told him to get me some pain medication. Like a good son, he said he would be here in thirty minutes. He's going to be so mad," Mukai said with a smile.

"You look great," Priscilla said. Mukai looked down at her outfit as if she had forgotten what she had put on. She wore a wrap-around skirt and matching top.

"Thanks, and you look gorgeous, as always," Mukai said, herding Priscilla and Rudo into the living room so they could hide and wait for Unashe.

Priscilla waved at the guests who waited patiently in the house, chatting in small groups. She was glad to see Unashe's colleagues from the bank and their wives. She walked over to where her sisters stood and hugged them. Vimbai had been staying with Rutendo for a few days.

Priscilla sat talking to her sisters when Mukai came back in the room.

"He's here. He's here," Mukai said softly.

"What about the cars?" Priscilla asked.

"I told him I was having a prayer meeting," Mukai whispered with a naughty smile.

Through the lace curtain, Priscilla saw Unashe walking in. He had a brown bag from the pharmacy in his hand, and just seeing his devotion to his mother filled her heart with overwhelming tenderness towards him. He looked so cool in his jeans and t-shirt. So amazing.

Her heart began to beat faster as he opened the door and she heard his footsteps. He turned the corner and everybody yelled "SURPRISE!"

He took a step back, staring at all the people in front of him, and scanned the room filled with balloons. Mukai ran to hug him.

"It's your party, son. Welcome back home!"

The group of excited family and friends started talking all at once and yelling their congratulations. Priscilla saw his face over his mother's shoulder and before he closed his eyes, his gaze lit on her briefly, sweetly.

"What is this about?" he asked after the long hug. The men walked over to shake his hand, and the women gave him hugs and kisses on the cheek.

Priscilla walked up to him and gave him a hug. Then she stepped back and let Rudo give him a hug, too.

Priscilla looked at Vimbai, and both their eyes held.

"Did you know about this?" he asked.

"Yes! Are you surprised?" Rudo asked between giggles.

"Of course I am," he said, still holding Rudo. He looked at Priscilla.

"You knew and never said a word?"

"It was meant to be a surprise. Your mother would have killed me if I said anything."

"And Vimbai knew, too?"

"Guilty," Vimbai said.

Unashe put Rudo down. "I'll be back to talk to you," he said to her as he made the rounds greeting people.

Vimbai took Priscilla aside. "It's all in your eyes. You still love him."

"Don't be silly," Priscilla said. "Let's go and help with the food."

Mukai had catered food brought in, and outside the fires heated up the *braii* to grill the meat. While the group had cold soft drinks or beer in bottles and cans, the men somehow gravitated towards the meat out in the back yard and started throwing in steaks, sausages and pork chops.

Priscilla watched Unashe walk outside with Vivian. There was always a woman in his life, and Vivian seemed to be lasting longer than the others. Vivian was dressed as casually as he was in slim black pants and striped shirt. Her braids were casually tied back, revealing her high cheekbones and intelligent brown eyes. She was more suited to him. Priscilla hated that she had overdressed in a red dress, the kind of dress Chamu and Lina approved of. She felt as if she was going to a wedding. Unashe must be laughing at her.

"Let's go out in the sun," Vimbai said. "I feel cold inside."

"All right," Priscilla said, looking at her sister with concern. Rudo and another little girl were watching *The Lion King* on video, so she left them alone and went to the gathering outside. It was a warm November day with a few clouds in the sky. The weather report had said that it was going to be partly cloudy with chances of rain, but the rain seemed to be elsewhere.

By the fires, Unashe was talking about how London had become just another Harare.

"You can't talk about anybody in the subway in Shona because chances are they can understand you," he said.

"Can you blame people for running away from this country? It's a mess," Tapiwa, another bank employee, said. "I'm surprised you came back, Unashe."

"This is home. As much as the pound is worth, that place is terrible to live, man! You don't have backyards like we do here, and just the way we are gathering having a party, which, by the way, I didn't want, is rare. Everybody is working searching for the mighty pound!"

"Was it that bad?" Tapiwa asked.

"I hated it. I'll try and make it here," Unashe said, taking a gulp of his drink.

Priscilla went to where Faith, the young woman she admired, sat with Joe's wife. She could see that she would not be able to talk to Unashe alone. He was surrounded and busy, and Vivian was the one getting his drinks and hanging onto his every word. Priscilla realized she was craving for moments alone with him when she didn't really have much to say to him. They had said all they could say, right?

Once, while they were outside, he did look up and she had seen something familiar in his eyes, or she thought she did. It was like seeing a picture that brought back favorite memories or places you wished you could visit. After a moment she turned her attention back to Faith, who was telling her about her business again.

Priscilla was very interested in that topic and it made it easier for her not focus on Unashe the rest of the time they were outside. She wished she wasn't so aware of him.

Later, without looking in Unashe's direction, Priscilla got up and went into the house to check on Rudo and give her some food. She saw her lying down awkwardly against the sofa.

"Rudo, come and eat," Priscilla called, but when she got close she realized Rudo was sleeping in front of the TV with a piece of cake stuck in her fingers. Priscilla sat on the couch next to Rudo.

Priscilla tried propping her up, but Rudo's head rolled back.

"Is she asleep?"

Stunned, Priscilla turned to see Unashe standing behind her. "Yes. When she sleeps she's gone to the world."

"That's like me. Here, let me take her to my old room," Unashe said.

Priscilla held her breath as Unashe's hands reached under Rudo and picked her up.

"Have you finished the grilling?" she asked.

"People are already attacking the meat. I think we'll eat outside since the sun sets later now."

He stood up with the sleeping girl in his arms.

"She weighs quite a bit. Do you carry her some-times?"

"I have to. She likes to fall asleep in my bedroom sometimes. Then I carry her to hers," Priscilla said, looking at Rudo. Her eyes went up to his face, and she caught him studying her.

"It's hard to imagine you as a mum. I mean I see you with her, but it's hard to grasp. You have done a good job. She's an angel."

"Thank you. She's the best," Priscilla whispered, overcome by emotion.

"Follow me," Unashe said and walked the passageway to his bedroom. Priscilla remembered it, of course.

"Should I put her under the blankets?" Unashe asked.

"Just the top one," Priscilla said, pulling it back. He immediately put Rudo down on the other blanket and pulled off her shoes. Rudo made a whimpering sound.

She's your baby, Priscilla thought, wondering if he felt something. It made her nervous that he might notice something, or feel something.

They both reached for the top blanket and froze. Unashe straightened up and let her pull it over the sleeping girl.

She stood up and he was still right there beside her, making her nerves tingle. They were alone in the house and the laughing voices outside seemed like they were a million miles away to Priscilla as she looked into his face. Unashe reached out and touched the side of her face, like a caress, then let go.

"Cilla," he said. The way he said her name went down her body like liquid lava. She felt weak inside.

"Yes," she said. She knew she should move away first, but she wanted to get lost in his eyes. She wanted his arms around her so much it made her heart stop.

"You really have changed," he said. His words hit her like a splash of cold water. She folded her arms in front of her chest defensively.

"Or maybe you were always the same, but I never knew," Unashe said.

"I don't know what you are talking about," Priscilla said.

"You look all expensive and fancy." The way he said it rankled Priscilla. He could see she didn't like his observations.

"That is ridiculous. What do you mean by that?"

"I remember when I used to be able to talk to you about anything. Now you seem so full of mystery. I guess marriage does that to you, or maybe it's time that changes people."

Priscilla didn't even know how to answer him. She glared at him angrily, but then she remembered Vimbai's words to her.

"You are so angry, Priscilla."

"No, Unashe. Life does that to you. You didn't really expect me to remain the same after six years?"

"No, I didn't. Anyway, let me get back to my guests. Vivian is probably wondering where I am."

She wanted to say more to him but she bit her tongue and looked down at her feet for a while. Then she glanced at him and asked, "Is she your new girlfriend?"

"Girlfriend?"

"That's what I said. She doesn't seem like your type."

Unashe laughed. "And who is my type?"

"Just answer my question."

"She's a nice lady. We don't know yet what our relationship is."

"Typical." Priscilla all but spat out the word.

"What's your problem?"

"I don't have a problem. *You* haven't changed, that's all." She pointed to his chest, restraining herself from beating it. She felt angry with him, but for the life of her couldn't really figure out why. Was she jealous? No. He could see and date anybody he wanted.

"I don't know what your problem is. Talking to you just messes up my mind. Vivian doesn't speak in riddles, and I enjoy her company. I don't know why you have a problem with that."

"I don't have a problem. If you enjoy her company so much, then what are you doing here with me? Just go."

Priscilla lifted her hand up to her face and sat on the bed. She made a big job of fixing Rudo's blanket. Rudo hadn't even moved during their conversation. Unashe shook his head and walked to the door, but Priscilla didn't look up to see him watching her for a while before he left the room.

CHAPTER 33
Mukadzi Akanaka—The Good Wife

Robert Chigoni sat in his office and looked at the photograph of his wife, Carol, and their children. His three children were beautiful, smart and well-adjusted individuals. His wife had been stricter on them than he was and made sure they worked hard at school and kept the right friends. Carol had even threatened violence to a girl who wanted to be friends with their oldest daughter, Nyarai. Robert recalled how Carol found out that Nyarai had been getting close to a classmate who had the wildest reputation in the school. Carol had gone to tell the girl to leave Nyarai alone or there would be trouble. Carol was not somebody who took anything lying down.

He looked at Carol's picture. He knew he couldn't call his wife pretty. No, Carol's beauty lay in her vitality and determination. She could be charming, but if crossed she could be lethal.

Robert had been thinking about Monica often ever since he saw her at Priscilla's house. As he leaned back in his chair his memories of her came flooding back.

When he met Monica almost thirty years ago, he had been dating Carol seriously for a few months. The moment Robert saw Monica he had fallen in love with her. At the time he had just started working for an insurance company and had purchased his first car, an old white Peugeot sedan. He drove to Chitungwiza to visit his uncle Mapopa, who had just opened a new store in an up-and-coming neighborhood. When he got to the store, his uncle was outside drinking beer and talking to some friends.

"Go in and grab a beer," his uncle had said. "Ask Monica, the new woman in there, to give you some food as well. You look hungry, young man. We have just eaten."

Robert walked into the store, where music blared from a tiny radio. There were two people sitting behind the counter, and one of them was the loveliest woman he had ever seen. Her smooth black afro framed a beautiful face with high cheekbones and full, soft lips. She had been cutting loaves of bread into halves so they could be sold at a lower price for the lower income customers.

"Can I help you?" She'd put the knife down.

"My name is Robert Chigoni. The owner is my uncle. He said you can give me some food and beer."

Monica nodded without meeting his eyes and walked away, leaving him speechless. She came back after a few minutes with sadza, meat and vegetables on a plate. She placed it on a counter and walked away again. She came back with a dish and a towel flung over her shoulder. She handed the dish to him so he could wash his hands. After he washed them, she handed him the towel and watched him dry his hands. He couldn't stop staring at her, but she wouldn't meet his eyes. He was too stunned to say anything but "thank you."

"Is Monica taking care of you?" Moses asked as he walked back into the store.

"Yes, she is."

"You can sit down and eat. So what do you think of this shop, young man?"

"It is a good business," Robert said, looking at the shelves stocked with food and household items.

"We were very lucky to find Monica. She's living with her relative right across from us, and she was looking for a job just as I opened the store. She's good, too, and is also doing sewing part time. I may even set her up right here in this shop."

Robert nodded.

Monica was busy cleaning the shelves while his uncle gave Robert the tour of the back offices and storage rooms. Robert wasn't paying much attention as his mind was on the beautiful woman with sad eyes at the front of the store.

Robert was happy when his uncle left and he found himself alone with Monica. He was not going to leave until he had learned more about her.

"What time do you finish work?"

"When I close the store," she replied, moving items around on the shelf until the tins were in perfect rows.

"What time is that?"

"Eight."

"How do you get home?"

"Walk."

"Can I take you home?"

"No."

Robert smiled when she said that. She looked down at the floor.

"I'll wait and take you home. I can't let you walk home alone at night," he said.

"I said I'll walk," Monica insisted. He could tell she hated even answering him. She clearly wanted to be left alone.

When she walked out of the store at 8:30 p.m., Robert was waiting outside, leaning against his car. Monica shook her head when she saw him and stood on the step, her handbag held in front of a red skirt and white blouse.

She stepped onto the road in her black shoes, and Robert was stunned when she walked right past him. He got into his car and started driving right beside her. The other cars hooted at him and swerved to avoid hitting him. After a few minutes of that Monica finally relented and opened the car door. She sat in the car, her bag held protectively in front of her chest.

"Fine. Just take me home."

Robert had smiled happily enjoying the fact that she sat in his car right next to him, angry or not.

"I don't usually do this, Monica, but you are hard to resist," Robert said.

"I am not interested in a boyfriend," she said as she sat primly as far from him as possible.

"Are you married?"

She kept quiet and looked out of the window.

When she felt his eyes on her instead of the road, she turned to him. "I don't want to talk to you."

Robert nodded and continued to drive in silence.

Far too quickly, they arrived at the house she lived in, right across from his uncle's house. She thanked him and got out. He watched her walk to the gate, open it with a key and walk into the house without a single glance in his direction.

Robert never gave up. His father liked to warn him not to rush. He would tell him not to test the depth of a river with both feet, but with Monica he had fallen in love and he was diving in head-first. Each day he would finish work at five and go home, bathe and change and drive all the way to Chitungwiza in time to pick her up from work. After five days she was starting to warm up to him. He took her to a band the next weekend at Queens Garden and to watch a movie. It was the first time she had seen a movie.

One day she finally agreed to visit him in his one-bedroom flat, and he was excited to show off his new furniture.

"I want to tell you something," Monica said, sitting down on the striped chairs.

"Wait. I'll give you a drink first," Robert said.

"No drink. Just listen. I'm enjoying your company, but I'm not what I seem to you," she began, leaning towards him. "I didn't want to have anything to do with you, but you persisted."

Robert walked up to her and sat right next to her.

"I have three children," she continued, looking down at her hands. "Hope is ten, Vimbai seven and Rutendo five."

Robert could not believe what he had just heard. Her story came out as silent tears rolled down her cheeks. She remained calm as she told him about Oliver and his new wife, Lindiwe, and her children living in what was her home.

"How could he do that?" Robert asked.

"I don't know. But you see now, Robert, you need to find yourself a nice untouched girl to marry who doesn't have children and a man in her past. I have too much to deal with."

"No, Monica. I want only you. I love you."

He reached out and kissed her. She resisted at first, but she had given in. That is how their affair had begun. He was getting ready to tell his parents about her, his future wife, when Oliver stormed into his uncle's store one evening.

Oliver arrived with his two brothers. Robert watched helplessly as Monica was dragged out of the store. She hadn't resisted, but her eyes had touched his briefly as Oliver grabbed her arm and held her to him.

"I have come for my wife. I heard there was a man trying to steal my wife. I will kill such a man!"

Robert shook his head to get rid of the memory. Had he been a coward? Should he have fought for Monica, even though she was still married to that monster of a man? He had not said a thing to stop Oliver and the other men he had come with.

He had not seen nor heard from her from that day. It was as if she had been a dream. Robert had been heart-broken for years, but eventually got back together with

Carol. He married Carol, who was jealous of the woman who had nearly stolen him. Carol was always suspicious of him even after all these years together. She still didn't trust him.

Seeing Priscilla had nearly driven him crazy with regrets, but also filled him with dread of what his wife could do. Carol was capable of anything, he knew that.

He and Monica had produced a child, a beautiful, wonderful girl as lovely as her mother had been when they met. Monica was still beautiful, still mysterious. He never knew what drove her, what made her live with a man like Oliver. He mostly believed that it wasn't love for the man, but love for her children that had allowed her to go back to him after he had treated her so badly.

Robert picked up the phone to dial Priscilla's number, but put it down for the fourth time. Her last words to him had been very wounding, but she had been right. He was a coward and he was weak. He had always done his job and made money, but when it came to emotional decisions he had just watched as Carol ran his life. The man who chased the young Monica until she gave in to him just didn't exist anymore. Could he bring him back? He couldn't live in fear. He had to speak to his daughter, explain, and plan the way forward.

Priscilla answered the phone at her house.

"Priscilla, this is Robert Chigoni," he said.

"Oh," Priscilla said. She sounded as excited as someone who had to clean cow dung.

"How are you?"

"Fine," she said.

Robert smiled. At least she was talking to him. Things would be fine.

"Can I talk to you? I know the last time I saw you I may have said things to hurt you, but it was the shock of seeing your mother and meeting your father."

"I don't have a father," Priscilla said, and her words cut him. He didn't know what to say for a while.

"Can I meet you for lunch today or tomorrow? I think we need to talk."

"I have a lot going on. My sister is very sick, and my daughter is upset."

"I am making an effort, Priscilla. Can you meet me halfway?"

"Fine. I can only come in today because Rudo has swimming. It'll be for a short time."

"You pick a restaurant," Robert said. Priscilla picked one and then put the phone down.

When Priscilla got to the restaurant in downtown Harare, Robert was already sitting at the table. She looked like her mother, but she was taller. She had gotten her height from his side of the family. His sisters were tall, athletic women with sons who were playing rugby for the national team.

"It's good to see you," Robert said.

The restaurant was busier than he would have liked, but he chose a table behind a potted plant. It was a popular restaurant, but since Priscilla had chosen it he had no choice but to accept it.

"Are you sure it is a good idea to meet in public?" Priscilla said putting her bag on an empty seat and sitting opposite him.

"It's fine."

They ordered their food and while they waited for it to arrive the waiter gave them cold drinks with straws.

"How is your mother?"

"She's fine, still in Glenview with her husband. I don't see her much."

"Because of what happened the last time?"

Priscilla nodded and took a sip of her drink.

"I'm sorry about what happened. It's not your fault."

"Tell that to Oliver."

"I didn't handle the whole situation that well."

"How do you handle such a situation well? I was just disappointed with you, and with my father, too. He hated me growing up. You rejected me when I was conceived."

"That is not true, Priscilla."

Priscilla just shrugged.

"I didn't know Moni . . . your mother was pregnant."

"Really? Weren't you sleeping with her?"

Robert shook his head, seemingly disgusted. "I was in love with her. I wanted to marry her."

Priscilla regarded him. She seemed surprised by his confession. "Tell me what happened, because she won't tell me anything."

Robert told her the story, as briefly as he could. "I watched Oliver drag her out of my life and I didn't do a thing."

Priscilla looked at him with very little sympathy. She had grown hard, and his story didn't move her. He had let his mother go to that monster of a husband.

"I regretted it, but at the same time my hands were tied."

"By what?"

"Monica was married to Oliver. I had no right to her."

"But he was living with another woman. He was married to Lindiwe."

"A man can have two wives," Robert reminded her.

"Legally?"

"Legally. They both belonged to him. Oliver had your sisters, and I think he would have done something to them."

Priscilla nodded. She didn't know what else to ask him that wouldn't invade his privacy.

"So now what? Am I your child? Do you accept me?"

"Of course I do! I am so happy you are here. I just wish I had known about you. Now I almost feel like it's too late. I can't save you from your childhood. You are all grown up. You don't need me."

"I do need you," Priscilla said, her wall of anger evaporating. "Ever since I found out I dreamed that you would be there for me and we could have a relationship. The reality was that you were out of reach, out of bounds."

"I'm sorry."

"It's fine. I'm a grown-up, married woman. Needing a father is no longer such a big deal. Chamu takes very good care of me and he loves me and I feel safe with him. I don't want to put your marriage in jeopardy, so if it is easier that we don't see each other again . . ."

"No, Priscilla. I want to find the best time to tell my wife. It's not like I cheated on her, but still she would take it very badly if she knew about you. I know it is something I'll have to tell her about, and soon. *Rine manyanga hari putirwe.* The truth always comes out, and I'd rather it came from me. I also want you to meet your brother and two sisters."

Priscilla smiled. Yeah, she did have a brother. What would that be like? "I look forward to meeting them one day," Priscilla said and looked at her watch.

"Do you have to go?" Robert asked.

"Yes. I have to pick up Rudo from swimming. I don't like to keep her waiting."

"My granddaughter." He took out his check book and started writing. Priscilla watched him with surprise.

"Please buy her something meaningful. One of these days I'll be able to tell her that it is from me, her grandfather."

Priscilla heard the sincerity in his voice and reached out and took the check. It was enough money to pay Rudo's private school fees for a year.

"Just do it for me, Priscilla. I know it doesn't make up for the years I missed in your life, but just do it for me."

Priscilla put the check in her purse and stood up. She gave her father a sad little smile and walked out of the restaurant. As she made her way down the stairs, she didn't see a woman in a blue suit follow her.

Priscilla had parked on the street, in front of a huge department store. She got her keys out of her bag and opened the door. She nearly had a heart attack when someone slammed closed her car door, bruising her hands instantly.

"What?" She turned and came face to face with a woman in a blue dress. Her heart started thudding, certain she was being mugged. She had always been so careful, but her mind had been miles away as she walked out of the restaurant. Women were robbed daily in Harare. This woman didn't look like a mugger, but Priscilla knew that you could not judge a thief by their appearance.

"I need to talk to you, miss," the woman said confidently, anger in her black eyes. Her voice was rough, like stone rubbing against steel.

"Do I know you?" Priscilla's heart rate was slowing down a smidgen. Her hand was on her chest, and she leaned into her car to get away from the fierce look on the woman's face.

"What were you doing with my husband? I saw you eating lunch with him in that restaurant. Are you planning on meeting him at a hotel now?"

It took a moment for Priscilla to put the pieces together. She had been eating lunch with Robert, so this had to be his wife. Carol.

"Who are you?"

"Carol Chigoni. You were with my husband, Robert Chigoni just now."

"Yes, I was," Priscilla said, relaxing a little. She wasn't his mistress, but being his daughter was probably worse in Carol's eyes. Carol seemed to grow angrier at her words.

"You want to die, young lady?"

"Why don't you ask him to explain? I'm not your husband's girlfriend, and never will be. I have to go."

Priscilla opened her door and Carol slammed it shut with her hip, a force that sent Priscilla reeling. Priscilla stood on the pavement, surprised that this woman would cause a scene right in the middle of the busy lunch crowd. People were turning to stare.

"You are not going anywhere unless you explain to me what is going on. You better tell me the truth. I don't treat bitches that sleep with my husband very kindly."

Priscilla sighed. This is what Robert had meant about his wife. She looked vicious, as if she could do a lot of damage to her. She could knock her to the ground and step on her vital organs, drawing blood and poking her eyes out. She was a tough-looking tall woman with large, expressive eyes. Her face was twisted in a snarl, ready to strike her. Priscilla had never fought anyone physically before and already felt the humiliation pour down her back.

"I'm not Robert's girlfriend." Priscilla watched Carol's face darken with anger.

"You are lying," she snarled. Priscilla tried not to cower from the woman's venomous anger. She didn't want her to see how much she terrified her.

"I'm not. Our relationship is innocent. You can go and ask him yourself. I have to go home to my husband and child, Mrs. Chigoni. Please step away from my car."

Priscilla had wanted to tell her the truth, but she knew it was not her place. Robert would have to deal with his wife.

"So why was he giving you a check?"

Priscilla's mouth opened, but she couldn't think of a word to say in her defence. She knew that in Carol's mind, Priscilla was guilty as charged.

"I want to see that check." Carol reached for her purse. Priscilla stopped her, then reached in her bag and pulled out the check. Carol grabbed it from her and her eyes widened when she saw the amount.

"That's a fortune! Why would he be giving you that much money?"

"Please ask him. You can take the check, but I tell you it is all innocent." This time Priscilla's voice trembled. She waited for Carol to strike her or put her hands on her throat. That's how violently angry the older woman looked.

"You are a lying slut. I'll find out the truth from him, and then you are both going to pay. Nobody makes a fool of me."

Carol stepped away from the car, but still had more threats to issue as she put the check in her bra.

"If I find out you are having an affair with my husband you will both pay very dearly. I can make people disappear. I can squash you until you are no more. *Hure!*"

Carol calling her a whore made Priscilla flinch like she had been slapped across her face. Priscilla nodded and got into her car. She was shaking and struggled to start the car. She drove away, and when she looked in her rear-view mirror Carol and her blue suit had disappeared. She realized in that instant that both Robert and Monica had not been lucky in their spouses. They would have been happier together.

CHAPTER 34
Zororo—Rest

After Unashe's party Vimbai seemed to deteriorate. The day Priscilla had the run-in with Carol she received a call that her sister was in her last days. She was rushed to the hospital at the end of November, but the doctors said there wasn't much they could do. Vimbai would have to go home and wait. Wait to die.

Priscilla went to visit her every day in Glenview. Oliver would be in the living room watching news as the sisters visited Vimbai in her bedroom. At the end of November, Vimbai slipped away, quietly, while Monica sat by her. She didn't make it to Christmas. Even though they had known that Vimbai's advanced AIDS was incurable and that she would die, the news was just as devastating.

The night Vimbai died Priscilla went to be with Monica. Chamu was driving back from Gweru, where he was checking the opening of another branch. She called Mukai, but Mukai gave her news that was just as distressing.

"Oh, Priscilla, I'm so sorry about Vimbai. I just can't come right now. Unashe was in an accident."

"What do you mean? Is he, is he . . ."

"He's fine. Just bruised and sore. They kept him in the hospital overnight but sent him home this morning. I just left him at the flat."

"Alone?"

"He sent me away. Said he's fine. I'll come to Glenview tomorrow."

After Priscilla hung up her heart felt battered and bruised. She had taken a walk and stood by the mango tree at the back of their house. Memories of her sister flooded back. When they were little, Priscilla liked to climb up trees and pass the juicy mangos down to a smiling Vimbai. She remembered how they would bite into the fruits and immediately the sweet juices would run down their throats like rivers of nectar.

Unashe's hurt and my sister is gone.

Oliver was being strange, and Priscilla decided to leave just before midnight when her aunts, uncles and other family members arrived. She told herself she had to get away from Oliver, but deep down she knew where she was really going.

She told herself to go home to her daughter but she found her car moving as if of its own accord towards Unashe's flat. In her grief, she just had to see him and make sure he was fine. Her mind glazed over what Chamu would think if he knew. She needed Unashe more than anything that night. She had never been to his place, but she knew where it was. She'd driven past the building often.

As the security guard let her in, she worried that he might have some woman there, maybe Vivian, massaging his wounds. She realized she didn't care. She wanted to escape the pain, and Unashe had that power. He could make her forget, even for a few minutes, even though they had fought the last time they spoke.

After a ride in the elevator to the sixth floor, she knocked on the door. There was no answer. Yes, that was what she got for just appearing without warning. She lifted her hand and knocked again.

Still nothing. With a sigh of regret and relief, Priscilla leaned her forehead on the cold wooden door. She turned away as tears filled her eyes. The sound of the door opening surprised her, and she turned to see Unashe's sleepy face.

"Cilla," Unashe said, surprised. He was wearing a loose fitting pair of jeans and a white T-shirt.

"Hi," she said and wiped the tears from her cheeks.

"What a surprise. Come in."

Priscilla walked in the room and turned to face him.

"What's wrong? Oh, baby, what's wrong?" he whispered, his voice soothing her. Unashe reached for her and she fell into his arms, sobbing. She just cried and clung to him like a lifeline, and they stood in the middle of the room for a long time. Finally, she moved away from him and asked for the bathroom. He could hear the water running in the sink but the door was locked.

"Cilla, what's wrong?"

"I'll be right there," she whispered, and then there was silence. Unashe looked out the window at the view of the city. He lived right at the top of the complex and could see the city lights from his living room and bedroom windows. The view did nothing to ease his worry. He hadn't really seen her since his surprise party, and that interaction with her left him feeling uneasy. He turned when she opened the door.

"Is it Vimbai?" he asked, his eyes getting moist. She nodded.

"Oh, no," he said. He walked to her again and guided her to the sofa. He helped her to his couch and sat next to her.

"I'm so sorry," he said. "She was a wonderful person."

Priscilla nodded and fell onto his chest, sobbing. He didn't know what to do. Since he came back this was the first real emotion he had seen from her. She always seemed so strong, taking everything in stride, living like a rich princess. He was still getting over the shock that she was even there with him. He gently put his hand on her hair and started stroking it.

"Can I get you anything?" Priscilla sat up slowly, her hands covering her face. He reached for her hands and pulled them back.

"Tell me what I can do to make you feel better," he said. "I want to help you."

"You already are. Were you sleeping? I'm sorry I just came from nowhere."

"Don't say that. I'm always here for you. Any time, day or night." She looked at him, reading his eyes and believing what he was saying though not wanting to analyze its implications. She wanted to hold on to his face so the pain that was right there close to the surface would go away.

The silence was deep; she could hear a plane flying over his flat and hear the clouds shifting up in the sky. They were alone in his house. Despite her pain, her loss, there was a prickling of something else. She longed to forget everything in Unashe's arms, she wanted to lose herself with him. But that was crazy; that was her survival instincts kicking in and messing up her mind. Unashe was not hers to take. She was already taken!

"I have to leave. I just wanted to see you. You look fine. Weren't you in an accident?" Priscilla looked at him from his head to his bare feet and back to his eyes.

"I'm fine. The doctors said I'll start to feel the pain tomorrow."

"How do you feel now?"

"Just a bit sore across my chest," he said and winced a little when he shifted in his seat. He could see her staring at his chest, and then she suddenly turned to him, knowing she must go but wanting to stay.

"I better go. I'm glad you are all right."

"I'm good. I'm sorry about Vimbai." She nodded. "You can stay here if you want," he said quickly.

Priscilla glanced around the bare living room. "You have a great place. I didn't realize these homes were so big. I like how simply you have decorated. How many bedrooms?"

"Three, and two bathrooms." He looked around, seeing it through her eyes. The townhouse was huge, but all he had in the living room was a set of sofas and his TV. There were two pictures on the walls and a plant that was in the corner. That was it.

"If I had known you were coming, I might have run to the store and bought a rug for the floor, added more pictures, bought a dining room table and added a bookshelf. Just to make it half as nice as your place."

Priscilla laughed. "I like it. It's just fine. Just how I would picture you would decorate."

Unashe smiled and they looked at each other intently. Finally he spoke. "I guess everybody is wondering where you are."

"Maybe. There is so much we have to do, to plan, but for a few minutes, I put it aside. That's why I came. It's overwhelming. And of course I was worried about you."

Priscilla stood up suddenly and Unashe jumped to his feet, nodding understanding. She looked at his face, but quickly looked away. Her heart raced at what went through her mind.

"Can you hold me again, please?"

Unashe stared at her as if he wanted to run away from her. She feared he would tell her she was crazy or scold her. Instead, he stepped closer and put his hands on her waist. Priscilla felt her knees weaken. Slowly, he pulled her even closer and she fell in his arms with the sweetest sigh. He held her like that for a long time. She wanted him to take this comfort thing to his bedroom, and she wanted him to kiss her like he used to. Her body molded to his.

He tried to pull back, but she tightened her arms around him, drowning in his masculine scent and strength.

She wanted him to run his hands down her body, pull her head back and cover her mouth with his own, but he didn't. Finally, she stepped back then smiled.

"So you didn't have a woman in here?"

Unashe smiled and rubbed his eyes. She was always talking about him and some woman.

"I'm not sleeping around. Can't trust most of these women," he said. His voice was different. Maybe he did feel something for her.

"Wise decision," she said, and then looked at him one more time.

"Thank you," she said.

"For what?" She just smiled.

"Let me take you to your car," he said.

"It's fine, Unashe. Go back to sleep. We'll see you at the funeral." She put her hand on the door handle and looked at him. She watched as he reached over and put his hand on her cheek. He leaned over slowly and kissed her gently on her lips. Just like their first kiss.

Priscilla pushed him away and their eyes locked. Then without warning she pulled his head down again and kissed him deeply, hungrily, and let go just as quickly. She slipped out of his house before he could catch his breath.

It rained heavily the week after Vimbai was laid to rest.

After Vimbai's funeral, the family had more to deal with. Priscilla spent hours having a heated debate with her mother and sisters about Vimbai's children. Gilbert's family wouldn't let them go. They couldn't agree on what to do about the innocent orphans, whether to fight Gilbert's family or let them do as they pleased.

As Priscilla left Monica and Oliver's house, she had a lot on her mind. It had started to rain again and the sound of the drops and her thoughts seemed to fight for space in her mind.

Priscilla still had to deal with Oliver's anger towards her. Her mind was filled with so many problems that she felt like a pressure cooker about to burst. She'd learned that Oliver wanted to cut her off legally. He planned to call a meeting with all of their relatives and publicly denounce her. He wanted her to remove his name from her birth certificate.

Robert Chigoni called her and told her about the problems he was having with Carol. Carol insisted that he have nothing to do with Priscilla. Carol was angry, but he was biding his time before he decided what to do. Priscilla swallowed that bit of information like a bitter pill.

And then there was Unashe. She was slowly sinking back into her old foolish self. Thinking of him as she drove, dreaming of him when she slept. Remembering the kiss like it had brought her to life, when she didn't know she had been half alive. How could that be? And yet, Chamu was even dearer. So much more wonderful than before. Taking care of her. Showering her with gifts and giving her a position at the bank.

How could she want to risk all that for a man who had left her and forgotten about her. Many days she almost drove over to his house but, for what? What did she want to happen? Unashe was moving on with his life, as he rightly should be. Shouldn't she?

With that difficult thought floating in her head, she drove right by Unashe's huge building. She refused to turn to look in the direction of his flat, no matter how tempted she was.

When she got home, her mind was whirling. She knew she had to make many decisions with her life as she parked her Mercedes and got out. She knew that at some point she had to leave the bank and start something on her own or go back to programming. She had been out of the game so long she might have to go back to school first. The job Chamu had for her was secretarial. It was only for a few days a week, and meant she still had the rest of the week to fill. With what? Since Vimbai died she really wanted to find ways to increase awareness about AIDS, maybe make that something the bank could focus on. She would talk to Chamu about it.

The house, as usual, was quiet; even the noise of the rain didn't penetrate the walls. Rudo was at school, and Chamu was at the office.

She picked up the mail that was on the kitchen table and scanned through the letters quickly. Most of them were bills that she would take care of later, but she was surprised when she saw a letter addressed to her in a handwriting she had never seen. She opened it and when she unfolded the lined paper, she saw two pictures: one of Chamu, a woman and two little boys, and another one of Chamu standing next to the same woman. Puzzled, she held them in one hand then began to read the shocking letter.

Priscilla,

I am writing to tell you that your husband has another wife and family. I am the wife. I got tired of hearing about how much he loves you and how he buys you fancy homes, so now it's time to come out in the open. Chamu told me not to tell anyone, but I got sick and tired of being the secret wife. Why should you think you are the only one while I suffer in silence? If you don't believe me ask Lina, or anybody else in his family. They all know about me, and Chamu still comes to me. I don't care what he does if he knows I told you, but fair is fair. You are not the only one he loves. In fact I have given him sons and you haven't, so I can tell you now that he loves me more than you.

From the other wife, Rosemary Tengani.

CHAPTER 35
Muroora—Daughter-in-Law

The rain had stopped when Priscilla drove to Lina's house after reading the letter three times. So Chamu had another wife. As shocked as she felt, it somehow made sense in her world of lies and secrets. *You reap what you sow.*

A conversation she had had with her friend Faith a few months ago stood out in her mind.

"Do you have family at Hartman House? I saw Chamu at the swimming gala there."

"Oh, no. Not that I know of. Our daughter is at Chisipite Junior. You must be mistaken."

"You are right. That's what I thought."

It was him, Priscilla thought now. *He had gone to see his little sons. Why didn't I suspect anything? Why didn't anybody tell me?*

What incensed her was the fact that Lina knew about it and definitely enjoyed it. She couldn't help recalling the way Lina had treated her when she first went to meet the family. Is that why the family was so cold to her? Did they prefer Rosemary?

As she turned towards Lina's street, Sidney's voice came back to her sharp and clear as if he whispered in her ear. Had Chamu's brother known all along too?

"You think you know him so well, don't you?"

She remembered the day he had behaved so strangely, acting as if he was interested in her and the innuendos that felt like darts to her mind. She recalled the look on his face, and now the realization made her feel naked and afraid. He had known, too, and somehow tried to warn her.

"She's bathing," the maid told Priscilla after she had walked into the kitchen. What she really wanted to do was to go in that bathtub and pull her out, but she sat impatiently on the sofa until Lina walked into the living room, fully dressed. She smelled of lavender soap and expensive perfume.

"Priscilla, what a wonderful surprise. You haven't been to visit in a long time," Lina said, extending her hand to greet her.

"I need you to take me to meet Rosemary," Priscilla said straightaway, standing up and folding her arms in front of her chest. Lina gave a small smile that had a wicked edge to it as she clasped her hands together.

"Who is Rosemary?" she asked.

"Don't play with me. You know who she is. I would like to go and see her today, and you better take me now!"

The two women stared at each other for a few seconds.

"Fine. I'm glad the truth is finally out. I was sick of seeing how you were dominating my son and my grand-children's money," Lina said, her chin help up.

Priscilla didn't respond, but bit her lip so hard it began to hurt.

"I'm not going to take you there. You can go and meet my real daughter-in-law by yourself."

"Why did your son do it?"

"He can tell you himself. I never wanted him to marry you, Priscilla. You are not good for my son, or good enough."

Priscilla swallowed her words like medicine from hell. How long was she going to go on without learning the truth?

"Her house is not far from here. After Main Street you turn into Fox Run, and then you will see her road on the left."

Priscilla walked away and got into her car, her fury making her tremble. It was almost time to go and pick up Rudo from piano lessons, but she had to finish this business. She wanted to see Rosemary for herself.

She followed Lina's directions, and it drove her crazy thinking that Lina was probably on the phone warning Rosemary. The house was so close to Lina's they could practically borrow salt and sugar from each other.

After pressing the intercom, the electric gate opened and revealed a stunning double-story house. It paled compared to the mansion Priscilla lived in, but it was a beautiful house with well-manicured gardens and a pool. Two little boys stopped riding their bikes and ran inside when they saw the car drive in.

A tall woman in a blue skirt and white top came to meet her. Priscilla stepped out of her car slowly and walked towards the woman she had just seen in the photos. At closer glance, Priscilla could see her face. She had almost the same skin tone as hers and was very attractive and curvaceous. Her hair was in chin length braids and she wore a loose-fitting top over a matching full skirt. By all accounts, she looked like somebody she might have been friends with or even worked with. But she was married to her husband? How could that be?

"Are you Rosemary?"

"Yes," she replied and lifted her chin a little higher. Her eyes already looked ready for battle. Priscilla knew that Lina had called her. The gate had opened as if she was expecting her.

"I got your letter," Priscilla said, taking it out of her purse. "Did you write this?"

"Yes, I did."

Rosemary looked angry as she lifted her head towards her. "I was with him first."

"I'm not here to fight with you," Priscilla said. "I never knew you existed."

"I guessed as much."

"Why didn't you tell me before?" Priscilla turned as the two boys came to see what was going on.

"Chamu, Winston, go in the house," Rosemary called to them. They disappeared around the corner, giggling.

"You weren't supposed to know anything. Chamu was protecting you," Rosemary said.

"Those are his children?"

"Yes, and another one is on the way," Rosemary said, tilting her chin up again and proudly putting her hand on her stomach. Priscilla almost threw up right there as the implication of her words sank in.

"Don't look so disgusted, Priscilla." Rosemary spat her name. "He slept with me almost every day before he came home to you. I got tired of seeing you on TV, Chamu thanking you for helping make his company a success while I hung out in the shadows like his whore. If I could get away with it, I would have killed you! Well, no more! I will not be a back-door wife when I'm the one having his sons and taking care of his mother while all you do is worry about your own mother and sisters."

Her words felt like a slap. Rosemary's hatred was enough to kill. The seven years of her marriage flashed before her eyes like a dream. All of it had been nothing. She wasn't married to Chamu. She had been living in sin with him while inside she longed for somebody else.

"Please open the gate for me. I'm leaving." Priscilla turned away from Rosemary and stumbled to her car. She started the engine and started reversing with Rosemary looking on. She knew Rosemary and Lina would probably laugh at her and rejoice that she was miserable. Her heart was racing as strong drops of rain began to fall on her windshield like tears from heaven. She merged with the Saturday traffic, but she was in such a daze she didn't even know how she got home.

Home. This wasn't her home anymore. After composing herself, Priscilla picked up Rudo. When she got home she told the maid to feed Rudo. Then she went to the bedroom and straight to Chamu's walk-in wardrobe, looking for more clues to his secret life. She had never scrutinized his bank statements or opened any of his letters. She had trusted him completely. There were too many papers in his office, all business-related.

That's probably where he keeps his secrets, Priscilla thought, looking at the locked safe. *How well do I know Chamu? What else has he been keeping from me?*

Priscilla went to Rudo's room. She was playing alone in her bedroom with her dolls. Her uniform was neatly folded on her bed and she had put her on her favorite shorts and t-shirt.

"Hey, sweetie," Priscilla said.

"Mummy, what are we going to do this weekend? You said we can go and watch a movie."

"We'll go, sweetie. How would you like to go and stay with Aunt Mukai?" Priscilla asked.

"Can I take my dolls and keyboard?"

"Yes. Go and tell *Sisi* to pack you a bag and I'm going to pack mine," Priscilla said and went to her room.

Priscilla pulled out a suitcase and started looking for what she would take with her. She took down five outfits and some shoes, then took her photo albums and her favorite books. She packed her laptop, and when she was about to close the bag she heard her door open and looked up as Chamu walked in.

"What are you doing?"

Priscilla stared at Chamu as if seeing him for the very first time. She hadn't heard a car drive in at all. She could see the strange light in his eyes and was frightened. She should have just left without packing anything. Lina must have warned him and he left the office to stop her.

"I'm packing," Priscilla said, trying to keep her voice calm as she closed the suitcase.

"Where do you think you are going?"

"I know all about your other wife, Chamu," Priscilla told him in a matter-of-fact voice.

"She means nothing to me," Chamu interrupted, waving his arms about.

"What! That's why you are having a football team of kids with her?"

"You didn't want to have my children."

"I can't believe you are saying that. So you think what you did was fine?"

"No. I'm sorry. I won't see her again."

Priscilla stared at him in disbelief. He wouldn't see her again. As if she was some girlfriend he had at school. She scowled at him, stunned. "You can have her move in here, which is what she wants. I'm leaving you!"

"You will never leave me! Where will you live? Where will you work?" He sneered at her.

Priscilla shook her head. "That's how you wanted me, isn't't? Totally dependent on you."

"You can never leave and have the kind of life I can give you. That bag you are packing is mine, and those clothes are mine."

Priscilla pushed the suitcase to the floor and the clothes tumbled out. She walked up to him. "You can have them all. I'm going."

He slapped her. "You are mine, too!"

The slap produced hard and fast tears and her face stung. Nobody, not even Oliver, had ever hit her like this. She touched her cheek and looked at Chamu as if he was some monster. She could see in his eyes that he was dangerous. She felt very scared.

"I'll never let you go, Priscilla. You will be dead and buried before I let any other man have what is mine."

CHAPTER 36
Tiza—Escape

Priscilla couldn't believe her life had spiralled so out of control. As she panicked, she remembered the tales her grandmother used to tell her when she was little, of girls who were greedy and suffered the consequences.

She slammed on the hard oak doors, but she knew that nobody was going to come to her rescue.

"Rudo," she screamed, but nobody came. She ran to the window and saw Chamu drive away. She could see Rudo's head peeking from the back seat. By the time she opened the sliding doors the car disappeared out the gate.

"Oh, no! He has my baby. He's crazy! Mad!" Priscilla picked up her cell phone and dialled Unashe's number, her hands trembling.

No answer.

Breathing heavily, she dialled again.

"Hello," Unashe answered finally.

"Unashe. He has lost his mind," she cried, her voice filled with fear.

"Who? What? Slow down."

"He took my baby! Chamu took my baby."

"What are you talking about? Took her where?"

"Just find her. Find her!"

"Where are you?"

"He locked me in the bedroom. You have to find her. He's gone crazy. I want to leave him, but he says he'll hurt Rudo if I do."

"Why would he hurt his own child?"

"It's not his baby. He knows it's not his baby."

Unashe was silent.

"Then who . . ."

Priscilla could sense by his silence that he had already added it up. She didn't care what Unashe thought at that time. She had to get him moving to get her child from the monster she was married to.

"She's yours, Unashe. Please save her. He took her somewhere . . . maybe his mother's. Find her and then come and get me!"

"Where does his mother live?" He asked the question calmly, but there was an undertone of rage in his voice. She gave him the address and hung up. She tried the window. There were no burglar bars, and it would be hard to get out from the second floor, but she had to try. Somehow she knew that Chamu was serious about killing her.

Unashe picked up his keys and rushed out of the office. Priscilla's words had his head spinning. *Rudo's my child. Rudo's my child.*

Priscilla tried the balcony, but she could see herself falling and breaking her bones if she tried to jump. What use would she be if she lay dying on the grass below?

She wandered if she should call the police, but what could she say? That her husband had kidnapped their daughter and locked her in the bedroom. Everybody knew and respected Chamu. In her cell phone she found the number for the nearest police station. She dialled it.

"I am locked in my house. Can you please come and help me out?"

"Where are you located?"

Priscilla gave the tired-sounding sergeant her address and answered questions that didn't seem necessary. She almost screamed when he finally said, "We don't have a car right now, but when we get one we will be sure to send it to your house."

She was pacing like a crazy woman, ready to tear her hair out as she imagined the worst happening to Rudo. She wanted her daughter safe from the man she considered her father! She wanted to leave this crazy house and never return.

She called Unashe again after ten minutes.

"Where are you?" When he spoke she barely recognized his voice.

"I have her with me. You were right. She was with your mother-in-law, and I had to fight to get her back. Rudo is fine, but a little scared. Can you get out of the house? I think Chamu is on his way over there. If you can get out, go to the shopping center."

"I'm going to try," Priscilla muttered and hung up the phone. She was terrified that Chamu would arrive any minute. She got to the French doors and opened them. There was nowhere to step from the balcony. She knew she would have to tie something together to make a rope to climb down.

Frantically she pulled the silken sheets off the bed and tied them to the poles as tightly as she could. She kept watching the gate, afraid that Chamu would drive up at any second and kill her. She threw her purse and back-pack to the ground. She climbed over the railing with her heart beating with fear and held on to the sheet. She slid down fast, bruising her hands, and landed on the grass with a painful thud.

For a second she lay there, dazed, and then got up and ran past the house. The maid was nowhere in sight. Had Chamu sent everybody away? The house was locked, so she couldn't even open the electric gate.

Running fast, she made her way to the gate. The walls and the gate were made in a way that thieves couldn't get in or out easily. She had to find a way out.

On the other side of the city, Unashe was fighting traffic to get to Priscilla. He hadn't had much time to think about what was really going on as he drove through

Seventh Street. Rudo sat in the backseat, worried and tense. He could tell she was confused and terrified.

He tried hard to think of something to say to the child. "Don't worry, Rudo. We are going to get Mummy."

"Daddy was shouting at her," she said.

Unashe gritted his teeth and gripped the steering wheel tighter. Now that he knew the truth about Chamu he realized they had been played like pieces on a chessboard, their lives maneuvered by a dangerous man who would stop at nothing to get what he wanted. Unashe was worried about Priscilla. Was she still in that house? Unashe had tried her phone, but it kept going to voice mail.

He had to get around the traffic. He would go insane if he had to stay put in one place waiting for the light to change five or more times before he could pass. Angrily he drove over the ridge, and the man who was selling wares on the side of the road had to jump out of the way. He squeezed past cars and fought his way to the front of the line. When the light turned green he sped uncaringly past the other annoyed and frazzled motorists. He had to get to Priscilla. He couldn't let her down. But what if he was too late?

Priscilla tried to climb the wall, but there was nothing to hold on to. She couldn't even see the top of the brick wall lined with jagged glass. She ran to the pond and grabbed one of the chairs, breathing hysterically. Before she could climb out, she heard a car. She leaned against the wall and only breathed again when she heard the car go past their gate. There was only one other house on the other side. She wanted to call out for help, but when she looked over the motorists were driving into their yard and disappeared over the bend.

Priscilla threw her purse forward and then used her sweater to block the glass so she could heave herself up. Finally, she jumped over and cut herself in the bushes. She landed in the mud. Not feeling any pain, she picked up her bag and started running down the street. The guards who sat at their posts stared at her and she waved at them as she walked past. They recognized her and waved back, though they looked puzzled.

What if they tell Chamu that I have just walked out?

She had a long way to go. After crossing the main street, she was on the side of the road that was close to some bushes and tall grass. She had never walked down that way.

Priscilla was angry that there was no pedestrian path, just a jagged mass of red soil filled with stones and puddles of water. Keeping herself in the bushes, she panted and felt the sweat of fear and exhaustion drench her clothes and pour down her body. She could see the sign for the shopping center. It had always seemed so close by car, but she wasn't getting there fast enough.

Over the bend, she saw the front of Chamu's car coming and she dove into the bushes and lay down as flat as she could, grass tickling her nose. She was scared she would hear him stop, but the car continued to move. When it disappeared down the road, Priscilla scrambled up and started to sprint.

Chamu arrived at the guard post that protected the ten families that lived in the enclosed neighborhood. The guard looked like he wanted to say something, but Chamu waved him off and quickly drove to the house.

Lina had called him about Unashe taking Rudo. Chamu was livid, and he was ready to take out all his anger on Priscilla. He opened the gate and drove into the deserted house. The maid and the gardener had been told to leave; he wanted no one witnessing what he might have to do to save his family. The first thing he saw was the bed sheet hanging from their bedroom balcony. Fury spread through his body like wildfire as he parked the car and ran to the house. He opened the door with the bunch of keys he had collected and ran upstairs.

"Priscilla! Priscilla! You better not do anything stupid!"

He got to the bedroom door and unlocked that as well. He already knew what to expect. The room was empty. He was furious. He should have tied her up! He should have thought things through; now Priscilla and Rudo were both gone. Rosemary would pay for this.

Chamu walked to the balcony where she had made her escape. She couldn't be far. She had to have walked because her car had to be in the garage. He had taken all the keys. The only thing he realized he had forgotten was her cell phone!

"Damn her to hell," Chamu growled as he ran down the stairs.

Unashe felt like he died a few times while he stood waiting for Priscilla. There was no sign of her in the shopping center. There were about five different stores, and he was scared to even go in and check in case she would need his help outside.

"Where are you?" He tried her phone again. Still no luck. The images of Chamu hurting her filled his mind and engulfed him in fear and dread. He almost sagged with relief when he saw her appear on the road, her clothes covered in mud. He started the engine and drove to meet her.

Priscilla ran and knocked on the window.

"Where have you been?" He opened the door and started the car at the same time.

"Let's go. I saw him," she whispered and looked back at Rudo, who looked at her with wide, terrified eyes. She looked haggard and terrified.

"Come, baby," she said, holding out her hands, and Rudo climbed over the seat and sat in her lap.

"What's wrong with your hands?" Rudo was looking at her scratched and bleeding hands. "Where are we going?"

"We are going on a holiday. Don't worry, baby. Mummy is here," Priscilla said.

"Why was Daddy shouting? Is he angry with us?"

"No. Everything is fine," Priscilla said and finally looked at Unashe. He gave her a meaningful glance, but continued to drive in silence.

CHAPTER 37

Waifungei—What Were You Thinking?

"She's sleeping. Can we stop so I can put her in the backseat?" Priscilla asked.

"I'll stop in Rusape when we get petrol," Unashe replied. She noted the coldness in his tone, but decided not to say anything. Silently she looked out the window at the shadowed scenery that flew by. Unashe was driving very fast. They reached the town in twenty minutes and Unashe parked in front of a petrol station.

"I'll come round and get her," he said, opening the door and telling the garage attendant to fill up the car. He came round to her side and gently pulled Rudo from Priscilla's tired arms. Rudo continued to sleep, and put her arms around his neck when he picked her up.

Priscilla watched him take a deep breath before moving to the back seat and placing her on the seat as if she were a baby.

He pulled off his jacket and placed it on her. Priscilla blinked back the tears, staring at the roof of the car.

After the tank was full, Unashe paid the attendant, came back and sat heavily in his seat.

Unashe started the car then turned to face her. "Do you really think Chamu would harm you?"

"Yes. You better call your mother and warn her not to tell anyone where we are," Priscilla said.

"She wouldn't tell him," he said.

"You never know. They do talk to each other," Priscilla said, but Unashe already had his cell phone out and was dialing the number. He sighed heavily and left a message.

"She's home, and her mobile went straight to voicemail. I'm worried we won't have any signal along the way," he said.

"It should be fine." Priscilla sighed. Unashe didn't want to talk. His silence hurt. Even though she deserved his censure, she would have preferred if he shouted and screamed at her.

The drive began again and somehow Priscilla managed to sleep, even though she had nightmares. When she woke, they were still on the road. She had a moment of panic.

"We are still on the way," Unashe said tiredly.

Priscilla looked back at the seat and saw that Rudo was still sleeping. They had torn out of the city and never looked back. Unashe had explained to her that he had the keys to a cottage his mother owned in Inyanga. It seemed like the best place to go and lay low while they figured out a plan. Priscilla wanted to leave the country if possible. In her heart, she knew that Chamu was capable of killing all three of them. She was not going to take the chance and stay in town like a sitting duck.

After several more miles, Unashe drove off the main road and onto a dirt road that curved up a mountain.

Priscilla felt like every shadow from the trees was going to attack them.

She looked at Unashe, but he wasn't offering any comfort. He had his own anger and fear to deal with.

They passed several houses with dark windows and finally Unashe turned into a house that sat at the end of a lane of trees.

"Here we are," Unashe said. "I'll open the house, then I'll come and get you."

"Don't leave me, please," Priscilla cried, looking around in the dark.

"He's not here," Unashe said. "I really doubt he would come all the way here."

Priscilla just stared at him, the car light illuminating the fear in her eyes.

"All right, here are the keys. I'll carry Rudo in."

She grabbed her bag and they made their way through the chilly night. Priscilla got the key into the door and opened it easily enough.

Unashe flipped the light switch with one of his hands. Priscilla felt better at the sight that greeted her. It was a lovely room with comfortable dark green sofas, a huge fireplace and a TV. It was fashionable but sparsely furnished. The sofas were separated by two pots with flowers and a tall reading lamp. Priscilla took in the two paintings on the walls as she closed the door and locked it.

"Come this way," Unashe said and walked down the passage to the first door. Priscilla opened it, and there was a freshly made bed and a fireplace in that room, too.

Priscilla pulled back the covers and Unashe laid Rudo on the bed and covered her.

"This girl can sleep," he said, looking down at her.

"Through anything, thank God," Priscilla said. They both stood looking at her, until suddenly Unashe just turned and walked out of the bedroom. Priscilla didn't turn, but her heart was tuned to the sound of his footsteps fading down the passage.

When Priscilla finally followed him, he was in the living room. She watched him light the match to the logs that were already laid out for the fire.

The fire started small at the bottom of the tinder, and then slowly began to eat up the dried wood. Unashe remained crouched there for a while, watching the flames grow, inhaling some of the smoke. Priscilla stood watching the fire, too, then walked closer to its warmth. She looked at his tired, handsome face. She wanted to reach out and stroke the tired lines, to stroke his head. She folded her arms across her chest instead.

"Would you like some tea?" he asked, still not looking her way.

She nodded, and he stood up and went to the kitchen. Priscilla pulled one of the dining room chairs over and sat by the fire. She pulled her trousers up and saw the cut she had received when she escaped from the house.

How did Chamu react when he saw she was gone? Surely he didn't just accept defeat. He probably went to her mother's or even her sister's house hoping to find her. He probably went and broke down the door at Unashe's flat. She shivered just imagining what he could be plotting. "What's wrong?"

"I'm just trying to figure out what Chamu is doing to find us," she said.

"Don't worry about him for now. You are safe here."

Unashe looked around the living room. The fire had already made the comfortable place cozier, the crackling sound and smells filling the quiet room.

"It's a nice place," Priscilla said. "You've been here before?"

"Yes. We came for a weekend with friends."

Priscilla swallowed at the bitter news of his life without her and his unfriendly tone. She bent her head to examine the wound on her leg.

Unashe walked out of the room again and she felt like the door had been left open to let the cold in. Priscilla put her arms around herself.

"Let's see?"

Priscilla looked up to see Unashe holding a first aid box. He pulled one of the footstools over and sat down opposite her. Methodically he took out a tube of antiseptic medicine, a swab of cotton and some clear solution.

"What's that?" Priscilla asked.

"I need to clean that out. It might get infected," Unashe said.

"Will it hurt?"

"Stop being a baby."

Unashe picked up her leg and held her calf in his hand while he applied the solution. Priscilla winced in pain, and Unashe shook his head as if he was disgusted at

315

her lack of backbone. She felt her heart warm at the gentle expression on his face. When he looked at her, she felt like his eyes were looking deep into her soul even though he was asking about her leg.

"How does it feel?"

"It's fine. I know this stuff works. I use it on Rudo all the time," Priscilla said.

"Rudo," Unashe said, then began putting the items back in the box.

Priscilla didn't know what to say. She looked at him as he stood and shook his head, the anger returning to his eyes.

"I really thought you had done all you could to make me hate you, but this, Priscilla, is the lowest you could ever go!"

Priscilla flinched at his words. She knew he would be angry, but she didn't at all guess he would have this rage.

"I wanted to tell you," Priscilla said.

"But what?" Unashe gritted the words out of his mouth. Priscilla went back to the day she had kicked him out of her life. She remembered her anger back then; his was ten times worse than hers. He was an inferno. It scared her more than she wanted to show, but she knew that she had no leg to stand on. Nothing she could say could excuse what she had done.

"You did that to her after how your father treated you? And now this monster you married kidnapped her."

Priscilla knew she deserved his tongue-lashing. She had put Rudo's life in danger for what? For security? To hide her shame of being pregnant without a husband? To live like a pampered housewife as if she had not begged her father to go to school so she could study and get a job? She had not been true to herself. She had sold out for a Mercedes, and she was paying the price. The lifestyle that she had worn was starting to hurt and terrify her; hopefully she had tossed it away in time, no matter how shiny it had been.

"I found out after you had left, and I thought Chantel was carrying your child, too!"

"That was another one of your husband's schemes," Unashe said with a bitter twist to his mouth. Her heart froze at his statement. She wanted him to look at her with favor as he had done before, but his eyes glittered with disappointment and anger. Would his heart ever be repaired?

"What are you talking about?"

"He paid Chantel to lie to you. And you bought it, didn't you?"

"He what? He-he-," Priscilla covered her mouth in shock. She felt dizzy.

"How could you believe her?"

Priscilla shook her head, stunned. She grew angry at his accusations. "How could I not? You were planning to leave me anyway."

"We could have gone together. You could have followed me."

"I never heard you once say those words, Unashe. You just couldn't wait to leave, could you? To start school so you could make money and drive fancy cars. Your plans did not include me."

"I was doing all that for you. I wanted to be a man worthy of you! I still wanted to be with you, but you almost wanted to kill me. You, Cilla, chased me away and never came to say goodbye. I hoped until the last minute that you would come, or at least talk to me. I was a fool."

Priscilla looked at his face. She was breathing heavily. "I thought Chantel was telling the truth, Unashe."

"I never wanted anybody else but you," Unashe said. "But you, you couldn't wait to marry some rich man with the fancy cars and give him *my* child." Unashe punched his chest to emphasize his point.

"I had no choice."

"You married him before I had even started school in England. I had just been gone for what, a month, and already I heard you were getting married. When were you seeing Chamu? While I was with you?"

"He was our client."

"And I guess you were impressed with all his money and Mercedes Benzes, right? I heard he used to come and take you to lunch." Unashe's tone was accusing, his voice full of disgust.

Priscilla stood up angrily, knocking the chair down.

"I don't need to listen to your junk," she spat at him. He stood up and pushed her into her seat.

"You will listen until I'm through." Unashe spoke close to her face as he held her arms.

"Let me go," she cried, fighting to break free, more from his hurting eyes than his grip.

"I'll let you go when you have finished explaining. We are not going to stay here forever, and tonight I want some answers."

They stared at each other like two adversaries. Their anger was as thick as a block of ice, visible and determined.

"I'm tired, Unashe. Tired and terrified. Just leave me alone."

Unashe let go of her arms as tears filled her eyes and poured down her cheeks.

"I'm sorry, Cilla," he said, straightening up and rubbing his head, something he did when he was puzzled or thoughtful. "I'm trying to understand how I missed six years with my daughter. How could I not have known just by looking at her? How could my heart not have known she was my flesh and blood?"

"I'm so sorry, too. I made a huge mistake from the moment Chantel came to see me. I did everything I could to forget you."

He looked deep into her eyes. "Did you?"

Priscilla shook her head. "Not even for a minute."

He leaned close to her, their foreheads touching. He stroked her hair and Priscilla closed her eyes, lost in another world. The ice around her heart melted.

"Mummy!" The sound of Rudo screaming for her made them pull apart and scramble to the bedroom.

Both of them were relieved to discover she had just been having a nightmare. As Priscilla hugged her and soothed her, Unashe watched helplessly. In his heart, he knew that he would die for his child, the amazing little girl he had only known about for a few hours.

After Rudo settled down Priscilla went to take a bath to wash away the sweat and mud on her body. Unashe remained in the living room. She dressed in a wrinkled pair of slacks from her backpack and sat by the dressing table, smoothing her hair back. She still wanted to talk to Unashe. She wanted to know if Mukai had called back. When she got to the living room, the fire burned brightly but Unashe wasn't there. Two cups of tea sat untouched on the table. She walked to the other bedroom, her heart beating wildly. She knocked gently.

"Yeah," he said. Priscilla turned the door handle and walked in. Unashe's shirt was unbuttoned and hung loosely over his smart trousers. She tried very hard not to stare at his chest.

"You are limping. How's the leg?" He crossed his arms over his chest but didn't make a move to button his shirt.

"It stings, but I'm a wimp when it comes to pain," she said, her mind foggy, still stuck on his unbuttoned shirt.

"How did you deliver a baby?"

"With horrible screams," she said with an embarrassed smile. Unashe shook his head as if to clear it of disturbing thoughts.

"How did you hurt your leg?" he asked instead.

"I jumped over the wall. I think I cut myself in the bushes or the glass. I wasn't thinking."

"You had to jump over the wall? It's hard to believe Chamu would lock you in like a prisoner." Unashe shook his head again and sat on the bed. Priscilla remained where she was, though her body wanted her to walk up to him and hold him. She desperately needed him to tell her everything was going to be all right and that he didn't hate her for keeping the truth from him.

"He took all the keys, Unashe, and locked me in the bedroom. He said he would kill me if I left. I don't even know who he is anymore."

"Did you tell him you would leave him?"

"Yes."

"Why?"

"He's married with two children and another one on the way."

"Didn't you know?"

"No. I never suspected."

"Did his family know?"

"I think they all did. His mother didn't like me from the moment we met. She prefers the other woman. Rosemary."

Priscilla watched him digest the information. "It has been quite a couple of months. You came back, Vimbai got sick . . ."

"It must be tough."

"We all make our beds, right? Right now I don't have a job. I haven't really worked at the bank since Vimbai, you know . . . and I never got my business started. I lost all my independence."

"You can get it back. It'll be fine," Unashe said. "I'm sure now you will want to get your house back. How can you live anywhere else after living in that palace?"

"It's a beautiful house, but it has become a prison to me. I'm glad to be out of there." Priscilla noticed Unashe liked her answer. "I was never after money, Unashe."

"I didn't say that. Listen, forget it. Knowing the truth is always best, and I had a run-in with your mother-in-law when I went to get Rudo. She's something else."

"Thank God you got her. What happened?"

"She let me in the gate, but when I asked for Rudo she started shouting at me. Rudo came and Lina told her to go to her bedroom. I had to push Lina out of the way to grab Rudo. It was not pretty."

"I don't care what you had to do to get her as long as you did," Priscilla said with determination. "Thank you for getting her. I'll never forget it."

"You said the right words to make me move fast," Unashe said, and Priscilla looked away.

"Is she still sleeping?"

"Yes. I better get back to her." Priscilla moved back, then winced again in pain as she bumped into the wall. Unashe jumped up and walked to her, his hand on her shoulder.

"What is it?"

"I hurt all over. I bruised my side, too," Priscilla muttered with a grimace. Having him that close made it hard for her to breathe. She held her side. Unashe grasped her hand and moved it aside.

"Is it here?" he asked. Priscilla nodded, biting her lip. She lifted her shirt a little and he saw the dark bruise below her ribs.

"It looks pretty bad," he said. All Priscilla managed to do was nod her head. Unashe put her top back down but he remained close to her, his hands on his side.

Without thinking, she put her hand on his chest, feeling his heart beat beneath her fingers. Unashe held her hand tightly but, after a few seconds, moved it away.

"This is not a good idea," he said. Priscilla nodded, eyes closed and head bowed.

"I better get back to Rudo. You sleep well."

"Good night."

Priscilla walked out of the room, feeling humiliated. She got into bed next to Rudo, but it was several hours before she fell asleep.

CHAPTER 38
Zuva Rekuyeuka—Memorable Day

Priscilla opened her eyes with a fright. Chamu stood over her bed. He leaned towards her, madness in his eyes.

"You thought you could run away from me?" he demanded angrily.

Priscilla shook her head, sitting up in bed. She pressed her back against the wall as he leaned towards her, arms stretched out. He put his hands around her neck and began to squeeze, his face tightened in rage. She tried to scream, but no sound came.

"Unashe! Unashe! Help me." Her silent calls went unanswered.

Priscilla woke up suddenly with a gasp, cold dread in her chest. Her body was drenched with sweat.

It was a dream. Chamu is not here. It's all right.

Priscilla stroked her neck as the pain she had felt in her dream faded. It seemed so real, and fear filled her whole being like an iron cloak of darkness.

All the memories of the past few days came rushing back.

"How did my life become such a mess?" she asked herself. Priscilla looked at her bed partner. She winced, pulling out of her daughter's awkward embrace, and went to the bathroom. She washed her face and looked in the mirror. She did look like somebody who had been through hell. Her eyes were puffy. She had a faint bruise where Chamu had slapped her. Her hair stood on end as if she had received an electric shock. She brushed it back with her fingers and tied it in a ponytail.

She walked into the living room and Unashe was already there watching the early TV show.

"Good morning," she said, standing behind one of the sofas.

"Hey." He looked up at her, his eyes alert. As usual he managed to make her pulse beat quicker with just one look. She took in his eyes, nose and lips, loving every detail of his face, secure that he was there, strong and dependable, even though he was angry with her.

"How did you sleep?"

"I had nightmares, and Rudo was playing with my hair in her sleep," she said, walking up to the fire. It warmed the room but added more than the heat. It added color and sounds and smells that were comforting and earthy. She looked out the window. The house was nestled behind gum trees and thick bushes that hid it from the street. She couldn't even see the next house, but saw the dirt driveway that led to the road winding up the mountain.

"I was thinking we could go to the Troutback Inn and have breakfast, ride some horses and check out the ducks," Unashe said.

"It looks warm enough," Priscilla said, and looked down at herself. "But I look terrible."

"No. You look beautiful," Unashe said, his eyes on her face.

Troutback Inn was one of the more popular hotels in this busy holiday resort town. Companies liked to host conferences and couples and families liked to get away from the city and enjoy the lush green landscape with hidden, secret waterfalls at every turn.

Even though it wasn't yet winter, it was chilly that morning. Priscilla enjoyed the warmth of the fire as they walked into the lobby crowded with guests.

"Can I go over there, Mummy?" Rudo asked, pointing to the fire.

"In a minute. Let's buy you another warm sweater," Priscilla said. They bought her an expensive hand-knitted cream sweater. Priscilla bought a matching one and Unashe bought a denim jacket. Everything was expensive at the holiday resort, but they were cold and would pay anything to keep warm. Unashe paid by check.

They walked to the dining room where a fire was blazing in the grate and looked out towards the lake beyond the glass and the sloping green grass and tennis courts.

"I remember that, Mummy. Daddy taught me to play tennis here," Rudo said, pointing outside.

"Yes," Priscilla said, looking at Unashe's stony expression. She whispered an apology to him, but he just walked away. Rudo wandered to the fire alone.

"Don't throw anything inside," Priscilla called to her and turned to follow Unashe, who had moved to sit on the chairs. He was shaking his head at her.

"Is she always drawn to the fire?"

"Aren't all children?"

"I don't know anything about her. She's so grown."

Priscilla couldn't mistake the pain in his voice. It was in the way he cleared his throat and turned his eyes away from her.

"She loves your fire truck," Priscilla blurted out, and then winced.

Unashe smiled. "Yeah. Ma says she has it. I used to play with that thing until I was laughed at in high school."

"Her Barbie dolls ride in it all the time," Priscilla said and laughed. Unashe smiled.

"She also loves peanuts like you. If I don't watch her she could eat a whole peanut butter tin."

Unashe smiled again, and the pain faded a little from his eyes.

They ate breakfast and Rudo went and sat right in front of the fire alone while Priscilla and Unashe talked. He wanted to know a lot about her, from the day she was conceived.

"When did you find out you were pregnant?"

"After you were gone."

"Oh."

"I couldn't believe it. I always had a low opinion of girls who got pregnant out of wedlock. Oliver had a name for them I won't repeat. I was scared and humiliated. No man to speak of and there I was, pregnant, just as my father had predicted I would be."

"I should've been there for you," Unashe said. "I wish I had known."

"I know. Chamu came in and just took charge of everything and within two months I was walking down the aisle."

"That's exactly what he wanted," Unashe said.

"He couldn't have known about us, could he?" Priscilla said.

"He knew everything about you. Chantel told me how he paid her to do what she did and even contributed to my studies overseas. Chamu knew about us somehow, and he knew about Chantel. I even think that's why he offered me a job, to keep his enemy close, so to speak."

Priscilla stopped eating. She felt like she had been punched in the stomach again. This time the blow nearly knocked her over.

"You really think so?"

"That's what happened. I've known for a while, but I didn't want to ruin your marriage," Unashe said with a twisted, ironic smile.

"I'm not his wife and never was," Priscilla said, then looked at Rudo who had turned to look at them. She waved at her.

"She is very intuitive. She knows something big is going on and we need to talk. She is a great child, Una."

"I can see that. But she thinks Chamu is her father."

They stared at each other. Priscilla couldn't think of a thing to say after that. They completed their meal in silence.

After eating, they walked outside in the sun. It was warmer outside as the sun shone down on them. They went to the pond where ducks waddled in the water and gazed at them for a while before Rudo noticed the pony. They got Rudo a pony ride and Unashe walked right by her side. He turned to Priscilla as they walked.

"Have you seen this waterfall hidden behind a mountain?"

"No. When we were here we just went to the casino," Priscilla said.

Rudo wanted to see it, so they got in the car and drove several kilometres before they reached a deserted area with a bumpy dirt road. Unashe had to go very slowly up the winding road, and Priscilla feared their car would not make it.

"It's worse in the rainy season," Unashe said. "Cars get stuck here a lot."

"Are you sure this is the right road? There aren't even any signs."

"I think I'm sure," Unashe said.

"You think so?" Priscilla teased.

Finally, they arrived at the top of the winding road after passing a game park, a lodge and a village, and, true enough, they were not lost. There were a few cars parked and a man and a woman selling souvenirs. Priscilla bought a hand-carved elephant and then followed Unashe and Rudo.

As they walked down the path they could hear gushing water.

"Listen," Unashe said to Rudo.

"I can hear it," Rudo said excitedly. "Is it like Victoria Falls?"

"It's a little smaller, but just as nice. Do you want to see it?"

"Yes," Rudo said happily. Her smile had always reminded her of Unashe. She had his love for life, his infectious grin and generous heart.

"Come, I'll carry you on my back," Unashe said then they started the steep, meandering descent to the waterfall.

They trekked for a while where they could hear the water but couldn't see it. They met three people returning from viewing the waterfall, but otherwise they were very alone. At last, all its beauty and glory was revealed to them and both Rudo and Priscilla gasped. Unashe looked at them with a smile.

They watched the water gush down rocks from where they stood, making its way down to an unseen bottom. They moved around carefully, enjoying the view from different angles.

"You like it," Unashe said, putting Rudo down. Priscilla could see his pride at having brought them, as if he had made the waterfall just for them. She loved him even more.

"Do you want to go over there?" Unashe pointed to some rocks that the water didn't reach.

"I'll fall," Rudo cried, holding on to Unashe.

"Don't worry, I'll hold on to you," he reassured her. Priscilla looked at the two of them, her heart warm and sad at the same time.

There was a lot to be talked about, but now wasn't the time to think about the future. She was going to enjoy their first day as a family and hope for many more.

They found a nice, smooth rock and then sat down sunning themselves like lazy lizards.

They were silent for many minutes, but soon felt the chill as the sun went behind a cloud. It seemed as if their nice day had been taken away and replaced by something from an ominous movie.

"Time to go home. It looks like there are a lot of clouds forming," Unashe said, getting up.

It had suddenly become dark, a light was turned off in the heavens, and Priscilla had a horrible feeling of getting back to reality and leaving their dreams behind on that waterfall.

CHAPTER 39
Rima—Darkness

The clouds covered the sky like a thick, suffocating, icy-cold blanket. The warmth of the day was gone, taking with it the joy Priscilla had felt in her heart.

"Let's stop by this Pine Tree Inn. They have these warm, sweet scones and jam that I know you'll like," Unashe said as they drove away from the waterfall.

"And tea?"

"Yes," Unashe said and took off towards another dirt road. This place was not as popular as Troutback Inn, but had its own charm and privacy. They entered the dining room where another fire blazed.

"I also told them to make us a packed dinner and more scones for breakfast tomorrow," Unashe said as they sat down.

"Thanks. How long do you think we should stay here?" Priscilla asked.

"One more day. Tomorrow afternoon we can drive back to Harare and I'll take you to my friend's house," Unashe said once Rudo was talking to a little white boy with curly red hair and a million freckles. They were getting along really well though she wasn't sure if the parents liked it or not. They kept glancing at the children with stiff expressions. The mother called the boy over, but the boy refused to come. Rudo had a knack for getting along with people, and the little boy was enjoying her company. Priscilla concluded that he didn't see color yet. His parents would teach him.

"I would like to be as far from Chamu as possible. How long can we stay in hiding? What do I do after a week? A month?"

"Then you get a lawyer to tell him that it's over," Unashe said.

"I hope it'll be that simple. How can I start my life from scratch while you still work for him?"

"I forgot to tell you. I resigned a month ago. After I learned about Chantel, I knew I wanted to leave. I also think he is under investigation for fraud. There is a lot you don't know about Chamu."

Priscilla's eyes widened at the surprising information Unashe was telling her. Would she ever learn everything about Chamu?

"He is also very dangerous," Priscilla added, shivering. "I just have a cold, hard feeling that won't go away. I don't think he can stand the humiliation of being divorced."

"You are his trophy wife. Everybody in the city knew that. They envied him."

"I'm surprised he would go to such lengths to keep me when he has another wife. I want to tell myself that he doesn't care if I leave him, but I remember the look on his face when he slapped me."

"He what? I need to get my hands on him," Unashe thundered.

"It's not too bad," Priscilla said, but her eyes filled with tears.

"He's crazy," Unashe said then regarded her for a while. When he spoke, she could tell he was trying to make her feel better. "But in some strange way I can understand his temporary madness. When you dumped me, I thought I would lose my mind. That moment when you were angry . . ."

Unashe reached over and covered her hands. Slowly he picked them up and brought them to his lips and kissed the center of her hand. Priscilla felt the warmth spreading from her hand to her heart and then to the tips of her toes.

"I've missed you so much," Priscilla said, and looked up and saw Rudo staring at them. "I missed you every day."

"I missed you. When I saw Rudo the first time, I wished she were mine. It's a miracle to me that she actually is."

"She's all yours."

The drive back to the house was quiet as Rudo lay in Priscilla's arms again. The car overflowed with the sweet aroma of the warm scones and jam they had ordered.

Outside it was already getting dark though it was only 4:30 p.m. They got to the house and Unashe started another fire while Priscilla put the food in the kitchen. Rudo found a game of checkers and played against

Unashe. He let her win and she was excited. She asked Priscilla to play against Unashe. Their game was tough, and eventually Unashe won.

"I'll challenge you tomorrow," Priscilla said, getting up and beginning to put their dinner on their plates.

"I think someone needs to go to sleep," Priscilla said when she saw Rudo yawning.

"Do I have school tomorrow?" Rudo asked. Priscilla looked at Unashe. He was already the daddy, and Priscilla naturally gave him the respect.

"You will go next week. Right now, you are having a holiday. A special holiday."

They ate together in front of the fire. Rudo chatted a lot and Priscilla let her tell Unashe all about school, piano lessons and dance. She could tell that Unashe felt left out, especially when Rudo spoke of her trip to Disney with Daddy. Every now and then she glanced at Unashe and their eyes connected, filled with warm sincere messages they knew they couldn't hide anymore. Priscilla had just put the dishes in the kitchen when she sensed something.

Both Priscilla and Unashe were surprised when they heard a car drive just outside the house. Unashe had just told Rudo it was bedtime.

"Who's that?" Priscilla asked. Her heart was already racing.

"Maybe it's Mum. I left a message for her again when we were at Troutback Inn," he said. Priscilla ran to the window and peered outside at the silver twin cab.

"I don't know who it is," she said, but the way her heart was beating, she had an idea. Unashe saw the fear in her eyes and ran to lock the door. The air in the room became charged with terrifying electricity.

"Rudo, I want you to go and hide in the wardrobe and don't come out until your mum tells you, okay?" he said.

Rudo ran to Priscilla in fear.

"Go quickly, Rudo. Don't come out until I come to get you. This is very serious." Priscilla had to push her. Rudo ran with tears streaming down her face.

"You go, too, Priscilla. I'll deal with him," Unashe said.

"No." Priscilla shook her head, fear in every fiber of her being.

"Go now!" Unashe's look demanded submission, and Priscilla went to make sure Rudo was hiding. She found her in the wardrobe and Priscilla gave her a kiss.

"I love you, Rudo," Priscilla whispered. She jumped when she heard Chamu yell.

"Where is she? Where is my wife?"

She stood up. "Stay here. Don't move," he commanded and left the bedroom. She was not going to run away from this evil. She had to face him.

When she reached the living room, her heart stopped. Chamu pointed a gun at Unashe's head, the same gun she had seen him packing for shooting practice. Unashe had backed away, holding his hands up. His pained expression grew when he saw Priscilla walk into the room.

"Chamu, don't do this," Priscilla begged, shaking her head. "Let's talk about it."

"There's nothing to talk about. He's going to die, and so are you!"

Priscilla lifted her shaking hand to him.

"Take me. Leave him alone," Priscilla whimpered.

"I told you to stay away," Unashe said.

"Shut up, you two! You make me sick. You thought you could get away and have your little affair without getting caught, didn't you?" Priscilla shook her head, as much to say no and partly to shake off what surely was a nightmare.

"Nothing, nothing happened," she said.

"I gave you everything, and this is how you thank me? And you . . ." Chamu looked at Unashe. "Why didn't you stay in England? You couldn't keep your hands off my woman. I should have killed you back then."

Priscilla had never seen Chamu look like this. He was crying and fearsome at the same time.

"Let's take this outside. Let Priscilla live. She will go back to you," Unashe said.

Chamu laughed a cold, hard laugh. "You can't give her to me. She was always meant to be mine, but you had to try to steal her from me. Nobody else is going to have her now. She will die mine. Mine, do you hear me?"

"Yes," Priscilla sobbed, seeing her life flash before her eyes. She was trembling so much she thought she would have a heart attack. She was going to die. He was going to kill her and Rudo.

Oh, God, please help me.

He pointed the gun at Priscilla. In the same moment Unashe jumped quickly towards Chamu; as he was about to reach him the gun went off. As if in a horror movie Unashe saw Priscilla clutch her stomach and fall to the floor, blood gushing through her fingers.

There was no time to help her. The two men fought for the gun with grunts and curses. They both fell into the TV and knocked the whole cabinet down with a loud crash, stunning them for a second. The battle for the gun continued. Chamu managed to gain the upper hand, and with a grunt aimed the gun towards Unashe. Unashe held his ground and tripped Chamu. Both men fell, and the gun tumbled towards the door.

Scrambling on their knees, they dashed for the gun and with both hands on it continued the fight to survive. After the struggle by the front door, the gun went off and both men fell still on the floor. Priscilla never saw what happened, as she lay motionless on the floor.

CHAPTER 40
Gamuchira—Accept

Monica held Rudo in the back seat of Mukai's car. The child still had nightmares, hearing gunshots in her dreams and flinching at the slightest sound. The doctors said it would take some time for her to recover from the trauma. She needed a lot of love, and that was exactly what Monica was going to provide. It was just perfect because Max and Chipo, Vimbai's children, were now living with Monica, too. They managed to distract Rudo. It was now weeks since the horrific event in the Inyanga Mountains, but Rudo was only slowly shedding the anguish from her eyes.

The newspapers and Zimbabwe's only TV station, ZBC, had just months before celebrated Chamu and Priscilla and the opening of Primehouse Bank. Now they were full of another story. The morning headline had left Monica feeling sick.

RICH BUSINESSMAN INVOLVED IN SHOOTING IN THE MOUNTAINS. WIFE SHOT AFTER AFFAIR WITH COUSIN.

Monica's life had come under scrutiny, neighbors and family adding fuel to the fire that was blazing all around them. Stories about Oliver and Monica were now being talked about at bus terminals and tea breaks. Even Robert's name came up in the newspapers, so that secret was now fully out. But she didn't care. She still had God loving her and she still had her children. She didn't need her neighbors' approval, and she didn't worry about their stares and whispers. Still, shootings were so rare in Zimbabwe that this particular one had been huge news. Chamu being a household name made the story even bigger.

They drove in silence to the hospital, both women in grief and torment. Mukai was still getting used to seeing Rudo as her granddaughter, and Monica was trying to get used to that idea, too. Neither of them knew what was happening right in front of their eyes. Mukai had not even seen her son falling for Priscilla right under her nose! If only she had known, she might have saved them the tragedy that had become their lives.

They reached the private hospital and took the lift to the intensive care unit on the second floor. Mukai looked at her phone as it beeped.

"It's one of my clients. Now I check this thing all the time," Mukai said to Monica.

"Since that time . . ." Monica said. She couldn't bring herself to say what happened.

"I never used to check messages because it's usually clients. Many people don't leave messages. I wish I had checked it . . ."

"It's not your fault, Mukai. Nobody knew what was happening or that he would do anything," Monica said.

"I even gave Chamu the directions. The last thing he told me was that he was going to Inyanga and he would explain. After that I never checked my phone, and I don't have an answering machine at home."

Mukai looked at Rudo and decided to change the subject.

"We are almost there," Mukai said instead. Rudo didn't respond.

They reached the reception where nurses in white uniforms and caps stood talking, holding boards. The senior nurse greeted them kindly. Monica held some flowers and Mukai held a bag with magazines and some fruit.

Mukai looked inside the room through the glass. She didn't know what to think as she saw Unashe sitting on the bed beside Priscilla. She remembered the fear she felt as she drove towards Inyanga with Unashe's friends and the police they had collected from the Inganga police station.

Seeing them brought back the fear she felt when she realized the big mistake she had made. By the time she got to the house there was a forbidding silence in the mountains. They opened the door and were greeted by a scene that still terrified Mukai to this day. Unashe sat on the ground, holding a limp and still Priscilla in his arms. He was covered in blood and tears. Chamu lay in his own blood on the floor not far from them, his gun not far from his hands.

Mukai shook her head to clear it, and then looked inside again. What kind of life awaited these two young people, Mukai wondered.

Priscilla opened her eyes and looked at Unashe's face.

"It's you again," she said groggily.

"I'm not leaving you ever again," he said, tears in his eyes. In the days when Priscilla was unresponsive, he had cried more times than he had ever cried in his life.

"What happened?"

"He shot you, then we fought for the gun and I shot him," Unashe repeated. Every time she woke up she wanted to know what happened. Her reality and dreams were all confused.

"He's dead?"

Unashe nodded.

Priscilla looked aside tears falling on her pillow. Unashe felt so grateful. It was incredible that she was alive. Doctors rarely had to treat gunshot wounds, so this had been a horrific experience for everybody at the hospital. Specialists had been called, and the miracle was that the bullet had done very little damage to her vital organs. Now the concern was infection.

"I need to sleep. Go, please," Priscilla said. Unashe was shocked. He hadn't expected her to chase him away again. Unashe went outside and gave his mother a hug. Rudo was standing beside Monica, holding her hand.

"Hello, Rudo," Unashe said. Rudo just looked at him. Monica walked into the hospital room with Rudo. Unashe feared that Rudo would probably always associate him with the nightmare in the mountains. It broke his heart to look at her and not be able to pick her up and show her that he was her father, that he loved her and that he would do anything to protect her and her mother.

God give me patience, Unashe said to himself. He turned to his mother.

"How is she?" Mukai asked.

"She sent me away," Unashe replied, unable to hide the pain from his mother. "She almost died, Ma."

Mukai put her hand on his shoulder. No matter how tall and big he looked, he was still her one-and-only little boy, and she hurt seeing the pain in his eyes. There was nothing more to say about the whole situation. They had talked about it for weeks. "Why didn't you come to me, son? I would have given you my blessing six years ago."

"We were scared of the family's reaction," he said.

Unashe tried to explain as they prayed for Priscilla's life. Unashe's life had flashed ahead of him, bleak and miserable without the love of his life. He did not want to live without her.

"Give her time," Mukai said.

"I don't know what I'll do if I lose her, Mum. I was a foolish boy. She's everything to me."

Mukai couldn't even understand that kind of love, but Monica did. Oliver was as obsessed with Monica as

Unashe was with Priscilla. What was it about these women that they had more than one man willing to kill for them, but she had none? There was this vulnerability and delicacy in their beauty that made men want to protect them, want to perform the impossible for them, and yet for the wrong man it made them want to hurt them, as in the case of Oliver and Chamu. Chamu wanted to devour Priscilla, make her his property at whatever cost. Even the cost of his own life.

Unashe turned and looked into the room and saw Priscilla's smile as she held her daughter on her bed, carefully so as not to upset her healing gunshot wound.

Mukai smiled seeing her granddaughter, love welling up inside of her.

She turned and saw Robert Chigoni walking down the passageway towards them. A young girl dressed in jeans and running shoes walked beside him. This was going to be an interesting visit.

Priscilla looked up at the door as Robert walked in. She looked at the girl next to him and her confusion grew. Robert greeted Monica and Rudo before turning to Priscilla.

"How are you? I came as soon as I heard you were awake," Robert said.

"You have been here before?" Priscilla laced her fingers with Rudo's.

"Every day," he said and turned to the shy young girl behind him. There was something familiar about her. Priscilla felt like she had met her before.

"This is my oldest . . . my second daughter," Robert said, clearing his throat.

"Nyarai, this is your older sister, Priscilla," Robert said. Nyarai walked forward and shook Priscilla's hand. She had tears in her eyes.

"I nearly didn't meet you," Nyarai said, smiling through her tears.

"It's good to meet you," Priscilla said and smiled weakly.

"We want you to come home when you are discharged. Carol, well, she would like to meet you properly, now," Robert said. Priscilla had to swallow the knowledge that his wife had changed so drastically.

"I'll have to see," Priscilla said, and then turned to Nyarai. "So what do you do?"

"I'm at university in Philadelphia. I'm studying computer science," she said. "I came home for summer break."

Priscilla waited for the twinge of jealousy, but it didn't come. She just smiled and asked a few more questions. Still, she did envy Robert and his "oldest" daughter's relationship. She talked to him like a friend and even leaned against him as if for protection. He was her father, too.

While Robert talked to Priscilla, Monica came in with some disturbing news. Priscilla could see it in her face.

"What's wrong, Ma?"

"Somebody else just insisted on seeing you. I told him no."

"Who?"

"Sidney."

Priscilla felt her heart beat faster. What was Chamu's brother doing here? They had given the nurses strict instructions not to send in any of Chamu's family. Lina had wanted to come in, but probably to kill her, not see how she was doing. The only other people she had been forced to talk to were the police and investigators.

"I'll see him," Priscilla said.

"No, Pri," Monica insisted.

"It's okay, Ma."

Sidney walked in looking sad and worn out, though he wore a dark suit that made his handsome features more distinguished. The tie seemed to be choking him, though. Robert and Nyarai walked out.

"How are you?" Sidney looked at the room filled with flowers and baskets of fruit.

"I think I'm going to live," Priscilla replied quietly. She felt uncomfortable when their eyes met briefly.

"I'm sorry about what happened to you."

"It's a sad time for everybody. Sorry about . . ."

"If only I had told you the truth, none of this would have happened," Sidney said.

"Don't blame yourself, Sidney. I remember you tried to tell me in your own way."

"Brother Chamu didn't want us to tell you anything. He said it was his life and he could do whatever he wanted."

"Thank you for coming, Sid," Priscilla said as a way of dismissal. "I really need to rest."

Sidney shifted uncomfortably on his feet, hands in his pocket.

"I know this is not a good time," Sidney began, a strange light entering his eyes. Priscilla somehow knew she didn't like what he was going to say. She felt her defences go up and her wound begin to throb.

"What is it, Sidney?"

"I just want you to know that I'm here for you, if you need me. I can take care of you and in time, when the time is right, I hope you will be able to love me just as much as I have always loved you."

Through his speech, Priscilla started to feel light headed. Was he crazy? His brother was barely cold in his grave and now he was declaring his love. The audacity!

"Sidney. I wish you the best in your life, but I don't think we can ever speak again. I'm feeling weak. Please leave." Though her voice was weak, the meaning was clear in her eyes.

Sidney walked out just two minutes after he entered her hospital room, but Monica was worried. Monica walked in and watched tears roll out of her daughter's eyes.

"What did he want?"

"I don't know. But I hope I never see any of them again."

"You won't."

Eventually Monica sent everybody home so Priscilla could rest. Rudo lay by her bed, stroking her hair and giving her little kisses. When Unashe asked if he could come in she sent a simple message to him.

"No."

CHAPTER 41
Batira—Hold On

Unashe had gone out of his mind in the week Priscilla refused to see him. He played squash, jogged, anything to stop the madness from creeping in. He had to speak to investigators sent by Lina, but they all knew that this was an open-and-shut case of self-defense. Chamu had followed them to Inyanga with the intention of killing them.

Lina told reporters that she would not rest until the people responsible for her son's death were behind bars. To Unashe's way of thinking, Lina and Chamu could only blame themselves.

A few days before she would be discharged from the hospital, Unashe forced his way into Priscilla's room. She was lying alone on the bed watching the TV set he had sent for her.

"Cilla, we have to talk," he said, closing the door behind him. She looked at him like he was one of the nurses coming to poke her with a needle or give her tasteless medicine.

He sat right on her bed and forced her to look at him. Their eyes held for a while and he saw the coldness melt away to be replaced by tears. He tried to hold her but she pushed him away with the little strength that she had.

"Please don't keep me away from you," he begged, his eyes beseeching her. They stared at each other for a minute.

"I can't be with you, Unashe. Don't you see?"

"What do you mean?"

"Every time we get together something happens. We both nearly died."

"But we didn't die."

"How can we live happily together knowing Chamu died at our hands?" Priscilla said.

"He would have killed both of us, and Rudo, too. I don't even know how I survived."

Priscilla lifted her hands and touched his cheek, savoring the prickly sensation of his rough chin where a beard was coming out. She looked into his liquid brown eyes.

"You were so brave. I was so scared. I heard you fought him when he held the gun. He could have killed you," she said.

"He could have. I didn't think he was that crazy, but I was looking at a crazy man that night," Unashe said. Priscilla didn't say anything. She sighed, closing her eyes for a moment. Unashe was so close, so real, so incredible. Was she dreaming?

"But why did somebody have to die for us to be together?" Priscilla's hand was still on his cheek. She dropped it.

"I don't know. I can't explain it. I'm not happy with what happened, either. I'm not happy that he died at my hand."

"I know. I can't think of it, but you can still see Rudo. I'm going to tell her the truth soon," Priscilla said. Unashe felt cold dread fill his heart.

"She is your daughter and you love her, I can tell. You should get to know each other, but I can't be part of your life, Una. I think it's time we really said goodbye, for good."

"Are you serious?" he said, vacillating between anger and shock.

"We should let it go, Unashe. I need you to help me let it all go. Please help me do this."

Unashe stood up and slowly rubbed his head in disbelief. He looked out her window for answers in the wind. As if in a daze, he just walked out the door without looking back. Priscilla watched the door close slowly, and then closed her eyes.

"Don't leave," Priscilla sobbed into her pillow, and when he didn't come back she began to panic. Priscilla remembered reading somewhere that there are three kinds of people in the world: those who make things happen, those who watch things happen and those who wonder what happened. She was tired of wondering what had happened to her life. She had to take control. She had to make her own decisions. Starting now.

She put on her gown and, pulling her IV along on its stand, she opened the door to her room. Unashe wasn't in sight. She walked slowly down the empty passageway.

When she got to the visitors area she nearly sobbed with relief. Unashe sat in one of the chairs, his head in his hands. He looked up when she got close.

His eyes stared questioningly at hers.

"I can't do it," Priscilla said.

"What?" Standing up, he walked towards her. "You should be in bed."

"I can't."

"I need you. I wasn't going to leave. Is that bad? I didn't follow your orders this time," Unashe said, taking her hands.

"Never follow my orders. I never make any sense," she sobbed. He gently put her head on his chest where she could feel his heart beating.

He put his arms around her, and this time he wasn't going to let her go.

ABOUT THE AUTHOR

For Miriam, the love of storytelling came at a young age. She remembers her grandmother, Theresa, sitting on a *rukukwe* and telling her and her siblings stories that began with *Paivepo*, which means Once Upon a Time. Her desire to construct a make-believe world grew as she spent hours creating elaborate stories with her brother, Michael, at the age of eight. Next came the hours spent drawing and writing comic books. In high school, Miriam wrote many stories and novels longhand in the school exercise books and she enjoyed sharing these only with close friends. She had her first short story published in *Drum Magazine* in South Africa when she was in college. She also wrote for many magazines including *Parade*, *Mahogany Magazine* in Zimbabwe, and *Jive* in the USA, before writing her first novel. Her first published novel, *Show Me The Sun*, is available in bookstores around the world. For more information, you can visit her website at *www.miriamshumba.com*.

2010 Mass Market Titles

January

Show Me The Sun
Miriam Shumba
ISBN: 978-158571-405-6
$6.99

Promises of Forever
Celya Bowers
ISBN: 978-1-58571-380-6
$6.99

February

Love Out Of Order
Nicole Green
ISBN: 978-1-58571-381-3
$6.99

Unclear and Present Danger
Michele Cameron
ISBN: 978-158571-408-7
$6.99

March

Stolen Jewels
Michele Sudler
ISBN: 978-158571-409-4
$6.99

Not Quite Right
Tammy Williams
ISBN: 978-158571-410-0
$6.99

April

Oak Bluffs
Joan Early
ISBN: 978-1-58571-379-0
$6.99

Crossing The Line
Bernice Layton
ISBN: 978-158571-412-4
$6.99

How To Kill Your Husband
Keith Walker
ISBN: 978-158571-421-6
$6.99

May

The Business of Love
Cheris F. Hodges
ISBN: 978-158571-373-8
$6.99

Wayward Dreams
Gail McFarland
ISBN: 978-158571-422-3
$6.99

June

The Doctor's Wife
Mildred Riley
ISBN: 978-158571-424-7
$6.99

Mixed Reality
Chamein Canton
ISBN: 978-158571-423-0
$6.99

2010 Mass Market Titles (continued)
July

Blue Interlude
Keisha Mennefee
ISBN: 978-158571-378-3
$6.99

Always You
Crystal Hubbard
ISBN: 978-158571-371-4
$6.99

Unbeweavable
Katrina Spencer
ISBN: 978-158571-426-1
$6.99

August

Small Sensations
Crystal V. Rhodes
ISBN: 978-158571-376-9
$6.99

Let's Get It On
Dyanne Davis
ISBN: 978-158571-416-2
$6.99

September

Unconditional
A.C. Arthur
ISBN: 978-158571-413-1
$6.99

Swan
Africa Fine
ISBN: 978-158571-377-6
$6.99$6.99

October

Friends in Need
Joan Early
ISBN:978-1-58571-428-5
$6.99

Against the Wind
Gwynne Forster
ISBN:978-158571-429-2
$6.99

That Which Has Horns
Miriam Shumba
ISBN:978-1-58571-430-8
$6.99

November

A Good Dude
Keith Walker
ISBN:978-1-58571-431-5
$6.99

Reye's Gold
Ruthie Robinson
ISBN:978-1-58571-432-2
$6.99

December

Still Waters...
Crystal V. Rhodes
ISBN:978-1-58571-433-9
$6.99

Burn
Crystal Hubbard
ISBN: 978-1-58571-406-3
$6.99

Other Genesis Press, Inc. Titles

2 Good	Celya Bowers	$6.99
A Dangerous Deception	J.M. Jeffries	$8.95
A Dangerous Love	J.M. Jeffries	$8.95
A Dangerous Obsession	J.M. Jeffries	$8.95
A Drummer's Beat to Mend	Kei Swanson	$9.95
A Happy Life	Charlotte Harris	$9.95
A Heart's Awakening	Veronica Parker	$9.95
A Lark on the Wing	Phyliss Hamilton	$9.95
A Love of Her Own	Cheris F. Hodges	$9.95
A Love to Cherish	Beverly Clark	$8.95
A Place Like Home	Alicia Wiggins	$6.99
A Risk of Rain	Dar Tomlinson	$8.95
A Taste of Temptation	Reneé Alexis	$9.95
A Twist of Fate	Beverly Clark	$8.95
A Voice Behind Thunder	Carrie Elizabeth Greene	$6.99
A Will to Love	Angie Daniels	$9.95
Acquisitions	Kimberley White	$8.95
Across	Carol Payne	$12.95
After the Vows	Leslie Esdaile	$10.95
(Summer Anthology)	T.T. Henderson	
	Jacqueline Thomas	
Again, My Love	Kayla Perrin	$10.95
Against the Wind	Gwynne Forster	$8.95
All I Ask	Barbara Keaton	$8.95
All I'll Ever Need	Mildred Riley	$6.99
Always You	Crystal Hubbard	$6.99
Ambrosia	T.T. Henderson	$8.95
An Unfinished Love Affair	Barbara Keaton	$8.95
And Then Came You	Dorothy Elizabeth Love	$8.95
Angel's Paradise	Janice Angelique	$9.95
Another Memory	Pamela Ridley	$6.99
Anything But Love	Celya Bowers	$6.99
At Last	Lisa G. Riley	$8.95
Best Foot Forward	Michele Sudler	$6.99
Best of Friends	Natalie Dunbar	$8.95
Best of Luck Elsewhere	Trisha Haddad	$6.99
Beyond the Rapture	Beverly Clark	$9.95
Blame It on Paradise	Crystal Hubbard	$6.99
Blaze	Barbara Keaton	$9.95
Blindsided	Tammy Williams	$6.99
Bliss, Inc.	Chamein Canton	$6.99
Blood Lust	J.M.Jeffries	$9.95

Other Genesis Press, Inc. Titles (continued)

Other Genesis Press, Inc. Titles (continued)

Other Genesis Press, Inc. Titles (continued)

Other Genesis Press, Inc. Titles (continued)

Naked Soul	Gwynne Forster	$8.95
Never Say Never	Michele Cameron	$6.99
Next to Last Chance	Louisa Dixon	$24.95
No Apologies	Seressia Glass	$8.95
No Commitment Required	Seressia Glass	$8.95
No Regrets	Mildred E. Riley	$8.95
Not His Type	Chamein Canton	$6.99
Nowhere to Run	Gay G. Gunn	$10.95
O Bed! O Breakfast!	Rob Kuehnle	$14.95
Object of His Desire	A.C. Arthur	$8.95
Office Policy	A.C. Arthur	$9.95
Once in a Blue Moon	Dorianne Cole	$9.95
One Day at a Time	Bella McFarland	$8.95
One of These Days	Michele Sudler	$9.95
Outside Chance	Louisa Dixon	$24.95
Passion	T.T. Henderson	$10.95
Passion's Blood	Cherif Fortin	$22.95
Passion's Furies	AlTonya Washington	$6.99
Passion's Journey	Wanda Y. Thomas	$8.95
Past Promises	Jahmel West	$8.95
Path of Fire	T.T. Henderson	$8.95
Path of Thorns	Annetta P. Lee	$9.95
Peace Be Still	Colette Haywood	$12.95
Picture Perfect	Reon Carter	$8.95
Playing for Keeps	Stephanie Salinas	$8.95
Pride & Joi	Gay G. Gunn	$8.95
Promises Made	Bernice Layton	$6.99
Promises to Keep	Alicia Wiggins	$8.95
Quiet Storm	Donna Hill	$10.95
Reckless Surrender	Rochelle Alers	$6.95
Red Polka Dot in a World Full of Plaid	Varian Johnson	$12.95
Red Sky	Renee Alexis	$6.99
Reluctant Captive	Joyce Jackson	$8.95
Rendezvous With Fate	Jeanne Sumerix	$8.95
Revelations	Cheris F. Hodges	$8.95
Rivers of the Soul	Leslie Esdaile	$8.95
Rocky Mountain Romance	Kathleen Suzanne	$8.95
Rooms of the Heart	Donna Hill	$8.95
Rough on Rats and Tough on Cats	Chris Parker	$12.95
Save Me	Africa Fine	$6.99

Other Genesis Press, Inc. Titles (continued)

Secret Library Vol. 1	Nina Sheridan	$18.95
Secret Library Vol. 2	Cassandra Colt	$8.95
Secret Thunder	Annetta P. Lee	$9.95
Shades of Brown	Denise Becker	$8.95
Shades of Desire	Monica White	$8.95
Shadows in the Moonlight	Jeanne Sumerix	$8.95
Sin	Crystal Rhodes	$8.95
Singing A Song...	Crystal Rhodes	$6.99
Six O'Clock	Katrina Spencer	$6.99
Small Whispers	Annetta P. Lee	$6.99
So Amazing	Sinclair LeBeau	$8.95
Somebody's Someone	Sinclair LeBeau	$8.95
Someone to Love	Alicia Wiggins	$8.95
Song in the Park	Martin Brant	$15.95
Soul Eyes	Wayne L. Wilson	$12.95
Soul to Soul	Donna Hill	$8.95
Southern Comfort	J.M. Jeffries	$8.95
Southern Fried Standards	S.R. Maddox	$6.99
Still the Storm	Sharon Robinson	$8.95
Still Waters Run Deep	Leslie Esdaile	$8.95
Stolen Memories	Michele Sudler	$6.99
Stories to Excite You	Anna Forrest/Divine	$14.95
Storm	Pamela Leigh Starr	$6.99
Subtle Secrets	Wanda Y. Thomas	$8.95
Suddenly You	Crystal Hubbard	$9.95
Sweet Repercussions	Kimberley White	$9.95
Sweet Sensations	Gwyneth Bolton	$9.95
Sweet Tomorrows	Kimberly White	$8.95
Taken by You	Dorothy Elizabeth Love	$9.95
Tattooed Tears	T. T. Henderson	$8.95
Tempting Faith	Crystal Hubbard	$6.99
The Color Line	Lizzette Grayson Carter	$9.95
The Color of Trouble	Dyanne Davis	$8.95
The Disappearance of Allison Jones	Kayla Perrin	$5.95
The Fires Within	Beverly Clark	$9.95
The Foursome	Celya Bowers	$6.99
The Honey Dipper's Legacy	Myra Pannell-Allen	$14.95
The Joker's Love Tune	Sidney Rickman	$15.95
The Little Pretender	Barbara Cartland	$10.95
The Love We Had	Natalie Dunbar	$8.95
The Man Who Could Fly	Bob & Milana Beamon	$18.95

Other Genesis Press, Inc. Titles (continued)

ESCAPE WITH INDIGO !!!!

Join Indigo Book Club©
It's simple, easy and secure.

Sign up and receive the new
releases
every month + Free shipping
and
20% off the cover price.

Visit us online at
www.genesis-press.com or
call 1-888-INDIGO-1

Order Form

Mail to: Genesis Press, Inc.
P.O. Box 101
Columbus, MS 39703

Name _____
Address _____
City/State _____ Zip _____
Telephone _____

Ship to (if different from above)
Name _____
Address _____
City/State _____ Zip _____
Telephone _____

Credit Card Information
Credit Card # _____ ☐ Visa ☐ Mastercard
Expiration Date (mm/yy) _____ ☐ AmEx ☐ Discover

Qty.	Author	Title	Price	Total

Use this order

form, or call

1-888-INDIGO-1

Total for books	_____
Shipping and handling:	
$5 first two books,	
$1 each additional book	_____
Total S & H	_____
Total amount enclosed	_____

Mississippi residents add 7% sales tax